A Product of the System:

Out for Self Series, Part 1

A Product of the System:

Out for Self Series, Part 1

Ms. Michel Moore

www.urbanbooks.net

Urban Books, LLC
300 Farmingdale Road, NY-Route 109
Farmingdale, NY 11735

A Product of the System: Out for Self Series, Part 1

ISBN 13: 978-1-62286-663-2
ISBN 10: 1-62286-663-0

First Trade Paperback Printing June 2018
Printed in the United States of America

10 9 8 7 6 5 4 3 2 1

Distributed by Kensington Publishing Corp.
Submit orders to:
Customer Service
400 Hahn Road
Westminster, MD 21157-4627
Phone: 1-800-733-3000
Fax: 1-800-659-2436

A Product of the System:

Out for Self Series, Part 1

by

Ms. Michel Moore

Who Is Da Daddy?

"Damn, will y'all hurry the hell up and snatch this little crumb-begging bastard up out of me!" Ms. Simone Harris was twenty-three years old, unmarried, and uneducated. Lying on the cold, steel delivery table with her legs cocked open wide enough for a UPS truck to drive inside, she screamed, "I don't know how much more of this pain I can stand! Yank on his big head if you have to!"

Simone's all-of-a-sudden Bible-toting, strict, holier-than-thou, also unwed mother had cast a rebellious Simone out years ago. She left her to basically get that shit how she lived, which, for the teen, was straight out scurvy. Done deal. Real talk. Simone had no respect for anyone, not even herself.

The exhausted night nurse on duty was at the end of a long, tiring shift. She was fed up, losing patience with the young girl's disrespectful demeanor. Taking a damp, cool cloth, she placed it on the back of Simone's neck. Attempting to ease some of the tension in the room, she tried reasoning with her. "Listen here, miss, I know that it hurts to some degree, but you don't have to carry on like that," she scolded. "Now try to relax and get control of yourself."

"How your old ass gonna tell me how to act?" Simone shouted out. "You ain't got no big baby dangling half out your pussy. So stop playing around and get this over. Why is it taking so long?"

Simone was out of breath from pushing. Even against the doctor's constant demands to calm down and not to force the baby out so fast, she refused. Simone was caught up with doing her own thing. In between each and every heavy pant she took, she found the time to curse. She berated the very nurses and doctors that were helping to bring her obviously unloved son into the world.

"Young lady, please, you have to take it easy," the doctor pleaded repeatedly. "You might injure your child."

"What about *me* and the way this freaking baby done injured *my* perfect ass?" Simone shrieked out in agony, still talking cash shit. "Is anybody concerned about *that?*"

Thank God for everyone on staff. Two or three more good pushes and several dozen insults later, Terrell Dion Harris was finally born. After the fatigued doctor went through the ritual of hitting the baby's tender behind and cutting the cord, the nurse held him up to his mother's face for her to get her first look at her son.

"It's a healthy baby boy." The doctors and nurses smiled with pride having brought another child safely into the world.

When Simone wiped the sweat from her eyes, seeing little Terrell, she went ballistic. "Bitch, is you nuts or something? Why the fuck is you dripping all that mucus crap all on me?" She not once took notice of the baby's dark, wavy hair or his tiny slanted eyes that were slightly opened. There was no counting of fingers or toes, just flat-out bugging. "Why don't you go do your job and clean his butt off before you bring him the hell over here? Don't nobody wanna be seeing all that slimy stuff."

"You should be ashamed of yourself for the way you're behaving," the nurse belted out in response. "I pity the man who fathered this innocent child. You're a disgrace to parents everywhere."

"Just do your steppin' fetchin' job, Nurse Old Ass, before I crawl outta this bed and smack you."

The entire delivery staff momentarily stood speechless at the young mother's rudeness. The nurse shook her head as she went about her way and cleaned the innocent newborn off. As Simone waited to hold her baby, she got increasingly angry thinking about the Ballers Shot Callers Cabaret that she would certainly miss that night. All the real true players in Detroit were gonna be flossing at that motherfucker, and here she was stuck up in a hospital room with a damn baby that she felt had stretched her womb ten sizes out of shape and caused her to gain at least thirty-eight pounds. When Simone finally held her barely minutes-old son in her arms, she looked at him and giggled with relief. From his light, bright caramel skin to the shape of his upper lip, he was the spitting image of her and only her. Hallelujah, Jesus, and praise the Lord. There was not one thing about little baby Terrell that resembled his father, not one of them, not even his forehead. Then she softly whispered in his small ear with a huge grin on her face. "Game on, li'l man. You about to make your momma some real paper now. Me and you ain't gonna want for shit out in these streets."

Chapter One

"Girl, trust and believe when I tell you thangs is straight lovely for a pretty bitch like me. I just can't believe how dumb and naive these assholes are in this freaking city. I swear to God, I have never, *ever* in my twenty-five years of living in the Murder Mitten seen two bigger fools walking the face of this earth than Joey and Kamal's simple behinds. They must have been born without brains. I know that I'm the shit and all, but, damn!"

Simone was sitting back, styling and profiling on her brand-new plush cream leather couch, with both feet kicked up on the matching marble coffee table. She was like a Supreme Court chief justice judge residing on the bench holding court as she passed her own personal observations and views on different ghetto bullshit. Sporting the latest clothes, a new Lexus in the driveway, plenty of jewelry, and two dudes on her line, Simone was on top of the world and her game . . . so she thought. Having given birth to a bouncing seven-pound baby boy a little over two years ago, her body was finally back in tip-top perfect shape. All the weight she'd gained during her pregnancy managed to stay put in the right places and was toned. Ms. Thang was what many old-school players referred to as a "brick house." Simone was completely convinced, hands-down, no questions asked, that she was the shit, and no one—man nor beast—could tell her any different. Even if they tried, it wouldn't do any good. Her self-esteem was seriously stuck on arrogant.

"Them crazy busters ain't got a clue about nothing. They gonna both hustle to take care of me and Li'l T for the next eighteen years, regardless. Flat-the-fuck-out." Moving her shoulder-length hair out of her face, she smirked as the tightly twisted blunt made its way around the room to her. Simone placed it up to her nose, sniffing the strong, funky aroma. "Hell, yeah. This dat true shit." She then put it up to her lips, inhaling deeply several good times, holding the smoke in until she started to choke. Simone tried her best to gain hold of her composure, taking full advantage of the blunt being in her possession. "You watch and see." She hit it once again and started gagging. "The game is on! Ain't no nigga around that ain't gonna serve me and my needs."

Her friend stared at her all of fifteen seconds before she started to complain. "Damn, bitch! Why you gotsta hog all the weed and shit?" Chari started laughing as she snatched the blunt out of Simone's hand and protested. "Other people wanna get high too. Shit!"

Chari was one of Simone's best friends in the entire world and godmother to her son, Li'l T. The two girls had been hanging out with each other ever since the fourth grade at McManor Elementary, when Chari's family moved to the projects from Grove Hill, a small town located in rural Alabama, right outside of Mobile.

While Simone was high yellow in skin tone, with shoulder-length, golden-brown hair and brown eyes, Chari was just the opposite. The hot Alabama sun had been generous with touching her already-extra-dark chocolate complexion. Chari wore short dreadlocked hair, and her skin was overly cursed with acne, which always brought constant ridicule from the fellas as well as most of the females she would encounter. Her best friend, Simone, didn't make it any better by always behaving like she was the real showstopper. Chari was content in playing the background position and was disgustingly loyal to Simone. She didn't mind playing the demeaning role that she was assigned in life. Chari admired her friend and loved listening to her brag about her so-called *skills*. It often passed the time away while they were getting fucked up. But the truth be told, deep down inside, Chari really felt sorrow for her misguided friend.

Simone struggled to talk, still choking as she laughed at Chari. "Be past careful, girl; don't be burning up my shit with them ashes." She made sure to watch her friend like a hawk. It took her two long solid months of begging and major ass kissing to get her new furniture. No matter how much crap she talked, bottom line, she knew her furniture would have to last for some time to come. No telling when Simone's money train would pull out of the station, leaving her high and dry and flat broke, looking for the next man in line to pick up the slack.

Out of the clear blue sky, Simone jumped up, running over to look out the huge picture window. With the rattling noise of the metallic blinds in her ear, she carefully searched the block for any signs of movement. After peeking out, scanning the premises and not seeing jack, she went back and plopped her body on the couch. The weed had taken over, having Simone posted on paranoid status, thinking that she was hearing things.

"Dang, I swear a bitch thought I heard somebody calling my name," Simone snickered as she finished her speech. "These trees must got me gone. Anyway, Chari, now, like I was saying, as long as I got Li'l T, then a bitch gonna get tore off, that's a given. You feel me? In between Joey damn near furnishing this crib and Kamal paying my car note on a monthly basis, I'm tight. Please believe."

***

Simone's tiny son had taken his first steps, celebrated two birthdays, and was smart for his age but was still somewhat confused over which one of his mommy's boyfriends, who always took turns sleeping in her bed and lying on top of her, was his true biological father. Simone taught Li'l T to call both of them Da-Da, and while not fully understanding one way or the other, he did as he was told. Joey and Kamal both showed Li'l T unconditional love whenever they would be around, and that was all that mattered to him in his little corner of the world.

The entire nine months of Simone's pregnancy, from conception to delivery, she had both Joey and Kamal running around catering to her every whim or desire. Whether it was an all-expense-paid shopping spree at the local upscale mall or fresh shrimp and lobster meals, it was done. Trips to the day spa to get a full-body massage, including her swollen feet being rubbed, Simone had them both going in circles to please her. She constantly reminded them the reason she was so fat and uncomfortable was that she was carrying their seed. Simone was out cold rolling the dice in the potentially fatal game she was playing. When she got the results from her ultrasound, she, unfortunately, found out it was going to be a boy she would give birth to. She had to think quickly to maintain the game that she had started. The closer her due date got, the pressure was building. Joey or Kamal didn't have any children, making Simone's baby their first. She knew for a fact each of them would most certainly want his firstborn son to bear his name and carry on their family legacy. In any other normal situation when a female was pregnant, married or not, naming the baby was no big deal. Yet, nothing was ever easy when it came to Simone and her fast-paced, confusion-filled life.

After weeks of thinking and scheming, she devised the perfect cover to secure her future. She explained to the two devoted expectant fathers that she wanted to name the baby Terrell Harris. That would be after her loving father, who had tragically passed away when she was just a little girl. She even managed to shed a few tears, looking sincere as a fuck when she told the sad, fictitious lie to each one. The crazy reality was, Simone never once met her father or even knew who the buster was, for that matter. She acted her ass off royally, deserving an Academy Award for Best Dramatic Performance in a Baby Daddy Lie.

Touchdown! After all the plotting that Simone went through, it paid off, working like a charm. It had to. Her cash flow and everyday survival depended on it. Joey was the first one to give in to her emotional request (code name for *lie*). He was easy. His devotion for Simone was true. The things that he did for her and Li'l T were strictly out of love. The day that Simone and the baby were due to be released from the hospital, Joey spent more than a couple of thousand on bottles, diapers, and cases of formula. He purchased a brass canopy crib fit for a little prince and enough clothes for an entire room full of babies. Joey vowed that his son would want for nothing. Simone, being the woman that carried his seed, would, of course, reap the benefits, receiving the same treatment as their son. She was undeniably living on easy street.

Joey offered to marry Simone so they could be a real family, but she flat-out refused the proposal after finding out that Joey's elderly parents would be living with them. There was no way that Joey was going to leave his folks, who were both sickly and needed him. They'd made sure to give him the best education they could afford. Always taking him to museums, art galleries, and other cultural events to ensure that he was well rounded and responsible, Joey's parents gave him everything they had. Now was his time to repay their loyalty, and the type of man he was, doing that was not a problem but a privilege.

Kamal, on the other hand, was stubborn, meaning Simone had some heavy begging to do to finally change his one-track sinister mind. He wanted the baby named Kamal Isa Jeffries Jr., after him. Period. Point-blank. He was way on the other side of the meter from Joey when it came to showing any form of compassion. If enough money was involved, he'd smack up, spit on, and rob his own dying grandmother of her last gasping breath. He was spiteful, stingy, and hard-nosed.

Simone believed the fact that both his parents were drug addicts caused him to be so mean-spirited. Late one night after getting overly intoxicated, Kamal even let it slip out that he and his younger sister were both born crack babies, which definitely explained his mind-set. She was happy that she'd never met either one of his parents, knowing they were the reason for most of his erratic behavior. A loose cannon from first conception, Simone would always have to bring her A-game when dealing with Kamal. The hustle was rough as hell, but the final payoff was always fucking gravy. Simone always got her way, even if it took an ass kicking to make it happen.

"Girl, what you gonna tell Li'l T when he gets older and shit? He's gonna want to know the truth, then what you gonna say?" Chari was honestly concerned for her godchild's well-being and safety as she reached on the table, putting the blunt in the ashtray. She adjusted her body in the chair, relaxing as she stared at Simone so she could hear her friend's response clearly to the question. "Then what?"

"Don't worry about all that. By the time that bullshit jumps off, please believe, I should be pushing a brand-new car every season, living in a plush, lavish condo uptown, and my pockets on swoll. Let me run this, Chari!" Simone rolled her eyes while sucking her teeth, twisting her neck. "Just get ready to ride in that new Lex, all right, bitch?"

Chari hated to doubt her girl or her skills, but she knew that Simone was living foul as a motherfucker, and misery was lurking around the corner, waiting to pounce on her. "I ain't mad at you. Simone, I swear to God," Chari insisted, raising her left hand up. "I'm just worried about Li'l T and how his feelings will be hurt when this lie hits the fan." Her facial expression was full of doom as she frowned at the thought of the outcome: *Everything in the dark comes to the light sooner or later.*

"All right, Ms. Worried. Stop sending all them bad vibes my way. You blowing my dang-gone high. How about I see if I can get a babysitter, and we go down to the club tonight?" Simone was trying to change the subject and get Chari off her back. "You need to loosen the hell up."

"You right, Simone. I know I'm tripping." Chari tried to act as if she was done with the subject. "I'm gonna call Prayer's behind and see if that jealous Negro she lives with will let her hang out."

Both girls gave each other a high five as they clowned their friend. "Yeah, he do be acting like her damn daddy," Simone laughed as Chari grabbed her cell phone out of her purse and started to dial Prayer.

"But for real, for real. I do wish I had a man like Prayer's. He really loves her." Chari smiled.

"Whatever," Simone replied with a sarcastic tone as she picked up the cordless phone off the charger, disappearing into the kitchen. She then swung open her well-stocked stainless steel refrigerator, checking how many juice boxes Li'l T had left while calling her young neighbor, Yvette, who lived just across the street with her nosy foster mother.

Any time Simone needed a babysitter on short notice, the impressionable girl was Johnny-on-the-spot and eager to please. Yvette looked up to her fly neighbor Simone. With all the high-priced cars and trucks that frequently pulled in and out of the driveway, and not to forget all the designer hand-me-downs Simone spoiled her with, Yvette loved being at the house. Whether it was washing dishes, cleaning Li'l T's toy-filled room, changing his dirty Pull-Ups, or braiding his hair, the orphaned teenager would rush right over to do her undeserving hero a favor, despite her foster mother's disapproving glances. Ms. Holmes seemed to have a third eye when it came to seeing Simone for what she truly was: trouble brewing.

"Hey, Simone," Chari yelled into the kitchen, "Prayer said that ol' boy is out of town, so she'll be over in about an hour or so." Chari was always happy when all three of them went clubbin'. It gave her someone to talk to when Simone would pull one of her all-too-famous disappearing acts and turn into a ghost. Simone was good for meeting some wannabe ballin' dude at the bar, getting invited to VIP, and leaving her friends' ass out to dry.

"Oh, dig that. That's tight. Yvette's young behind is on her way over, so let me get Li'l T up from his nap. Plus, I have to call Joey and see if he's going to hang out tonight or what." Simone came back into the living room, starting to gather up stuff to put in an oversized Coach purse, which doubled as her son's overnight bag.

"Dang gee, Simone, I thought, you, me, and Prayer were just hanging tonight," Chari questioned with a disapproving frown plastered on her face.

Simone did a double take at her girl, immediately stopping dead in her tracks. Steam appeared to be rising from her head as she leered maliciously at Chari. "Listen, you big crybaby, if Joey and his boys show up down at the club, we all three gonna get free drinks." Simone threw Li'l T's stuff down on the coffee table out of frustration. "So unless you got some other fools to sponsor our black asses, shut the fuck up and get ya behind ready. How 'bout that!" The room grew silent as Simone stormed out, marching into the bedroom to get her son up and ready to go over to Yvette's.

That bitch must be freakin' nuts! Simone thought as she harshly shook Li'l T awake from his peaceful nap. It was no way in Miami heat hell that Ms. Simone was going to let any opportunity to eat, drink, or party on someone else's fat pockets slip by. If Chari wanted to stay home and miss out on the fun, then so be it. That would be her fucking loss. Simone was about her business when it came to getting over. If it was ladies free before ten o'clock, then you better know that Simone was walking in at nine fifty-nine on the nose. She was always down for whatever, especially when it wasn't costing her a damn thang.

"Hey, wake up, Terrell." She grabbed his little arms.

"Yes, Mommy." Li'l T began to cry from being instantly snatched out of his teddy-bear, candy-land dreams.

"Come the hell on and help Mommy get your things so you can go bye-bye with Yvette."

Li'l T was still half-asleep as Simone stood him on his feet, forcing him to walk on his own. Still considered just a baby, he wanted to fall out on the floor, whine, and kick about being too sleepy to move but was wise enough to know that his mother, Simone, didn't play that shit and would smack his hand, or better yet, his behind.

Li'l T would have been considered a blessing and godsend to most parents, but to his mother, she saw him in a much different light: a meal ticket! The two baby books Simone kept with both Joey and Kamal's names listed as the "daddy" was proof positive of that messy, underhanded shit.

Misunderstood Chari, still motionless, alone in the living room, finally quietly sat back in the chair without muttering a single solitary word as she listened to Simone bark orders to her son. She knew, once again, that her friend was right about the night.

I guess the fellas should come. Free is free!

Chapter Two

It was almost eight o'clock in the evening when Prayer was pulling up in the long, gravel-filled driveway, bouncing her man Drake's, brand-new, triple-black Range Rover that was sitting on 22s. The sounds were on bump, causing the windows in Simone's house to vibrate from the bass while all the neighborhood kids stood wide-eyed and amazed at the spinners. They swarmed around to gawk while dancing to the sounds of the music playing. It was a typical scene out of a deep-down-in-the-dirty rap video with everyone snapping their fingers, even Granny.

"Ooow weee! That's my truck!" one kid yelled.

"No, it ain't; it's mine!" screamed the next.

Chari happily ran on the porch and out to the sidewalk greeting Prayer. "Damn, chick, when did y'all get this? This shit is hot to death! Y'all two done moved up in the world like George and Weezy!"

"Girl, stop bugging. It ain't nothing but another crazy bill to pay." Prayer laughed, stepping out of the truck. "Another way for Drake's crazy ass to floss. You know how he do."

Chari completely tuned out her friend trying to downplay the sweet ride she was gripping and continued to jock. No matter what Prayer said to Chari trying to change the subject from the new truck, they both had to agree that it was the shit, and Drake had truly outdone himself this time. Prayer never bragged about her house, wardrobe, or money. She didn't have to. Her shit spoke for itself. This female didn't have to put on airs of superiority or degrade the next person to make herself feel better. She was living her life the way Simone dreamed about, which is probably the reason the two hardly ever got along. Simone was secretly bitter and insecure when it came to Prayer, who was equally as pretty as Simone but carried herself with a lot more class.

"Girl, stop all that fooling and come give me a hug." Prayer opened her arms, running toward Chari. They both smiled as Chari continued praising her girl. Prayer was rocking a pair of bright white hip-huggers that showed off her shape, a tight-fitting tank top with flashy rhinestones across the chest that spelled out "Diva," and a pair of raw gator sandals. Her toes were perfectly manicured to match her nails. She had a Christian Dior purse on her shoulder, and her hair was fierce. The girl stayed on point and couldn't be faded.

"Now, *that's* what's really up, Prayer. You keep you some fly gear on ya butt." Chari waved her hand around, snapping her fingers twice as the two walked up the stairs, entering Simone's front doorway.

Simone had been standing in the bedroom window, watching Prayer pull up, fuming with hatred from the whip Prayer was driving and the way Chari, who she thought was her private flunky, was kissing Prayer's ass. Simone wanted to see exactly what Prayer was wearing so she could try her best to outshine her. She tore through her closet like a tornado, searching for an outfit that would make both Chari and Prayer jealous. Unfortunately, the last few days that Simone tried on her clothes, nothing seemed to fit the way she liked for them to.

Damn, I need some new gear! Them hoes done seen most of this shit. Forget Li'l T. From now on out, I'm buying for self!

Simone snatched up her phone off the bed, dialing Joey's cell number. After three or four rings, he answered.

"Yeah, what's good, Simone, baby?"

"What took you so long? It was about to go to voice mail." Simone rolled her eyes to the top of the ceiling as she paced the room. Her frustration in not finding an outfit was getting taken out unfairly on an innocent Joey.

"Is something wrong with my li'l man?" he quizzed. "Is my son missing his old dude? Put him on the phone."

"Naw, nigga. Don't play yourself. He ain't even here. Yvette just came and swooped his little bad butt and took him across the street. She's keeping him until I get back."

"Where is you going?" Joey instantly got pissed. "And why you calling me going off? What the fuck is your problem?"

"What, now I can't call you unless it's about my son?" Simone whined, sensing Joey's anger.

"Don't you mean *our* fucking son?"

"Whatever, Joey! You know what the hell I mean."

Simone was now offended and started yelling at him. "Me, Chari, and Prayer's stuck-up ass are going out later, and I ain't got shit to wear. Most of this stuff I got is way too tight." Simone quickly eyeballed her clothes. "You always talking about you love me and your son so damn much, then why a bitch ain't got no gear? Can you tell me that?"

"What did you just say?"

"You heard me, Joey. I ain't gonna repeat my damn self."

"Hold the fuck up! Is *that* why you blowing up my phone, 'cause you can't decide what to wear tonight to some club?"

"And?"

"Damn, Simone, why you have to act so fucking childish all the time? That shit ain't even cute."

"Oh, and I guess I'm acting childish when a bitch be on her knees sucking your little dick too, huh?"

"Dig that. You got jokes and shit," Joey huffed as he grabbed his nuts. "Ain't shit little about this monster in my pants!"

"Naw, that ain't no joke, boy. You think you just gonna keep knocking the value off my body and a bitch don't get shit outta the deal except a soaking wet pussy?"

"What you mean nothing? Simone, who do you think paid for that new, expensive furniture your ass over there par-laying on? The fucking couch fairy?"

Simone sighed. "Damn! Why don't you stop tripping?"

"Naw, Simone, let's keep it real," Joey insisted. "Didn't I just buy your ungrateful butt $450 worth of stuff?"

"When? What you talking about?"

"You know the fuck when! Don't play dumb. Down at ya girl's spot from around the way. Don't front."

"Oh, that shit don't count. Nigga, you wanted to see my fine ass poured into those panties and hookups."

"However you want to put it, Simone, a guy still dropped that loot! So be easy and chill the hell out."

Joey and his crew were posted at the park, enjoying the summer sights of females running around half-naked. From the tiny shorts that barely covered their butt cheeks to the thin material tops that showed their braless breasts bouncing up and down, the guys were in heaven. Most days, it was like being in a strip club without the pole or high-priced, watered-down drinks. A brother didn't even have to come out his pockets to tip and still see plenty of ass. At Chandler Park, anything goes.

Joey was one of those rare exception-to-the-rules-type of brothers that a chick always daydreamed about but never actually ran into. No doubt, hell, yeah, he'd look; the guy was human, but he never crossed the line. Joey loved spending time with both Simone and his son, Li'l T, but he was growing increasingly tired of her out-of-the-blue tantrums and outrageous demands. Besides, his boys thought Simone was nothing more than a sac-chasin' slut and often made their feelings known. Joey constantly heard the rumors circulate about Simone and her wild behavior but still didn't care. He trusted her. She was, after all, the mother of his son. Simone often pressured him for money and gifts, but enough was enough! He was starting to feel like her little Do Boy.

When Joey originally met Simone at one of the after-hours spots she hung at, he was fully aware of the many challenges he would have to overcome to satisfy a woman like her. Even though he was stressed out much of the time, aggravated by Simone's sharp tongue and the barrage of insensitive words that flew out of her mouth, he genuinely loved her unconditionally.

Simone was glad that the huge flat-screen television in the living room was on the music channel, so her friends wouldn't be all up in her business while she was getting her beg on. "Listen, Joey, I ain't being childish, and don't talk to me like that either! I don't have shit to wear," she fumed. "I bet you rockin' some fresh gear. Do you want ya baby's momma walking around the streets looking busted?" Simone was trying to sound sexy as she slowly convinced him for some money to go shopping. "Please, daddy! I love you! I love you! I love you!"

"All right, then, Simone, I tell you what," Joey remorse-fully replied. "Meet me down at the club later and I'll give you some loot. Now, peace!"

***

Joey usually made Simone sweat it out a little bit longer before he would agree, but he had to rush her off the phone. He gave in a lot quicker when he spotted a caravan of six different-colored F-150s turn into the park's entrance. Simone and her bullshit had to be put on the shelf temporarily. Joey and his crew had been beefing on and off with these dudes all summer long over the Brewster Housing Projects and who could or could not sell drugs there. The uncontrolled violence was steadily increasing with each passing month. They all stayed on the six o'clock news doing ambush-style slayings. The trucks took their time cruising the perimeter of the main strip, giving everyone, especially the females, time to jock them. Joey and his boys perched back on their rides, trying to play it cool. Their hands were tightly gripped on their pistols, which were concealed by the oversized T-shirts that they wore. The hot, scorching sun beamed down, causing an already-tense situation to get even hotter.

All six trucks slowly pulled onto the main strip of the park and eased in the direction of Joey and his boys. Joey could feel his heart beating extra fast the closer they got. He cautiously kept his eyes focused on each dude that occupied the passenger's seats. If something was gonna jump, nine out of ten times, they'd be the shooter. The air was extremely dry, and there hadn't been a breeze blowing by in hours. Everything was still as if Mother Nature had advance warning of trouble.

"These fools act like they want some. Y'all fellas be on point," Joey advised his crew and his right-hand man, who stood by his side.

"I'm on it," Trevon whispered under his breath as he waited with anticipation. "They don't want none!"

The first five trucks eased past without incident. It was the first time that each crew really had the chance to get a good look at one another in the daylight. The driver in the last F-150, which was royal blue with gigantic tires making it sit higher than the others, took his time to mean mug Joey's entire crew while smiling, nodding his head to the music that he was pumping. His sinister grin showed off his gold fronts. He stared extra hard and winked his eye at Joey, and then—*Bam!* Everything from that point on went in serious slow motion. Chaos and havoc checked in, taking complete control over the normally quiet summer afternoon at the local park. The calm day was ruined.

Oh, shit! What the fuck!

Just as the truck had almost turned the bend, two guys rose up out of the flatbed and started shooting in the direction of Joey and his crew. One of them was huge in stature with long, thick cornrows that reached his shoulders. He and another skinny dude had fully automatic weapons and were spraying bullets into everything that moved, hopped, or skipped. Pandemonium took over the strip and the main park entrance as cars rushed out.

Joey and his boys barely had time to dive under their cars and take cover. With their faces pressed on the germ-infested pavement, each prayed not to get hit. The bullets were flying, hitting garbage cans, parked cars, and empty baby strollers that mothers had abandoned. As they searched for refuge from the terror that was taking place, Joey and his crew were trapped at a disadvantage, never having time to return fire.

Simone slammed the phone down. *Now, that's what's up! I knew that punk-ass nigga was gonna reconsider and give in. I just gotta play this shit off.*

Focusing back on the problem at hand, she glanced in the closet, finally deciding to put on a multicolored strapless sundress and a pair of slip-on Jimmy Choo mules. The hookup wasn't new, but Simone was gonna front anyway. After putting on her makeup, she did a double check in the full-length mirror, admiring herself once more before making her grand entrance to join her friends in the living room.

"Hey, Prayer, when did you get here? I didn't see you pull up. I was in the back talking to Joey's whining self. His crazy ass is trying to take me on a shopping spree." Simone was trying her best to sound convincing as she strolled in the room. "I told him that I was hanging out with my girls and would see him at the club later. That guy know he be sweating me."

Simone's acting job was amusing to Chari and Prayer. They had both seen the curtains in the bedroom moving before they came in, and they knew Simone was watching them like a hawk. Plus, Simone was not the quietest person in the world. Even with the television on, they could hear her begging Joey for money. They were her friends, so they let Simone keep her dignity and listened to her lies. They could have easily humiliated her, but Chari and Prayer weren't built like that. It was more Simone's cutthroat style to kick a person while they were down.

"Hey, Simone, I love this couch. This shit is butter soft. He's got good taste. Did Kamal pick this out by his self?" Prayer rubbed her hands across the leather material as she grinned, changing the subject.

"Hell, naw. Kamal's crazy behind ain't picked out nothing. Joey bought this for me. You know I got Kamal's behind on car note duty," Simone announced proudly, poking her chest outward. "Matter of fact, I'm thinking about upgrading from my Lexus, maybe getting a truck or something. What y'all two skanks think?"

Once again, Simone was fronting. Chari and Prayer looked at each other and smiled. They knew that their friend's tall tales were just beginning for the night.

"One day I'm gonna school y'all two on playing these cats. God put dudes on this earth to serve females like myself. Kamal and Joey are both running around here on my chain. Me and Li'l T is living hood rich." Simone continued talking cash shit, holding court again. "It's a hard job pimping these Negroes, but somebody has to."

Prayer, finally having had enough of Simone 101, cut her off in mid speech. There was only so much she could take of Simone's annoying voice and nonsense before she needed a stiff drink.

"In my opinion—"

"Girl, it's getting late. Let's be up and out." Prayer grabbed her purse and keys, heading toward the door. "I'm ready to get my dance on."

Chari was glad that Prayer suggested they break camp, and she followed her outside, leaving their girl Simone standing in the middle of the living room by herself.

Simone, being Simone, had to get the last word in. "I was 'bout to tell y'all hoes to hurry up," she informed them while grabbing her purse and locking the door before catching up.

"Just come on, girl." Prayer waved.

Chari ran across the lawn and up to the Range Rover, calling out shotgun like a little kid. Prayer clicked the remote, unlocked the doors, and started the truck, all in one movement. The music came on full blast as the girls climbed inside.

Simone was trying to act all high post and didn't even acknowledge the new truck. Although she was heated that she would have to play the back seat, she tried not to make a big deal about it. Fake-ass Simone really did wanna ride in Prayer and Drake's new truck. Who wouldn't? All bullshit aside, no doubt about it, the Range Rover was cold as a motherfucker—even the back seat. Holier-than-thou, good-hatin' ass, pissed-to-see-the-next-bitch-do-better Simone couldn't deny it even if she tried. But to let those simple, complimentary, ass-kissing words slip from her mouth for the next bitch to actually hear—especially Prayer? Oh, hell to the naw! Forget about it! Next!

Chapter Three

Joey and his friends slowly crawled from beneath their cars, checking to make sure that no one was hit. Even though they had their hands on their pistols, not one of them had expected them boys to open fire in broad daylight in the middle of a park, or be brazen enough to lie down in the back of a flatbed.

"Man, them dudes is crazy, doing that old gangsta-type shit out here with all these kids running around." Joey was heated as he looked over at the swings, thinking about the fact that his precious son could have been on them and killed by a stray bullet. "Them punk bitches got holes all up in my ride. And look at my motherfucking windshield!" He walked around his car and couldn't believe his eyes.

"You right, Joey. We gonna have to seriously deal with them cowards," his boy Trevon screamed, wiping the sweat off his forehead. "Who the fuck do they think they are, coming on our side of town with that crap?"

"Man, that shit was too close. We gotta sit down and figure out a plan that's gonna make them rat-ass busters catch it." Joey started brushing the dirt off his clothes and surveying the scuffs on his new Air Force Ones. He then reached his hand inside the car, putting the key in the ignition. "Let me see if this bitch gonna even crank."

After three good tries, the bullet-riddled car shockingly started. Joey smirked. "I'm gonna bounce to the crib, shower and change into something else, and switch rides.

Let's meet down at Bookies later on and start plotting on them fools. After this, a brother straight needs a drink. Besides, I gotta hook up with Simone anyhow."

His friends gave him a straight dirty foul look as soon as he mentioned Simone's name. Her name was the last one they wanted to hear right about now. Each knew she didn't truly give two hot shits about their homeboy. They started to call Joey out and talk mad shit about her, but they'd all had a rough afternoon and were ready to get out of Dodge before the police came around questioning everyone at the park.

On the way driving home, Joey couldn't help but to think about the driver of that royal-blue truck and the way he had looked at him. Something wasn't right with the whole way shit went down.

Joey turned his sounds down as he buried himself deep in his thoughts. *Damn, I know that guy from somewhere other than the streets, but where? I gotta figure that shit out! But right about now, the first thing on the agenda is to get home and change.*

The line for valet was twisted clear around the corner. Bookie's was off the chain. It seemed like everyone who was anyone was trying to post up in the club. The long wait gave the trio of women time to flirt with all the guys walking by and see who was driving what. That would cut down on time inside the club trying to figure out who was broke as shit and who was really getting that paper.

Even though Simone was pimping the backseat, she was still geeked. They were getting mad major props from all the fellas and cold-blooded animosity from the envious females.

"Damn, I have never waited this long for valet." Prayer shook her head while maintaining her place in line and a tight grip on the steering wheel. "It's obvious that it's crowded. Fuck this line!"

"Yeah, girl, it's packed in there. Do y'all chicks wanna head somewhere else?" Chari added her two cents.

Simone wasn't trying to hear none of that and was the first one to respond. "Dang, it ain't that long. Y'all should be happy. It's some ballers up in there. I'm 'bout to get my mack on, so y'all hoes chill!"

Simone was on a mission to convince Prayer and Chari to be a little bit more patient and go inside. Yeah, true enough, there were a few guys that went inside Bookies dressed to impress as if they were slinging that shit, so of course, that alone was reason enough for her to go in. Yet, first and foremost, Joey was gonna meet her in there, and there was no way in hell Simone was gonna miss out on getting the loot he'd promised her earlier. Simone was going inside the club to wait it out for her money even if it meant she had to jump out of the moving truck and go in that bitch solo.

After a few more minutes passed, the girls made it to the front of the line. Prayer had a bootleg mix CD blasting as they rocked their heads from side to side. All eyes were, without a doubt, on them. Simone was basking in all the status they were getting from pulling up in a pimped-out new ride. Prayer pumped the brakes repeatedly, causing the Range Rover to dance before they screeched to a halt. Part two of the *Dirty South* video was happening as everyone leaned with it to the sounds that were blaring

The guys working valet, as well as the people standing out front, were staring and smiling as the trio of ghetto diva superstars made their exit from the truck. Simone and Chari both stood beside the truck, holding shit down in the spotlight while waiting for Prayer to give the valet her keys.

"Here you go." Prayer slid him ten extra dollars to park her shit up front. "Put my truck at the doorway, sweetie!"

"Not a problem! Y'all ladies have a nice evening." The valet couldn't wipe the silly grin off his face as he watched the three walk away.

Chari, Simone, and Prayer marched to the front of the line with confidence. No sooner than the bouncer saw them approaching, he pushed open the door. They were all regulars at the club. The manager of Bookies knew that every time Simone was in the house, guys would buy her and her girls top-shelf drinks. He anxiously anticipated making a lot of money from the bar. She was good for business. Simone might have been reckless when it came to treating her friends with respect, but flat-out, she was a true hustler. No one could knock her ability to play the game.

When she put her mind to getting something, she usually achieved her goal. Simone was so good at talking junk, dudes would be popping bottles until their money ran low, and then she'd oftentimes abandon them where they stood, moving on to the next fool in a matter of minutes before the first asshole even knew what had happened.

The club was almost packed to capacity, and the crowd was hyped. Simone took the lead as they cut across the dance floor, making their way to the bar. Until Joey got there, she had to find another sucker to buy her a drink.

"Come on. Let's go to the other side of the room." Simone was smooth flowing in and out of the sea of people. "Hey, it looks like those guys who were bouncing that red BMW in front of us are standing over in the corner. I'm gonna see if I can get on."

"Dang, why don't you slow down?" Chari asked.

"Just hurry up before some other ho beats me to the punch." Simone frowned back at her friends.

Prayer was also trying to keep up with Simone and finally gave up. "Chari, forget chasing her ass to try to get a free drink from some losers. I ain't got time for that. I got us."

"Good looking out, Prayer. You can just order me an apple martini with two olives."

"That's sounds good as hell. I'm gonna get me one too." Prayer squeezed her small frame up to the bar to order both their drinks as she watched Simone push up on the guys, trying to work her magic.

Chari saw some people leaving one of the booths and quickly grabbed the table. She took a piece of tissue out of her purse and wiped it off. Just as she finished and was sitting down, Prayer was bringing over the drinks.

"They're busy as hell at the bar. I just took a napkin full of olives my damn self." She sat down and took a small sip, handing the other glass to Chari. "Damn, this is good."

Chari was preoccupied with staring at a dude that was sitting back at a table across the room. She knew he was out of her league, as fly as he appeared to be dressed, but that didn't stop her from checking him out. From his visible swag and demeanor, he was more Simone's type. Even though he seemed to be flirting back by smiling, Chari was so brainwashed by her girl she wasn't even sure what day it was most of the time when it came to men or relationships. Simone always had a bad habit of stepping in and coming between any guy that showed an interest in her, whether she truly wanted him or not.

Prayer nudged her friend's arm to bring her out of the trance she was in. "Earth to Chari, Earth calling Chari. Come in. Do you hear me? I repeat. Do you hear me?"

"I'm sorry, girl. I was paying attention to something else over there." Chari laughed as she nodded her head toward the guy.

"I feel you. He is a cutie," Prayer agreed.

The two of them sat back, enjoying the music, the atmosphere, and their drinks. Even though it was loud and crowded, they needed the time alone to recover from all of Simone's antics and insults.

"That chick is out of her rabbit-ass mind. How long does she think it's gonna take before that baby daddy shit hits the fan? She can't play the game forever," Chari said, talking about Simone.

Prayer took another sip of her drink, nodding her head in agreement with Chari. "You ain't never lied. Everything in the dark always comes to light. Karma will come around one fucking day, sneak up, and bite that ass every single time."

"I'm just scared for Li'l T because he's so innocent and didn't ask for or deserve any of this mess," Chari added.

"I just know when the shit does hit the fan, he's the one that's gonna suffer." Prayer regretfully shrugged her shoulders as she took another sip. "Simone's ass don't care. Ol' dumb bitch."

Both of the girls' calm and peaceful time came to an unfortunate halt when Simone found her way to the table. Her big BMW mission must have failed, because she was only holding a small glass of cheap wine, but she did have Joey and his boys in tow behind her, so her begging must have been cut short.

"I was wondering where y'all broke hoes were at." Simone was trying to be funny and show off in front of the fellas.

Neither Chari nor Prayer laughed at their so-called friend and her harsh comments. The true fact of the matter was Prayer held a master's degree in business management, pulling in a nice fat paycheck every week, and Chari was a full-time student who still managed to fit in a forty-hour week working at the local mall and vol-

unteered for several different children's charities. Both
girls had more money saved in their own personal bank
accounts than the one-track mind, unemployed Simone
begged from both of her baby daddies combined. Still,
she was their girl, so they put up with her. But you know
what they say: there's only so much a person can take,
then just like that, you snap. If they lived in the animal
kingdom, Simone's half-cooked ass would've been torn
apart and spit out in no time flat.

"We can all squeeze in here. Y'all slide over." Simone
pushed Prayer, who, along with Chari, obliged, making
room in the booth. They liked Joey much more than
they liked Kamal. Joey seemed to genuinely care about
Simone and Li'l T. Yeah, Joey did his dirt like all men do,
but he never tried to disrespect Simone in her face.

Now, Kamal was truly a horse of a different color. Any
time he and Simone would get into it and she got to running off at the mouth, he would kick her ass right on the
spot and take back most of the shit he'd bought her. Her
car would stay on repo from his ass. He didn't care if they
were out in public, in the middle of a busy street, or in
the crib chillin' alone on a Saturday night. It was nothing
to him. Kamal would drag Simone's name through the
mud on a regular with his family and friends. The fact
that she was his son's mother meant absolutely nothing
to Kamal if he was pissed off. Rest assured, he was the
number one poster child for Wife Beater of the Year. He
was legendary around Detroit for whooping a bitch's ass
at the drop of a dirty dime.

"What you ladies drinking this evening?" Joey was
being big spender and treating, just like Simone had
anticipated.

"Apple martinis with extra olives," Chari spoke up.

"Thanks, Joey." Prayer winked.

Simone didn't want to be left out or outdone with the gratitude, so she kissed Joey on his lips to show her appreciation. *Let's see these hoes top this!* she thought as she gave her girls a fake smile.

Joey waved his hand at the waitress several times before finally catching her attention. When she finally fought through the thirsty crowd, making it over to take their order, Simone tried to check her.

"Damn, is it that busy that you keep top-paying customers waiting all night?" Simone made sure to talk extra loud so everyone could hear her blatant attempt to humiliate the young girl. "You must be new."

Joey, Prayer, and Chari looked at Simone like she was crazy with three heads growing out of her neck. She still had half a drink left in her hand that she claimed the fool pushing the BMW bought her when she first came in, so there was no legitimate reason for her to trip or make a scene.

Trevon and the rest of the fellas shook their heads at Joey and laughed. He knew exactly what they were thinking and that they were 100 percent right. Simone had no class whatsoever. It was as if she was raised with no home training, to say the least. Joey didn't want to seem soft. Besides, Simone was out of order and needed a reality check in the worst type of way.

"Simone, why you gotta act such a loud, goddamn fool all the time? What the fuck is the matter with you? Are you high or something?" Joey was pissed off and read her the riot act. "We came here to relax and have a good time and shit. Why you gotta try to ruin it? We almost got killed this afternoon, and your ass worried about waiting ten minutes for a free drink? That's real fucked up!" Joey gave her a long, cold stare, taking a deep breath. "Damn!"

"Whatever." Simone frowned.

Joey then turned to the waitress, who was still standing there, overjoyed that he'd taken up for her. He tore off two crisp hundred-dollar bills, lightly closing them up in her hand. "Here you go, sweetheart. I'm sorry for all the confusion. Now, what's your name?"

"It's Tami." She blushed gleefully as she took the money.

"Well, Ms. Tami, with your cute self, let me get three apple martinis and double shots of Rémy for all the fellas." Joey rubbed her hand. "You can keep the change."

"Thank you. I'm very sorry it took me a while to get over here to you." Her eyes were glued on Joey. "Tonight is kinda packed and—"

Before the young girl could take a cop, she was stopped. "Naw, Tami, baby, thank you." He cut her off. "I know it's busy." Joey went out of his way to be extra nice, flirting with the waitress. He knew good and damn well that Simone would be pissed off to the nth degree.

Tami was happy as she bolted to place their orders, making sure to put a little extra shake in her ass, knowing that Joey was watching. The change from their bill would probably be her biggest tip all night.

Simone was fuming by this time. In a matter of moments, Joey had managed to flip the script on her. She was past being embarrassed, not only in front of Joey's boys, who she knew despised her, but worst of all, Chari and Prayer, the two that she always tried to front on. There was nothing left for her to do but sit there, stick her lips out, and pout like a small child.

As bad as Simone wanted to spit directly in his face and storm out, she couldn't. Joey hadn't given her that dough he'd promised her yet, so she had no choice but to chill. Heated as Simone was about getting disrespected right in her face, obtaining that cash revenue was still first on the agenda, so she tried to sit back and relax.

In no time flat, Tami came back with the drinks on a tray and set them down on the table, making sure to rub her breasts on Joey's arm as she bent over. Once again, Simone sucked it up, but not before throwing shade on the overfriendly, sassy female. Everyone saw the fury on Simone's face as they grabbed their glasses and started to get their buzz on. Each person at the table was happy that she was finally getting a tiny dose of her own medicine. The night had just started, and Simone had already accumulated strike one in Joey's book.

Prayer had heard what Joey said about almost getting killed, and she was concerned. Her man Drake was also deep off into the game. He was on a much higher level than hand-to-hand street sales, thank God, but the risk and odds of him getting knocked or murdered were just as high, if not higher.

"What do you mean you almost got killed?" She hated the violence that always came along with selling drugs, but that was the life that all three—Joey, Kamal, and even Drake—had chosen. The fast money was why Simone was attracted to both of her sons' fathers. Their personal safety came second to her finances. Yet, Prayer's relationship was built on pure love. She had met Drake back in kindergarten before crack was even born.

"Thanks for asking, Prayer. I'm glad someone around here cares if a person lives or dies." Joey made sure to look an already-aggravated Simone extra hard in her face. "It ain't nothing, Prayer. Some cats from the other side of town fell through the park today and called they selves lighting that bitch up."

Trevon threw his hands up and grinned, looking at Joey. "All that shooting and the only thing they killed was a few cars."

"Don't remind me," Joey fumed.

Everyone at the table busted out laughing, except a stone-faced Simone. Her cell phone started to ring. She quickly glanced down at the screen, seeing that it was Kamal.

"Ah, fuck," Simone mumbled under her breath as her heart started to skip a beat. There was no way she could answer the phone in Joey's face. Plus, Kamal would hear the music blasting in the background and bug out because she was at the club hanging without his permission. That type of trouble she didn't need or want, so she decidedly ignored his call.

Let Kamal's lunatic, hotheaded ass leave a freaking message, Simone thought as she sat next to Joey, still agitated by his straightforward act of putting her in her place.

Five minutes later, the phone rang again, but this time Simone didn't even bother to look at the screen. She just disregarded it altogether. *Things are already going bad enough this night. I ain't hardly in the mood for his crap too!* Simone sat straight up in her seat, tapping her fingernails on the table, waiting it out until she could find the perfect opportunity to get the cash that was promised.

Chapter Four

"Damn, Kamal! That shit at the park was off the chain!" Big Ace smiled as he rolled a blunt, thinking about the earlier violence.

"Yeah, you right. Did you see them little bitch-ass fools crawling under they rides like scared little girls?" Kamal was enjoying all the turmoil that he believed he and his crew had caused at the park.

"I'm about to turn on the television to see if that shit made the ten o'clock news," Big Ace announced excitedly as he clicked the remote. "I know it had to."

Kamal agreed with his boy and leaned back on the dingy plaid couch to see just who had suffered injuries from their rampage and assault. He opened a beer and lit a cigarette as he thought about the dude at the park earlier that called himself mean mugging him. The smoke from the Newport filled the air as Kamal squinted.

That nigga acted like he knew me and shit. Like the shit was personal and not fucking business. Where do I know that li'l faggot from?

After waiting fifteen minutes for the news to come on, they continued to watch the broadcast intensely for any mention, but they were disappointed.

"I can't believe that shit didn't make the news." Big Ace coughed as he passed the blunt to Kamal. "I know for a fact that I hit one of them motherfuckers!"

"Fuck it, dawg! It ain't nothing." Kamal inhaled a few good times before passing it back to his boy. "When we really break they asses off, that shit ain't gonna be local. That shit gonna be on CNN breaking news!"

"I'm tired of waiting. Them niggas should have known better than to try to set up camp in our territory." Big Ace slammed his fist in the wall, causing the loose paint chips to fall to the floor. "They got the game all fucked up. Them projects is ours! Nan one of them NFL hoes ain't get our approval to slang in that spot."

"Oh, please believe the hype. The clock is ticking on them hoes." Kamal grabbed his beer off the table, guzzling the rest of it down. "Damn! Speaking of hoes, let me call my baby momma and see where the hell she at. A nigga like me want some pussy."

Kamal rubbed his semi-hard dick with one hand as he dialed Simone's number. After the fourth ring, it was apparent that she wasn't answering. On the fifth ring, her voice mail clicked on, and an enraged Kamal went straight postal on her, using the harshest words he knew in his small vocabulary.

"Listen up, you rotten-mouthed bitch. I know you see my damn number. You best stop playing games with a pimp and call me the fuck back, or when I see you, I'm straight busting that ass!" Kamal was holding the phone in his face, tilting his head from side to side as he yelled into it. "Where the hell you got my son at this late anyway, tramp? Call me!"

Kamal flipped his cell phone closed, tossing it on the floor, causing the clip on the back to break in two. He then took his size 12 Tims, kicking over the two blue milk cartons that served as a makeshift coffee table. He shook his head, glancing slightly over at his boy with a facial expression of disgust. He'd had just about enough of Simone and her slutty ways. It was starting to take a serious toll on him. Although he tried to fuck everything that hopped, jumped, or skipped, he wanted her to be his and only his. Typical of most men in Detroit and every-fucking-where else, even when he would disappear, spending days and nights ripping and running the streets, he was hard on his girl, expecting loyalty.

"You know what, Big Ace? Simone is begging for me to stomp a mud hole in that ass. She be on some other type of bullshit," he complained, rubbing the two-inch long scar on the side of his face.

Big Ace was sick and tired of Kamal always going off on Simone, day after day. To him, it was nothing more than a waste of time. He knew Simone from way back when growing up in the projects, and he had always hated her and her arrogant ways. They weren't enemies growing up, but they sure weren't friends either. They played their little childhood Hide-'n-Go-Get-'Em games, but nowadays, Simone acted like her family never had roaches, never shared their meatless dinners, and didn't have their utilities shut off on the regular.

"For real, though. Kamal, man, no disrespect to ya son. You know a brother gots mad love for Li'l T, but forget Simone. You can't patrol that trick. That shit is in her blood. Her moms was an old-school whore when need be."

Big Ace was with Kamal the night that he'd first met Simone, or rather, won her in a craps game. The low-life guy whose arm she was proudly hanging on was over five thousand in the hole. That's when Mr. Smart-Ass came up with the bright idea to put his woman up for collateral. The out-of-luck gambler saw the way Kamal and every other Negro in the spot was checking her out and decided to take a chance. Three rolls of the dice later, Simone was standing on the other side of the room, property of Kamal. The fact that she would jump ship that easy or not even put up a fight about being disrespected like that by her man should've been a red flag to Kamal, but it was the complete opposite as he began parading his prize around town, even making her wifey. Big Ace tried to warn his boy about Simone from jump, but Kamal wouldn't listen. He had to have her. She and Big Ace had a strange back-in-the-day history, so he knew.

"Man, calm down," Big Ace wisely suggested.

"Dude, I'm telling you I be wan' to kill that bitch." Kamal looked up to the ceiling. "I ain't bullshitting."

"Dig this here. Let's go down to the club and find some real little freaks to get fucked up with." Big Ace tried his best to defuse his boy's anger. As he awaited Kamal's response, he leaped to his feet and started to dance. "Well, what about it, my nigga? How you gonna carry it? You with me or not, playboy?"

Kamal gave his boy some love and nodded. "You right, dude. Fuck that slutbag! Let's get clean and be out! I'll deal with Simone's slimy ass later."

"Good! Now *that's* what in the hell I'm talking about." Big Ace laughed.

After polishing off a second round of martinis, Simone, Chari, and Prayer started drinking shots with the fellas.

"Can you ladies handle drinking with the big dogs?" Joey was fucked up, slurring his words as he raised his glass high into the air. "This that shit ya rookies don't know jack about. That Hen Doggy Dog!"

The entire table was high out of their minds. All the guys were taking their shots like troopers, barking each time their glasses slammed down on the tabletop, while the ladies tried unsuccessfully to hang.

Simone had no choice after downing the third round. She was buzzing like everyone else and back to her normal annoying self. With her dress hiked up past her upper thigh, she was all over Joey, covering his face with kisses and rubbing her curvaceous body seductively on his. She wanted to make it perfectly clear to Tami the waitress and every other chick in the place that Joey was her meal ticket. So, point-blank, hands the fuck off! Anyone that crossed that line tonight would feel Simone's wrath.

The DJ had the crowd jumping and the dance floor packed. He was playing everything from rap and reggae to every slow song you or your momma could think of. When a couple of back-to-back old-school jams played, it was on.

"Hey, does anyone want to dance?" Chari was snapping her fingers, feeling good and lifted. She was ready to get her grind on and didn't care with whom. "Come on, Trevon. Get ya fine ass up and let's do the damn thang."

Trevon was on Front Street, blushing as he took her up on her offer, or rather, demand. He stood up while reaching for Chari's hand. She was busy trying to squeeze past her girl. Simone was resting her head on Joey's shoulder and sticking her tongue in his ear.

"Dang, excuse me. Can a bitch get past you two lovebirds?" Chari giggled as she made her way to the dance floor with Trevon close behind, being a typical man, watching her ass jiggle as she walked.

Simone was getting horny as hell and started rubbing on Joey's throbbing manhood. She was slowly moving her hips to the sound of the music.

"Girl, you better stop playing with a grown-ass man. Do you know what you doing?" His dick was jumping from the pressure of Simone's hand. "You gonna mess around and wake this monster all the way up."

"Yeah, I'm holding on to what's mine. *That's* what I'm doing. Is it a problem, Joey?" Simone licked her lips slowly as she tightened her grip. "And let him wake up! I got something for his ass!"

Joey put his hand on top of hers and moved his shit to the other side of his pants. "Do you want something else to drink, baby?" he affectionately asked. Joey was high, forgetting all about the incident that had happened earlier. His hookup was now hard as a brick, and Simone was wide open, acting as if anything goes. Joey wanted her good and faded so he could get some later without hearing her moan and groan about money.

Simone reached across the table, grabbing Prayer's glass, putting it up to her mouth. "Girl, let me have the rest of this until the waitress gets her slow, ugly self over here."

Prayer didn't have a chance to answer one way or another. Simone was already turning the glass up and slamming it down on the table. Prayer leaned over, putting her arm around Simone. "Listen, girl, you better slow the hell down and behave. Ya behind is way too twisted."

"Whatever, bitch. Stay outta my business. My man bought the drink for ya ass anyhow." Simone dismissed Prayer's legitimate, trying-to-be-a-friend concern.

"Oh, it's like that? You think I couldn't have afforded a five-dollar drink?" Prayer laughed out loud as she waved her diamond engagement ring in Simone's face. "I'm gonna give you a pass on that one, sweetie, 'cause now I see you're more fucked up than I thought."

"Yeah, Prayer, do you and let me do me."

"All right, then, playgirl, roll with it."

"Good! Then that's what's up," Simone hissed.

Prayer was wise and had stopped doing shots two rounds ago. She knew her limitations when it came to drinking. Besides, she had to drive home, and there was no way that she could get even a scratch on her man's new truck, especially hanging out with Simone's good-for-nothing, trifling behind. Drake, just like all of

Joey's crew, hated her. Prayer was glad he was occupied down in B-More on business, so she wouldn't have to get cursed out for spending time with her supposed-to-be friend and caught up in her madness. There was no two ways about it. Simone's name was mud all over town. East to west! North to south! Coast to motherfucking coast!

The music slowed down to a more relaxed pace as a heavily panting Chari finally showed back up to the table. Her face was sweating buckets of perspiration, and her clothes were drenched.

"Damn, it was hot out there! I need some H2O." She fanned herself with her hand, trying to catch her breath. "I'm getting too old to be dancing all hard like that!"

Joey started smiling while passing her a napkin. "It looks like you went swimming and shit. Where's my boy? Did you leave his ass backstroking in the river?"

Prayer, Simone, and Joey joined together in laughing relentlessly at an angry Chari.

"Forget y'all! I'm here to party, not sit around trying to look all cute. Y'all some haters," Chari barked at them.

"Come on, girl, don't trip. We were just playing. Now, come on, let's go to the bathroom and see if we can try to get your shit back together." Prayer got up, pulling an agitated Chari by the arm. "But for real, doe, you look a hot mess!" Prayer was still laughing as Chari continued wiping away the sweat as they merged in with the crowd and found their way to the crowded ladies' room.

With her girls out of the way, a drunken Simone started in on Joey. It didn't matter how many drinks she had in her; when it came to getting her money, Simone would always sober up quickly.

"When you gonna give me my dough?" she whined as she tried her best to manipulate Joey, who was watching her lips move and had one thing in mind. "You promised!" Simone took a sip of his drink and leaned back in the booth, not bothering to cover her mouth when she belched.

Joey overlooked Simone's obnoxious behavior and kept his mind on the bigger picture. "I got you. Don't worry. I got everything you need—and more." He was planning on getting some of Simone's famous head before the night ended. His dick was getting harder and harder. Simone, on the other hand, was starting to feel dizzy.

"Baby, I feel sick. I think I'm gonna throw up," she warned as she put her hand over her mouth, slightly gagging.

Joey jumped up without a second thought. "Well, don't do that shit on me! Why didn't you take ya drunk ass to the bathroom with ya girls?" He was getting fed up with her.

"I'm sorry, baby. Can you please help me to the bathroom? I don't think I can make it."

"Damn, come the fuck on." Joey snatched her up. "Why you always gotta be on that over-the-top crap constantly? Your ass should know better than to mix dark and light liquor."

As he complained loudly, the waitress emerged from the crowd, approaching the table. "Is everything all right?" Tami placed her hand on Joey's shoulder and winked. "Can I do something to help?"

Before Joey could part his lips to respond, a tipsy Simone answered for him. "Listen, chick. We good, all right? Now, for the record, this is my fuckin' man, you skank, two-dollar-tip-gettin' ho. And we don't need shit from ya ass but to keep running them drinks! Now, scram! And stop slow-stalking what's mine! Is we clear or what?" Not waiting for a reply, she kept talking mess. "All up in here looking like a scalawag."

Joey was tired of hearing Simone talk shit and roughly yanked her arm, dragging her toward the bathroom. "You better keep it moving!" she hissed back at the waitress as she held onto Joey's arm. "I mean it!"

"Come your silly ass on, Simone, before you fall the hell out on this floor." Joey tried his best to navigate through the sea of people that were packed into Bookies getting their groove on.

"I'm trying to keep up, Joey."

"Well, try harder."

"Stop bossing me around."

"Girl, shut up and come on. I ain't got time for this."

"What you got time for—that ugly little bucktoothed waitress that insists on riding ya dick?"

"Just come on!"

Joey felt relief when he saw the men's bathroom finally in sight. He was glad she had to throw up because that would mean five minutes of peaceful silence from the nagging sounds of hearing Simone run her big-ass, boisterous mouth.

Chapter Five

"Damn, cuz, this joint is packed." Kamal looked down at his clothes and knew that he was tight. He grinned as he checked his gold fronts out in the truck mirror. "I'm gonna find me a hot one tonight, for sure." Paying careful attention to his surroundings, Kamal then checked out all the cars and other trucks. "Damn, that black Range Rover parked up front is cold. I wonder who's bouncin' that motherfucker. I should check them rims in tonight."

"Dude, I feel you. It's a beast! But on another note, ain't nothing in that spot but wall-to-wall girls, waiting for their daddy." Big Ace smoothed his cornrows out. "I'm gonna be on it."

Kamal pulled his F-150 up on the curb across the street from the club, taking up two parking spaces. He was beefing with so many different cliques, getting blocked in wasn't an option. Just as they'd finished parking and were downing a fifth of gin and finishing off a blunt, two girls strolled past the truck on the way to the club and made sure to put extra pep in their step, hoping to entice the unknown occupants of the truck.

"Hey, baby, bring that phat ass over here!" Kamal was loud and rude as he dangled his body out the window. "Let me get ya number so I can hit them guts later," he blurted out, having the manners of a hog.

The females, who were disgusted, turned back, getting a good look at exactly who the driver was. After seeing Kamal's wicked face, the two immediately sped their pace up in entering the club doors.

"Ain't that those dudes from the park?" one girl asked the other as they paid the cover charge.

"Yeah, that's they crazy asses. That fool Kamal ain't no joke at all." She shook her head, thinking about the harm he could have caused from that park stunt. "He needs to be locked under the jail for that dumb shit him and his reckless crew pulled earlier. Instead, he chilling outside, showboating in his truck like he ain't did shit! That dude is pure evil."

"Girl, I just hope he don't start no mess in here."

"You ain't never lied."

"Damn, it's always some shit in the club."

The guys watched them disappear behind the doors and laughed as they continued to drink and pop Ecstasy pills.

"Man, fuck those freaks. Let's down the rest of this and go in there and find some *real* women," Big Ace reasoned with Kamal, his partner in crime.

After fighting a long line to get into the bathroom, Chari and Prayer took care of their business and were almost back at the table. Before they could maneuver their bodies through the crowd, something caught their attention. They stopped to listen to some girls who had just come in talking about a dude name Kamal, who had shot up the park earlier that day. Prayer and Chari stood in shock and disbelief, not fully comprehending what they'd just overheard.

"I just hope that it wasn't Simone's Kamal they're talking about," Chari whispered to Prayer, holding her arm tightly.

"Girl, you and me both!"

After continuing to listen, they found out that the dude drove a royal blue F-150 and had gold fronts. That was when they knew for a fact that it was, indeed, Kamal. But the most important thing that Chari and Prayer over-heard the two females say was that Kamal and his boy were parked right outside the club and would probably be coming in at any given moment.

"Oh my God! We gotta tell Simone this!" Chari ran across the dance floor toward the table, rudely bumping into people without offering one "excuse me" or "pardon me" on the way.

Prayer was trailing behind Chari, right on her heels, displaying the same disregard for others. "Hurry up, girl." Prayer's heart was pounding from fear. She was scared for Simone, herself, and everyone else in the club that might be caught in the middle of the pandemonium and turmoil if Kamal and Joey's paths crossed and they were forced to lock horns.

They were almost back at the table when the two came close to knocking down a chick that was dressed like a low-income whore on the prowl. The female and her girls acted like they wanted drama. If it had been any other time, Prayer and Chari would've stepped up and granted the bitches their wish, but they were busy trying to save Simone's ass, so they gave them a pass.

When they got to the table, they saw no Joey and no Simone. What they did find was Joey's boys ordering two bottles of Moët, kicking back.

"Hey, Trevon, where's Simone at?" Chari nervously questioned as she scanned the room.

"Simone who?" They laughed. "We don't know anybody named Simone."

Prayer was getting heated, pushing Trevon's shoulder hard. "Man, why don't y'all stop playing? For real, this is serious. Where are Simone and Joey at?"

The guys were rolling over laughing by this point, holding their stomachs. "Damn, Prayer, you trying to go all hard now? Don't front. You know you hate that sac-chaser as much as we do! That backstabber ain't hardly y'all friend!"

Chari and Prayer listened to the words coming out of Trevon's mouth and knew that a small portion of them would gain no better pleasure than seeing Simone suffer, getting what she finally deserved. As much as they would like to stand idly by and watch the fireworks that were sure to take place if Kamal and Joey bumped heads, they stood by their girl.

"Come on, y'all! Stop playing," Chari pleaded with tears in her eyes. "Where are they at?"

"Joey took her drunk, dirt-ball ass to the bathroom," Trevon finally decided to stop clowning long enough to say. "About ten minutes ago."

"We just came from that way, and we didn't see her," Chari yelled. "I need to talk to her. It's important!"

They had to put Simone up on what they'd just over-heard and find a way to get her out of the club. This night was turning out to be some more crazy bullshit in a long list of crap that Simone had tangled her friends up in.

"I just told you where the tramp went, so go look in there for the bitch and stop acting all federal questioning my black ass," Trevon shouted back.

"The line for the ladies' bathroom is too long." Joey hesitated for a second. "You gotta go in the men's. Ain't nobody in there. Come on."

"Joey, I can't go in there," Simone slurred.

"What ya ass gonna do? Throw up on the dance floor?"

"Naw, but—"

"But what?" Joey was getting frustrated.

"Okay, but stay in there with me." Simone's face was fire-engine red.

"I ain't gonna leave ya drunk ass open like that. How you gonna play me?"

Joey put his arms around his son's mother, helping her into the men's bathroom and finding an empty stall. Simone saw the toilet, and almost on cue, she started to spit up all the liquor that was in her system and what was left of her lunch and dinner. Joey was disgusted by the smell but continued to hold her hair out of her face. He firmly gripped it in a ponytail, rubbing her neck as she worshipped the white porcelain god. She didn't hold back one bit as she hawked.

"Thank you, sweetheart." Simone smiled as Joey helped her off the filthy floor.

"I swear I be trying to have you and Li'l T's back." He looked into her eyes. "Why you have to trip on a brother all the time? I let ya ungrateful butt stay up in my pockets. What else you want, huh?"

"I don't know." Simone shrugged her shoulders, regretful for some of her disrespectful actions as she turned the water on in the sink, leaning over to rinse her mouth out from the foul taste of vomit.

Joey was instantly mesmerized by Simone's ass bending over, and he felt his manhood rise again. He wrapped his arms tightly around her waist and slowly started grinding his dick against her. She closed her eyes and didn't protest his actions.

Simone turned to face him, grinning as she grabbed his hand, leading him back in the stall and shutting the door behind them. She unfastened his pants, massaging Joey's throbbing dick with one of her still wet hands while pulling her dress up with the other.

"Come get it, daddy," Simone teased eagerly. "I've been a bad girl, so punish me!"

Joey wasted no time, quickly bending her over, snatching her thong to the side, and ramming all nine inches inside of her warm, moist inners as she squirmed.

"Damn! Damn! Fuck me harder," she begged and pleaded as if they weren't in a public place.

Not showing Simone any mercy, he reached down, grabbing hold of her hair once more, making her scream out his name in pain and sensual passion repeatedly as her body jerked from the powerful force.

After ten minutes of a constant assault on Simone's sore pussy, Joey moaned and busted a nut, removing his still-hard dick. He wiped the head off with tissue and zipped his pants up.

"I'm gonna get some more of this when we get back to your crib." He spanked her on the ass.

Simone was shook up from all the pounding and leaned forward, throwing up again. Her once-flawless makeup and perfect hair was out of order and in serious need of attention that only a female could render.

"I'm 'bout to go get your friends so they can take you in the ladies' bathroom and try to help you." Joey kissed her gently on her forehead and left. "I'll be right back!"

Simone knew she was sick and surprisingly didn't argue. She sat down on the toilet and waited patiently for Joey to return with Chari and Prayer. Several guys came in to take a piss, and Simone didn't flinch or blink an eye. She was too excessively fucked up at that point to care even if Michael, Freddy, or Jason came in the place. One of them would have to kill and drag her body out for her to move.

"All right, player, let's break out." Kamal turned off the ignition and clicked the locks on the F-150.

"I'm right behind you, my dude." Big Ace climbed his 240-pound frame out of the truck and brushed the ashes from the blunt off his pants. "Time to get on."

"Well, then, let's get to it." Kamal threw his hands in the air as they approached Bookies' front door. There was no line outside, and security must've been on break.

An older guy and a woman were coming out and accidentally bumped into an already-high Kamal.

"Guy, is you insane or what? You betta watch ya step!"

"Sorry, friend. My mistake. I didn't see you." The man was overly apologetic, not wanting any trouble.

Kamal didn't give two hot melted shits about the man's remorse. He had to show his ass in front of a female, no matter what age, and hauled off, sucker-punching the man dead in his jaw, causing blood to squirt out. The man fell backward into his woman's arms, resulting in the pair hitting the pavement. The woman started to yell for the absent security but was quickly silenced by Kamal, who smacked her twice across her face.

"I'm not your damn friend, playboy. The next time you come out of a door, pay attention where the fuck you going. Ya follow?" he demanded, pointing downward as he towered over the injured man.

Big Ace and Kamal, showing no sympathy for the couple, went inside the club as they laughed hysterically at the man and his woman, who were both left stunned, shocked, and hurt by what had just taken place.

Once inside the packed walls, they were both patted down and searched for any weapons. The DJ was playing a new song from an up-and-coming rap artist from Detroit named Skillz, and the dance floor was packed. His latest song was causing the partiers to go insane. The club was dimly lit across the rest of the interior, including VIP, but the entrance where Kamal and Big Ace stood was well lighted with high-voltage bulbs. The two friends were immediately forced to take several good minutes trying to adjust their weed-reddened eyes to the sudden change from outside and take in the atmosphere.

***

Chari and Prayer bent the corner, running smack into Joey.

"Oh, snap, I was just coming back to the table to get one of y'all to help a brother out."

"Hey, Joey! Where's Simone?"

"Yeah, we were just looking for you and Simone," Prayer stated, trying not to look suspicious as she glanced over Joey's shoulder nervously.

"Well, you found me." He smirked. "But ya girl is in need of some serious assistance."

"What's wrong?" a puzzled Chari asked, eyeballing the entrance. "Where is she?"

"She's drunk and out of her rabbit. The women's bathroom was too crowded, so I had to take her to the men's." Joey's dick started to tingle, thinking about finishing up what he and Simone had started in the bathroom.

"Oh, that's why we didn't see her pass us." Prayer was, without a doubt, relieved that Simone hadn't stepped out front to get some air and run into Kamal's crazy self. That would've been undoubtedly another murder in The D off rip.

Joey shook off his short-lived daydream. "I left her sloppy ass in there calling Earl until I could locate one of you two to play nursemaid."

"Okay, thanks, Joey. We can handle it from here. We'll get Simone together and meet you back at the table." Chari forced a half smile.

Joey didn't respond to her words as a stern and treacherous expression suddenly graced his face. He was busy focusing on the front door.

Chari's eyes darted back in the direction of the door, and her heart fell to her feet. Kamal and his boy had just come in and were getting searched.

Prayer turned pale, and her mouth got dry, wishing that she had listened to her man, Drake, and not even hung out with Simone's bad-luck ass.

Joey's normally happy-go-lucky demeanor was quickly turning before the girls' eyes. He shuddered with apprehension. "I know that ain't that buster," Joey mumbled under his breath. His total attention was engulfed by Kamal's every movement. If Kamal blinked twice or even farted, Joey would've seen the air blow out of his ass. He was on the guy. Real talk.

Chari was panic-stricken, leaving Prayer and Joey standing there to make small talk. Without wasting any more time, she rushed into the bathroom.

"Simone! Simone!" she yelled in a frenzied manner as if the club itself was on fire. The few guys that were standing up taking a leak never missed a beat, because females were out cold these days and would say or do just about anything. Chari bursting in the men's john was just another part of a typical wild night at the club. They laughed as they left the bathroom.

"Where the hell are you at?" Chari yelled loudly. After looking on the floor and seeing her girl's sandals, she pushed open the stall door and snatched a worn-out Simone to her feet. "We gotta get the fuck out of here!"

"I know, Chari. I'm sick. I think I drank too much."

"Hold tight! Forget what you had to drink. You gonna be sick for real if you don't get your ass out of this bathroom and out of this club," Chari insisted. "You don't know what's going on!"

"Girl, slow ya roll. Just let me sit back down for a few more minutes." Simone stumbled backward, trying to reason with her frantic friend, who was seemingly scared to death.

"Listen good, Simone! Pay attention! I ain't playing around." Chari grabbed her girl's face, looking her dead in her bloodshot eyes, and delivered the harsh news. "Kamal and Big Ace just came in the club! They're here!"

"What?" Simone sobered up on the spot. "What the fuck did you just say?"

"You heard me! Kamal's ill-mannered ass is up at the front door getting searched by security as we speak."

"Oh my God." Simone paced the floor with big alligator tears forming in the corner of her eyes. "Where's Joey?" She was starting to hyperventilate, imagining the awful scenario that was about to become a reality.

"He's talking to Prayer near the front dance floor, but I saw him looking up at the door where Kamal and some big dude is standing."

"Why is he looking at him?" Simone agonized over what the answer could possibly be. "You think he know about Li'l T? Oh, shit! Why this gotta be happening? Outta all the clubs in the city, both they asses in here? What kinda bull is that?"

Chari shattered Simone's world, putting the final nail in the coffin for the night. "I don't know about that, but the other reason we came looking for you is that Kamal is the one they had the shoot-out with earlier at the park."

"What?" Simone put her hand up to her forehead.

"Me and Prayer just heard some chicks at the front door gossiping about it." Chari spoke fast. "And you know the way hoes talk. That shit is about to be all around the club."

"Oh, shit! You right. I gotta get out of here." Simone trembled with fear. "Damn, what am I gonna do now?"

The two girls paced around the men's bathroom.

"Let me go see if the coast is clear." Chari peeked out the door, terrified of what she might see.

Thank God there was no commotion going on. She saw Prayer and Joey ending their conversation, and she signaled for Prayer to come in the bathroom so they could somehow get Simone out of the club without drawing attention to them.

Time was ticking, and the trio had to come up with a plan quick. They could sneak out the back emergency exit to safety. Prayer went to ask the manager if he would do her a small favor and unlock it for them. If they could make it to the truck, they would be safe. The girls didn't have time to worry about Joey and his boys. They could hold their own. Bottom line, everyone had been searched before coming inside, so at least there wouldn't be any gunplay in the club.

Chapter Six

"Is the coast clear?" Simone looked around the corner of the back door exit with her shoes and purse in hand. "Is it straight? Is anybody out there?"

"Yeah, girl, I think it's tight, so come the fuck on and stop bullshitting." Chari had taken complete control of the situation, pulling Simone by her wrist as the two of them ran down the littered, broken-glass-filled alley. "Prayer is driving around to the other side to swoop us."

As much as Simone needed to move swiftly to get out of Dodge, she still found time to complain about running barefoot down the short distance. The girls didn't have time to be cute and keep any overpriced high heels on their feet. They had to keep that shit moving.

"I think I cut my baby toe on something," Simone whined as she climbed into the back of Prayer's truck, lying down across the rear seat.

"Girl, fuck your toe." Prayer peeled out, turning the corner on two wheels. "If any one of them dudes would've came to blows, the first ass that would have been stomped would've been your wannabe-slick butt."

Simone couldn't help herself, and she couldn't just let Prayer get the last word in. She sat up and started screaming. "Listen, bitch, I don't know who the—"

"Lay your dumb ass the fuck back down before one of them clueless idiots spot you and you get my man's new truck shot up." Prayer cut Simone off, not allowing her to get another word in. "You're too old to be still doing this teenage bullshit. I should've left you!"

Chari was bending over, wiping the dirt off her feet before she slipped her shoes back on. "Simone, she's right. You could've gotten one of us killed tonight. And you still don't know if Joey is gonna be all right. You know that Kamal stays strapped."

"Then that's on them, not me! I just hope they don't mention Li'l T." Simone sucked her teeth. "My phone bill is due next week and the water bill. Joey was supposed to give me some loot later on, plus a chick like me planned on getting that new fall collection of Kenneth Cole riding boots in every color. It's the wrong time of season for me to take a loss. And that's for fucking real!"

Prayer had enough of hearing Simone talking petty shit and slammed on the brakes, throwing the huge SUV into PARK mode, causing Simone to fall on the back floor of the truck. "Bitch!"

"What the fuck?" Simone moaned, holding her head that had bumped the side of the door.

"You know what? I'm 'bout tired of hearing your voice. Get your cold-blooded, callous ass out of this motherfucker and find another way home," Prayer hissed, turning around to face her so-called friend, who was dazed.

Chari was in shock at Prayer's demands and tried to be a mediator. "Come on, Prayer, we both know that she's wrong as hell, but she's still our girl. You can't just abandon her out here like that in the middle of the street."

"Oh, yes the fuck I can. I could care less." Prayer clicked the door locks and frowned. "Maybe Miss Big-n-Bad can catch a ride in the ambulance that one of her damn baby daddies will be passing by in, in a few fucking minutes."

"Don't say that," Chari argued at Prayer, not really knowing what was taking place back at the club. "That's not nice to even say. Joey is a good guy, and even though I can't stand Kamal, I don't want his evil ass hurt either."

"Yeah, don't say that, bitch. Why is you hating on my hustle like that and shit?" Simone finally got herself together.

"What you say?" Prayer hissed.

"For real doe, chick, stay outta mines!"

Prayer looked at Chari and smirked, pointing in the back seat of the huge SUV. "You see what I mean? This simple-minded trick tramp don't give two shits about nobody but her damn self. Fuck endangering innocent people. Let me hurry up and drop her no-good ass off back where I found her."

"Don't do me no favors." Simone sat straight up in the seat with no remorse and folded her arms, sucking her teeth while bucking out her eyes. "I'll find a damn way to the crib, and y'all bitches can really stop talking about me like I ain't here."

"Shut up, both of y'all," Chari yelled with frustration, banging on the dashboard. "Damn, shut up!"

With that exchange of words, Prayer restrained herself, putting the Range Rover back in DRIVE. She quickly hit a few dark, remote side streets before jumping on the expressway.

The ride to Simone's house was filled with silence. Prayer concentrated on the road as she wondered how Drake would react if he ever found out about the danger that Simone had put her in. Chari sat dumbfounded in the passenger's seat. Getting chills, she imagined what would be the deadly outcome if Kamal and Joey ever linked up. She silently asked God to watch over everyone back at the club, especially Joey. Simone wasn't the least bit worried about either man, just her game. She pulled out her cell phone and sent a text message to Joey, trying to explain her sudden disappearance. The rest of the time Simone spent trying to fix her hair and search her purse for a breath mint. Unlike the way going to the club, there was no music, no laughter, and no conversation. It was like being the only night watchman down at the local morgue.

I know this ain't the same fool from the park, but it sure as hell looks like him. Joey had the self-control of a predator as he watched every move that Kamal and Big Ace made, from them getting patted down and searched, to the Coke and rum they ordered from the far side of the crowded bar. Joey eyeballed the heavy-set chick stuffed in the cheap red dress that Big Ace rubbed on the ass. He was so mesmerized with them he even started to mimic their mannerisms, forgetting all about Simone and her girls that were still MIA in the bathroom.

"What's the deal, dude?" Trevon snapped Joey out of his trance. "Put a brother up on game."

Joey tightened his grip around the neck of the beer bottle he was holding down at his side. His apparent anger was written across his face. "You know them cats that was pushing them F-150s at the park?"

"Yeah, what about them?" Trevon immediately went on the defensive, scanning the crowded room. He bit his lower lip, awaiting his friend's answer.

"I think that's two of them silly-ass motherfuckers posted over there." Joey nodded his head toward the far left side of the noise-filled club. His teeth were clenched tightly as he spoke with fury. "The guy over there, standing near big girl in the red with the glass in her hand."

Trevon focused in on Big Ace and Kamal. As he joined his comrade in watching the dudes that were just hours earlier trying to take them out of the game permanently, he grew increasingly heated. "Are you sure?"

"Yeah, Tre, I'm sure. The big dude was one of the fucking shooters that raised up, and other homeboy with the mouth full of gold was pushing the blue truck. Trust me. That's them."

"Dawg, I'm 'bout to go over there and give both of they families something to do on Saturday morning." Trevon cracked his knuckles then rubbed his chin.

Joey held his boy's shoulder, trying to calm him down. He tried reasoning with him before things got out of hand.

"Hold up, Tre. Look around. This motherfucker is packed. Plus, we got Simone and her girls with us. We ain't trying to catch no case for them cowards or gamble on getting nobody else hurt. It's a right time and place for everything." Joey raised the now-warm bottle to his lips and took a swig. "Besides, them mark busters ain't seen us yet. I'm about to make a call to the rest of the fellas so they can get down here and post up at the front."

"Yeah, you right, Joey." Trevon grimaced. "But before the night is over, I'm gonna lay them fools down! I ain't gonna just let them come out to the park and gangsta us!"

"I feel you, but just chill out for a few and let me handle this." Joey reached on his waistband to get his cell phone. When he flipped it open, the screen read: ONE MESSAGE. He pushed the tiny envelope button on his phone and started scrolling down to retrieve the message: WENT HOME, STILL SICK.

Joey let out a big sigh of relief when he saw the text message from his son's mother. *Damn, that's one less thing in the mix to handle tonight. Simone's drunk ass would've just been in the way.* As much as they argued and fought like cats and dogs, he wanted to make sure that Simone was ghost and out of harm's way.

A calculated, masterminded Joey let his mind wander all of five seconds before he placed the call to his crew. He knew he'd have to do something quick to handle things before Trevon's fury and aggression blew up and things turned haywire.

Chapter Seven

Kamal gulped his drink down as he surveyed women who walked past. He was definitely way beyond being blasted. Coupled up with the blunt that they'd just finished and the Ecstasy pill he'd popped, he was gone.

"Damn, you got a big booty," Kamal slurred to one. "You wanna come home with a real big-dick pimp?" he questioned another with malice.

Big Ace was a little bit more chill with his high as he pushed up on a thick chick with her huge 38DDs damn near falling out of her dress. You could tell she was out of her shit, too, by the way she was throwing herself all on Big Ace, letting him grab her ass up in both hands. She didn't know him from Adam, but that didn't matter. Kamal and Big Ace had only been inside the club for less than fifteen minutes before the female made her move. Big Ace had everything that she wanted and found attractive in a man: an expensive iced-out chain, a pocket full of dough, and last but never least, a huge print bulging in his pants.

Leaning back on the bar, getting a little light-headed from the combination of all the chemicals in his system, Kamal reached his hand in his pocket, pulling out a semi-crushed pack of cigarettes. After taking one out and putting it in his mouth, he fumbled around, looking for his lighter.

"Hey, man, you got my shit?"

Preoccupied with the overzealous freak, Big Ace didn't hear his partner in crime. His mind was on one thing, and one thing only.

"Damn, nigga, get ya hands off that nut gobbler and see if you got my fire." Kamal was now sweating buckets, looking as if he was gonna fall out.

"Why I gotta be all that?" the female screamed back with her hands planted firmly on her hips.

"You'll be whatever the fuck I say you is." Kamal lunged at the girl, who didn't flinch or blink an eye.

"Try ya luck. I ain't scared of ya crazy ass." She giggled, dismissing him as she would a fly. "Please don't play yourself. You can't hardly even see straight." Homegirl was one of them serious throwback, hard-core project chicks that you only saw in the movies or read about in a good-ass book. Popping gum, way too much makeup painted on, and dirty feet, she ain't have shit, didn't know shit, and wasn't gonna never be shit. All she wanted in life was a big dick inside her every so often, a hot meal once or twice, and a few dollars at the end of the month when shit was tight for her and her three nappy-headed, illegitimate bastards. Well, tonight was that night, and trust, this female was fearing no man! She was ready to come to blows to make sure all her flirting and talking trash paid off. She had hungry mouths at home to feed.

Big Ace stepped in the middle, trying to avoid a scene, and put his arm around his boy. "Listen, dude, you about done had it for the evening. Why don't we jet? We can get some grub; then you can sober up and drop me and ol' girl here off at your crib so I can get my truck."

Kamal looked up and down at the female in the red dress and laughed out loud at her spunk. "I feel you, my dude! This one right here is a wildcat!" He gave Big Ace some love, still dissin' the chick on the humble.

"Yeah, I wanna hit this ho off with a li'l something something!" Big Ace informed his boy on the sly.

Kamal's mind drifted to the thought of getting with Simone later that night. Big Ace's taste was miles different from his. Neither this chick nor any of her big-boned side-kicks that were waving at him trying to get his attention could hold a candle to Simone. "All right, then, dawg. Do you then. It's all good with me."

"Yeah, dawg, you know how it is." Big Ace grinned as he rubbed his manhood. "She about ready for Big Daddy."

The female and Big Ace knew that Kamal was right. Ol' girl didn't even mind Kamal's ugly-spirited insults. It was all part of being "out there." They both planned on getting busy later if things went right, so why not cut out the preliminaries and get down to the business of freaking? Fair exchange was never a robbery. "Pink for green" was her motto.

After the female informed the rest of her sac-chasing friends that she'd hit a lick and was leaving with Big Ace and his boy, the trio started making their way toward the door. Kamal stopped, looking on the other side of the room. A strange feeling came over him. He thought that he was being watched.

For a brief second, Kamal's and Joey's sights locked across the smoke-filled club. Joey was burning a hole through Kamal with his eyes. This was gonna be it. The shit was gonna hit the fan. Simone's big, concocted web of deceit was now just a matter of seconds from being exposed to both men. She was going to wish she had not played the momma's baby/daddy's maybe games that she had.

Joey felt an adrenaline rush seeing Kamal off point from all the liquor he'd watched him and his boy drink. The thought of his car being shot up, his new sneakers being fucked up, and the memory of the sound of terri-fied parents and kids at the park earlier caused him to get an instant migraine.

An intoxicated Kamal paused, trying to regroup. For a hot moment in time, he kinda thought he recognized the dude at the booth, but he shook it off, thinking that he was faded and the X had him hallucinating.

Damn, I need to get some fresh air. I'm seeing things. He took a deep breath. *I gotta get out of this loud motherfucker and try to call Simone's whore ass back anyhow and see why she ain't picking up!*

"Where the hell are they going so damn quick?" Joey had to physically hold Trevon back as they leered at their two nemeses approaching the exit. "Why we just standing here like some suckers? They about to dip!"

"Shit, I know it's no way in hell that J-Rock, Mookie, or Looney Larry is out front posted yet." Joey rubbed his sweaty palms together.

"Fuck it! Let's roll after they asses." Trevon broke loose.

"Come on, Tre, think." Joey was about to break down the science that made him the leader as he stood in front of his hyper road dawg. "Do you really wanna run out of this crowded, witness-packed motherfucker with guns blazing?" Joey raised his eyebrow as he looked at Trevon with an expression that a father would give his son. "Do you wanna be a fool that spends all his stashed money fighting a no-win murder case, and then sits twenty–thirty behind the prison walls, wondering why the hell didn't I slow down and think?" He was on a roll with being the negotiator. "Your people ain't gonna put shit in your account, and that calling collect crap is a wrap off jump."

Trevon grabbed a napkin and wiped the perspiration off his bald head, finally realizing that Joey was making sense. "I guess you right, homeboy."

"I know I'm right." Joey signaled for the waitress to bring another round of shots. "Let them cowards live to see one more sunrise. Just like we just peeped they ass out in this club, they'll be out and about in another spot, and bet money, next time, we'll be ready."

Joey called his crew back, canceling his request to have the front door covered. He informed them that their targets were ghost, and he'd holler later. Joey then suggested they should just continue getting buzzed and try pretending that they didn't even spot Kamal and Big Ace. And considering the fact that Simone and her girlfriends were ghost, Joey could now openly talk shit and do a little harmless flirting with Tami. He made sure to text message his son's mother back before getting all the way loose, informing her that he'd be by her house later on about one or two.

For Simone, it was her lucky night so far, because both of Li'l T's fathers had dodged the bullet and were alive, safe and sound—for the time being.

Chapter Eight

Prayer exited the Lodge Freeway at Livernois and made a quick right onto Dexter. She then placed her tiny sandal on the gas pedal, flooring it until she saw Simone's block. It was a little after midnight, but you couldn't tell from the number of people that were out on Richton Street. It was bad enough the crackheads and drug addicts were out doing what they do, yet, flat-out, there was no legitimate reason for small kids to still be running around, unsupervised, playing dodge ball under the streetlights. In front of Simone's house, sitting on the curb, were some of the same children that had been outside ever since the girls left earlier to go to the club. Prayer had to blow her horn to avoid hitting some of the older, defiant ones. The sound of the truck's horn woke an exhausted, still-half-drunk Simone out of her sleep.

"Dang gee. Is we here already?" She wiped her red eyes and stretched. "That was fast as hell."

"Yeah, it was pretty fast," Chari added, looking back.

"Bitch, it wasn't fast enough. Now, get outta my man's truck and kick rocks," Prayer snarled with her mind still focused on Simone's disrespect of human life. She hit the door locks and pushed the volume button of the radio up on high. She was no longer in the mood to hear Simone's voice or snappy one-line comebacks.

Chari could tell that her friend was not trying to be bothered anymore with Simone, so she just waved her hand and turned completely back around in the seat so as not to jeopardize her ride home.

"Oh, so it's like that?" Simone cracked the door, placing her right leg outside. She dropped one of her shoes on the ground and searched the floor of the truck for the other. Simone then tried yelling over the sounds that were blasting out of the speakers. "Y'all sluts trying to go all hard and shit with a chick?"

After five or so seconds of waiting for a response and not getting one, Simone reached across the seat, grabbed her purse, and climbed out of the truck. The heels of her feet barely touched the concrete before Prayer burned rubber over Simone's shoe and down the crowded block out of sight, leaving her standing on the edge of the curb. Simone bent down, becoming enraged as she tried to pry her shoe's smashed heel out of the ground.

"That bitch," she mumbled angrily. "I oughta kick her prissy ass."

All the shots she'd done at the club still had her dizzy. When she leaned up, attempting to get herself together, Simone lost her balance. The neighborhood kids laughed at her misfortune as she staggered toward her walkway. Before she could put her key in the door, Simone heard a voice yelling her name.

"Simone! Simone!" The voice got louder and more demanding with each word. "You hear me calling you!"

Simone rolled her eyes to the top of her head, turning around to see Ms. Holmes walking down the sidewalk with Li'l T in her arms. "Yes, Ms. Holmes? What is it?" Simone held her composure the best she could.

"What do you mean? This is your son, isn't it?"

"And? So?"

"And just what time did you plan on coming to get him from my house? Whenever you felt like it?"

"I'm just getting home. Give me a break." Simone was quickly reaching her breaking point for the night.

"No, my dear, you give *me* a break and stop pawning your responsibility off on Yvette. He's your burden to bear."

"Yvette likes watching my son. Plus, I paid her little behind."

"If you call filling her head with all type of nonsense about not needing an education to make it in the world 'looking out for her,' then by all means, congratulations. You've succeeded." Ms. Holmes handed Simone her son. "Day after day I watch you and try to find some good in you, but I can't." She slowly shook her head. "It's no wonder that your own mother doesn't want any parts of you."

That was the straw that snapped the camel's back. Simone sat a sleepy Li'l T down in the lawn chair on the porch. She then placed her purse and keys in the empty flowerpot. All the people outside seemed to get quiet as the main attention was now focused on the argument. Ms. Holmes was one of the few neighbors on the block who had the awful misfortune of living in the same housing project Simone did when she was growing up. At one point back in the day, before Simone's mother got saved, she and Ms. Holmes played bridge and hung out together. That was then, but this was the here and now. Knowing Simone as a young girl didn't give her the right to disrespect her as a grown-ass woman, and not to mention on her own front steps—in front of everyone. "Respect ya elders" be damned. Ms. Holmes needed to be checked.

Simone felt her hand itching as she reached back all the way to Mother Africa and made contact with Ms. Holmes's wrinkled face, giving her the business. "Listen, you rumor-starting hag. I done had it up to here with you and all the commotion you keep going on this block."

Ms. Holmes lost her footing, falling to the ground. "I'm gonna call the authorities on you and your bastard son. You've got one hell of a nerve putting your hands on me."

"You've got some nerve always going from house to house telling people's personal business. What about *that?*" Simone felt no kind of sympathy for Ms. Holmes whatsoever. "It's no way in hell I should know all about Mrs. Reynolds's gas being shut off last week or poor old Mr. McKenzie getting fired for drinking on the job." Simone was just getting started. "Oh . . . son of a bitch, I almost forgot about the three abortions that Melody, the preacher's granddaughter, had this year."

Ms. Holmes was trying to get off the ground but was receiving no help from the crowd that had gathered. She was embarrassed that all the gossip she was spreading was now coming back to bite her in the ass. Once again, Karma was alive and well. "Is anyone gonna help me to my feet?" She grabbed for the nearest arm—Yvette, her foster child, who boldly snatched away.

The neighbors whose names Simone had shamelessly mentioned for all to hear disappeared into the dark, returning to their homes to face their demons. The others lowered their heads, hoping that they weren't next on the chopping block. Every-Sunday-churchgoing Patrice, who sucked dick for crack on the regular; Chubbs, the shy, stuttering midget that lived at the corner house who, was Patrice's best customer; and even nine-year-old Denise, who still pissed in the bed nightly, were terrified that their secrets would be blurted out next. No one was immune to the hard-edged sword of insults Simone was swinging. Everyone that made their way to the front of Simone's crib expecting a show got one that would definitely be the talk of the hood for several weeks to come.

"Ain't nobody out here giving a fuck if you crawl your ass back to your porch." Simone turned around, picked

Li'l T up in her arms, flung open her door, and stood sternly with her son posted on her hip. "Now, if you don't mind, I'm about to go in *my house*. The one that *I own—not rent*. So, everyone, please do me a huge favor and remove ya asses from my property before I make a call, and I don't mean the fucking crooked-ass police."

Slamming the door in the faces of her stunned neighbors, Simone carried a sleepy Li'l T to her room, laying him across her king-size bed. She had to use the bathroom and try to get herself together before she undressed him and put his pajamas on. Even with all the confusion that had taken place, Simone was still high. What she needed more than anything else was a good night's sleep.

Prayer turned the radio down as soon as they hit the next block over from Simone. "I can't take any more, Chari. I gotta cut that chick out of my life once and for all, for good."

"I know what you mean," Chari replied. "Each time I try to deal with her and all the drama she brings, I end up getting cursed out. I just hope Joey's okay."

"Well, this time is the last time for me hanging out with her. I don't know about you, but I have to look out for my best interest. Simone is always running off at the mouth, saying that she's strictly out for self. Well, ASAP, and so the fuck am I. I'm so over that bitch."

"Girl, I feel you. You know I do." Chari started to preach to her friend as she reminisced about the past. "It's just the fact that when I think about the way that Simone's mother just up and did a flip-flop on her, I kinda understand why she's so out cold with her shit."

"Okay, okay. Her old girl flipped out, turning her back on Simone's ass. Well, boo hoo for her. I'm all cried out. We all were born in the hood with a hard-luck story to tell."

Chari wasn't done trying to make excuses. "Yeah, Prayer, but it wasn't like any of us seen that situation unfolding. One day, Simone's mom, my mother, and a couple of other women were playing cards, and Ms. Harris just got up from the table and nutted up on everyone."

"Chari, trust me. I know the story, but damn!" Prayer turned the corner, jumping back down on the freeway.

"If my mother turned her back on me outta the blue, just like that . . ." Chari snapped her fingers. "I'd bug out too."

"Yet and still, her ass is still cut off. I'm done."

"I know, Prayer. I feel the exact same way. It's just that every single time I try to stay away, I miss Li'l T."

"Li'l T is sweet as pie; too sweet to be caught up in the middle of Simone and all her games. One day, Joey or Kamal gonna wise up and ask for a blood test. Then you know what, Chari? She's gonna be fucked for real!"

"For her sake and Li'l T, I hope that Joey's the father."

"Yeah, you right, girl. 'Cause to have a stupid bitch like Simone for a mother and Kamal's no-good ass for a daddy will fuck a grown motherfucker up, let alone a kid."

Simone came out of the bathroom with her robe on. The hot shower water spraying her worn body proved to be just what she needed after throwing up twice more. The house was silent as she walked into her bedroom, seeing Li'l T still fast asleep. Taking his tennis shoes and socks off, she tossed a sheet over him and quietly closed the door.

Simone decided to look out her front window and was amused and impressed with the way she had shut the block down for the night. *I guess they all in they little sugar shacks with hurt feelings, plotting on kicking Ms. Holmes square up her ass!*

Falling back onto the couch with a content smile plastered on her face, Simone reached for the television remote with one hand and a half-smoked blunt with the other. *Damn, this is what a bitch really needs.*

She was almost in total relax mode, feeling good and twisted, when her cell phone rang. *What does this psycho want now?* Realizing that it was crazy Kamal made her start to cough and choke.

"Hello," she gagged, sniffing her nose and pressing mute.

"Where the fuck you been?"

"Huh?"

"Don't 'huh' me, Simone. I said where the fuck you been? I called your punk ass earlier, and you didn't answer."

Simone coughed twice more before she could reply. "I was here, stretched out on the couch," she lied, playing it off. "I don't feel well. I've been asleep all evening. I took some cold medicine that has me drained."

"Oh, I was about to come over there and get off into ya ass. I thought you was out in them streets, giving my pussy away." Kamal belched into the phone, indicating that he'd been, and still was, drinking.

"Never that." Simone giggled to herself. "It's all about you and only you."

Kamal's manhood was back intact. Simone didn't have to worry about him storming over, causing a scene and taking her car out of the driveway like he usually did when things didn't go his way. "Dig dis here, baby. Me and Big Ace is out doing what niggas do. When I get finished, I'll be over there to hit them guts, so make sure Li'l T is knocked the fuck out, you hear me?"

Simone was stuck, not knowing what to say. Glancing over at the clock, she realized that it was damn near two in the morning, and Joey had texted her earlier telling her of his intentions to fall through also. *Shit!* She wanted to tell Kamal that she wasn't feeling up to him coming over but knew that he'd get suspicious and probably really kick her ass.

"Yeah, okay, but do me a favor and call me first so I can hear the doorbell. These pills got me exhausted." Simone knew she needed a heads-up just in case Joey was still over and she had to try to rush him out the door.

"Come on now. What the fuck I look like calling my woman, telling her I'm on my way? I'll be there when I get there, so be listening the hell out. You heard me?"

"Yeah, okay." She flipped her phone closed, praying that Kamal wouldn't show up. When he was locked up, the entire Li'l T situation had been easier to play off.

Simone was no fool, opening the cell back up and dialing Joey's number. She was trying to cover all bases. After two rings, he picked up.

"What up, doe?"

"Hey, Joey, what's up?" Simone was putting on her best *Damn, a bitch tired as hell, see you tomorrow* routine, but he wasn't buying it.

"You, sweetheart. They just called last call for alcohol. When me and the fellas down these last two rounds, I'll be on my way over so we can finish what we started."

"Baby, I'm still feeling sick as hell. I think I'm about to fall out. Just call me early in the morning."

"Don't worry. I'll stop by the 24-hour burger joint and grab you some hot tea and something to put on your stomach." Joey was genuinely concerned. "I'll be there in a few. Kiss my son for me until I get there. Peace."

"Fuck!" Simone screamed, tossing her phone beside her.

This was some crazy mess that she had tangled herself up in. Feeling her heartbeat increase with each minute and second that ticked by, Simone leaped to her feet and paced the floor, trying to figure out a quick solution. Under any normal circumstances, she could have Chari rush over no matter what time of day or night to cock block Joey or Kamal. They would get aggravated that they couldn't get loose with company in the house, and jet. This night was different. Somehow, the tables had turned, and Chari had all of a sudden grown balls, jumped ship, and was taking sides with Prayer. When she needed her the most, her doormat Chari wasn't there. Simone couldn't call either of her friends and come up with a sure-fire scheme to get her out of this bullshit that was about to jump off. They were both calling themselves pissed, so fuck 'em. And Yvette was totally out of the question.

Simone's stomach was doing flip-flops, causing her to rush back in the bathroom to spit up once more. "I ain't drinking shit else ever again in life," she repeated over and over as she stared into the mirror at her red, puffy eyes and tightened the belt on her robe. "That's why you off your game tonight, you dumb bitch."

There was nothing for her to do but sit on the couch and get high, waiting for whatever was gonna happen to happen. However the scenario played itself out, so be it. The whole baby daddy crap was getting on her last nerves anyway. Simone kicked her slippers off, rubbing her sore feet. The high-grade weed she was smoking had her wishing that she was *Bewitched* or that damn *I Dream of Jeannie*. That way, all she would have to do was twitch her nose or bob her head and she'd be somewhere chilling on an isolated tropical island instead of laid out on the couch in the heart of the ghetto, waiting to get her ass kicked or killed by one—or both—of Li'l T's fathers.

Times like this, when Simone was all alone and things were at their worst, she yearned for her mother, who was not trying to deal with her at all. The last time Simone tried calling her mom to invite her to Li'l T's very first birthday party, she got hung up on. The next day, when she made an attempt to call back, the telephone number was changed. If that was what being saved meant, turning your back on your own child, then Simone was glad to be what her mother often referred to her as: an outcast and a shepherd for Satan. After years of Simone plotting and scheming to get over, she was drained of any emotional feelings in her heart.

"Whatever either one of them suckers wanna do tonight, fuck it. Let 'em do it. I'm tired of playing the game." Simone closed her heavy eyelids, drifting off to sleep.

Chapter Nine

Ms. Holmes slowly wobbled through the mob of furious neighbors who watched her with disgust. Some wanted to knock her back on the ground, while others just turned their noses up as she passed. Her days of sitting on the front porch, backbiting, gossiping, and collecting stories, spreading them here and there, were now over. Simone had snatched her mask off. Ms. Holmes's true identity was revealed smack-dab in the middle of the street. Everyone was now shockingly aware of the snake that lived among them. The public embarrassment that Ms. Holmes intended to unleash on Simone had backfired. The tables had turned, and now she was the bad guy.

The people she'd befriended now felt betrayed and used. A group beatdown was the mentality of all. When she reached her house, placing her hand on the rusty railing, the screws gave way, causing her to slip once more, scraping her knee.

"This is all that no-good troublemaker's fault," Ms. Holmes moaned, practically crawling into her living room, getting her address book from her dresser. Picking up the telephone receiver, she started dialing. "I'll fix her little red wagon. She'll see."

Yvette sat on the couch with her arms folded. Watching every single movement that her foster mother made, she clenched her teeth with remorse for not sticking up for her idol, Simone.

"Why you keep picking on her all the time?"

"Listen here, young lady. Don't question me in my own house." Ms. Holmes waved the phone toward her and shouted across the room. "I don't know who in the hell you think you are. You're starting to get beside yourself. After I finish dealing with that damned Simone, maybe I'll call the folks at the agency about you!"

"Do what you feel," Yvette growled. "I'm done with running around here cooking and cleaning for your old self anyhow. I ain't no slave."

"What did you just say?"

"You heard me. I don't care."

"Get your ungrateful orphaned behind off my couch, go in the room I allow you to occupy, and go to bed!" Ms. Holmes hung the phone back up momentarily as she ranted at Yvette. "I'm not playing with you, either, or the next call I make is really gonna be to the social worker to pick you up first thing in the morning."

Yvette reluctantly made her way to her bedroom. *Dang gee, I wish I could go live with Simone.* After slamming the door as hard as she possibly could, she took off one of her gold earrings that Simone had blessed her with and pressed her ear to the door.

Why she hate Simone so much? Yvette wondered, listening to Ms. Holmes dial a phone number. *And who the hell she calling?*

"Simone isn't any good at all. She's a terrible mother and an all-out awful human. Little Terrell is left in my care days and days at a time." Ms. Holmes wasn't stretching the truth to the person at the other end of the conversation. She was outright lying through her teeth. "Sometimes that child is so filthy it takes two or three good hot baths to get some of that dirt off his behind. And that's not all. You should see the rags she dresses him in. Oh, Lord have mercy, I feel sorry for that little boy." She continued without even taking a second to breathe or giving the party on the other end a chance to respond to all the nasty lies she making up about Simone. "It's a crying shame. All I was trying to do was help that devil child, and she slapped me in my face."

The impressionable teen wanted to climb out the bedroom window and bang on Simone's door to put her hero up on exactly what Ms. Holmes was doing, but she was scared that the old bitch would keep her word and call the people on her next.

I hate her ass! I hate her!

Yvette had no way of knowing that Ms. Holmes had no intentions of giving up that monthly foster care check she was receiving on her behalf. Yvette being disrespectful or not didn't matter. That income wasn't getting out of Ms. Holmes's greedy hands.

She went on and on for a good twenty minutes or so nonstop before hanging up. She never shut up long enough for the other person to ask a question, leaving Yvette finally removing her ear from the door, going to bed confused and worried about what sort of chaos and turmoil tomorrow would bring.

Shortly after hanging up the phone, Ms. Holmes finally found time to put antibacterial cream on her knee and went into her room, climbing in her bed for the night.

Chapter Ten

Kamal and Big Ace were just finishing up with cheese-burger deluxe platters that they had ordered. Big Ace had his arm around Monique, the girl from the club. She wasn't like the fellas; she flossed out, ordering a top-of-the-line porterhouse steak, grits, and scrambled eggs. Big Ace was treating, so she decided to push the shit to the limit.

"Damn, big girl. You gonna eat all of that?" Kamal tore off a small piece of the menu and picked some meat out from between his teeth. "That's why ya ass swollen now!"

"Stay out of my business," Monique screamed at him, resting back in Big Ace's grip. "I still look good. Don't I, baby?"

Big Ace had already spent a few dollars on the greedy trick and didn't want to sour the deal, so he quickly agreed with her. "Girl, come on. You know you the shit. It's more of you to love." He kissed her on the cheek.

"That's what I'm talking about," Monique hissed, twist-ing her lip at Kamal. "So dig that fly shit."

"Man, control your big-ass bitch." Kamal cracked a smile after spitting the loosened meat particle on the carpeted restaurant floor. "She straight outta line."

Monique wasn't done yet. "Why you here chilling with us? Where's your bitch at anyhow?"

Kamal raised his shirt, revealing his gun, which was tucked nicely in his waistband. "This right here is my bitch. Now, what you know about this?"

"Oh, it's all good for me." Monique's voice became sarcastic in tone as she rubbed on Big Ace. "I like my shit hard, black, and shiny. And I guess you do too, huh?"

"Oh, you's one of them smart-mouthed, big-boned bitches." Kamal spit out another small piece of meat. "I'm all man. Ain't nothing soft about this right here!"

Monique was still persistent. "All right, then, I ain't mad at ya. I'm just saying, you want me to call one of my girls to hang out with us?"

Kamal looked her dead in her face and couldn't help but to burst out laughing. "You mean one of them skank dust-bunnies you was running with back at the club? You've gotta be out your mind for even saying that crazy shit!"

"Damn!" Big Ace smiled.

"What's wrong with my girls? You think you too good to roll with them or something?"

Big Ace had to join in on his boy's defense. "Monique, I ain't trying to front for ol' boy here," he said, pointing at Kamal. "And no disrespect, but you ain't the pick of the litter."

"Y'all ain't shit." She rolled her eyes as she reached for the dessert menu. "I'm getting this to go."

"Damn, ya ass still hungry?" Kamal rubbed his chin as he pulled out his cell phone.

"Didn't I tell you to mind your own?" Monique fumed.

"It's all good. I'm about to call my son's mother anyway. Maybe if you play your cards right with Big Ace, I'll let my girl take your wide ass to the gym with her."

The fellas laughed as Monique sucked her teeth, still checking out the menu. Kamal pushed redial, and Simone's name, which was locked in, blinked in the screen. Big Ace signaled the waitress so they could break camp.

***

"Come on, Trevon. You about ready to dip or what?" Joey stood up, calling Tami over to settle up the tab he'd started. "I got business to tend to. I told Simone I was gonna be over there when I leave, so I know she waiting up for a brother."

"Yeah, I'm 'bout ready," Trevon answered, waving a chick over that he'd met on the dance floor. "Just let me tell this female where to meet me at outside."

Joey paid Tami what he owed, plus a little bit more. She wrote her number down on a napkin and gave it to him, making it crystal clear that she was open and available when and if he was free. Joey took the number but knew he never planned on using it. Drunk or not; bossy or not; bitch or not; Simone was his girl, and he loved her to death. There was no way that he would or could just dis her like that. Fun was fun, but the night of games was over, and it was time to go home and tend to his sick wifey.

After the house lights came on, Joey and his crew made their way toward the door. After a lot of handshakes and politicking, they were in front of the club. Trevon was now with the chick and climbing into his ride. The hotel was their next stop of the night. Joey, of course, flying solo, had to swing by the all-night joint and grab some grub before going to his final destination for the night—Simone's.

Kamal hung up his cell phone, slightly grinning. "Her ass know what time it is."

"Who was that? Simone?" Big Ace inquired just outta fake-ass curiosity.

"Yeah, that was her." Kamal licked his lips. "She over at the crib sick. That's why she ain't pick up earlier." He was happy to offer his friend an explanation, considering the way he'd bugged out before at the spot.

"Oh, dig that." Big Ace was skeptical about Simone's flimsy excuse but shrugged his shoulders, not really caring one way or the other.

"Who is Simone?" Monique butted in after belching and not bothering to say "excuse me" or at least cover her mouth.

"That's my baby momma." Kamal sat back, stretching his arms. "The one that can give ya wild ass some tips on dressing and behaving like a ho supposed to."

"Who you talking about? Simone Harris that used to live near me? Boy, bye with all that."

"It depends where you live at," Kamal fired back, "with ya Inspector Gadget ass."

"I live around the way at the Truth Homes," Monique said proudly without hesitation.

"Oh, you mean the fucking projects?"

"Yeah, so?"

"Whoa! Slow ya roll." Big Ace threw his hands up, checking Kamal on trying to dis the projects. "Calm down with all the loud talk. I was born in them projects too. That was home for years and years."

"I'm sorry, sweetie." Monique hugged on him. "But ya boy been tripping all night and shit. I'm tired of his mouth. When we gonna bounce?"

Big Ace went in his pocket, revealing a thick knot, causing Monique's pussy to drip at the sight. He paid the bill, and they were out the door, making their way to the crowded parking lot.

Kamal suddenly stopped, glaring vindictively at Willy Dale, the local begging bum slumped over on the side of the restaurant's wall with a dirty cup clutched in his hand. The late-night regular customers were blessing him with spare change and empty bottles out of their cars.

Making his way closer to Willy Dale, Kamal raised his left Tim, kicking the less-than-fortunate man's hard-earned revenue across the lot, causing him to crawl around like a baby to recover all the cup's contents.

"Damn, dawg! Why you do that bullshit to ol' Willy Dale?" Big Ace asked, confused about his boy's actions.

"Man, fuck his homeless ass. I ain't got no love for these annoying motherfuckers out in these here streets! He a man like me and need to get that shit like I do—hard knocks instead of begging."

"You wrong as hell." Monique dug in her purse, revealing the fact for the first time all night that her mooching ass actually had a couple of dollars.

"Oh, dig that." Kamal called her out to Big Ace, changing the subject. "Her wide ass been holding out. This ho got a pocket full of dough! She should've been treating us."

Big Ace was tired of Kamal and all his foolish behavior. He put his arm around Monique, walking her off into the direction of the truck. She had her carryout bag in her hands and Big Ace's money on her mind. Climbing her mostly-breasts overweight body into the back cab of the truck, she mean mugged the back of Kamal's head as he pulled out of the lot, thinking about just how dumb he was. She wanted to haul off and slap him on the back of his neck, but she chilled.

I ain't even gonna put that nigga up on game. Monique's mind jumped back to the club. If her eyes weren't playing tricks on her from drinking too much, she was almost certain she'd seen Ms. Think-She-Better-Than-Everyone-Else-That-Still-Live-in-the-Projects Simone posted at a booth with Joey, the dude she thought was Simone's baby daddy. Monique knew for a fact that Simone's homegirls, Chari and Prayer, were definitely in the house. She almost had a run-in with the bitches in the middle of the nightclub, but they asses knew better and kept that shit on the high-post move. Monique started to giggle, settling in the seat as she thought about Kamal's stupidity.

Now this trying-to-go-for-hard, cock-blocking Negro wanna throw salt in my game. As much as I hate Simone, I would put him up on the bullshit, but considering how he acts, he got the shit coming. For-real for-real, I'm glad she giving his ass the straight-up motherfucking business! Forget even telling his rude ass that Simone is playing him! Good for her!

Kamal was on his way to get on the freeway. He positioned his seat back, getting comfortable for the long drive across town. "Hey, fat girl in the back seat, don't forget to strap them big titties of yours down. I don't need them gigantic twins slapping me on the back of my head while I'm driving."

"Go fuck yourself," Monique shouted. *Yup, good for her!*

"Damn, dude, shut up with all that crazy madness. We get the point," Big Ace interjected, fed up with Kamal's mouth.

Kamal knew his boy was heated and floored it so he could hurry up and drop Big Ace and Monique off at Big Ace's truck. Then he would double back and sleep at Simone's.

Joey did a triple take, getting a quick glance of a shiny royal-blue F-150 with rims going down the freeway ramp entrance as he was coming up the exit. *Naw, couldn't be,* he reasoned with himself, unknowingly turning into the 24-hour restaurant that Kamal had just moments earlier left. No sooner than he stepped out, he ran into a couple of females who had been hanging at the park when all the commotion jumped.

"What's up, Joey?" Karen shyly flirted.

"Oh, hey, Karen. What it do?"

"Just up here getting a sandwich to take home." She stuck her tongue out in a seductive manner. "You know how it go." Karen was one of those not-so-attractive females that had to go the extra mile to get a brother to notice her, so she always made it known that she was easy and had no problem with paying like she weighed.

"Yeah, I feel you." Joey acknowledged her pimping, backing up slightly so as not to encourage her.

"I'm glad you and your boys are all right from that stuff out at the park." Karen twirled her extra-long weave with her fingers, still trying to push up on Joey.

"Yeah, Karen, that was some pretty fucked-up shit."

"It really was," she agreed. "Two of them lunatics and Moneymaking Mo just left this bitch."

"Is Monique still out here setting folks up?"

"Come on, Joey. You know how she roll."

"Well, dig, I need to get this food and be out. I'll holler."

Joey saw a frantic Willy Dale over on the edge of the curb, chasing a crumpled-up dollar bill as he stepped inside. Any other time he would've given him a few bucks, but his mind was preoccupied. He couldn't believe what he'd just heard from Karen. First them busters were at Bookies, then at the restaurant. It was like they were all connected at the hip all of a sudden. He pulled out his cell phone, calling Trevon with the quickness.

"Hey, Tre, you not gonna believe this bullshit!"

"What's the deal, homie?"

"Guess what? Those guys was just up here."

"Up where?" Trevon questioned. "Where you at?"

"I'm up here at The Midtown Grill grabbing Simone's sick behind some food."

"Is they still there? Did they see you?" Trevon was busy throwing his white tee back on. He and the girl he'd met at the club were already half-undressed, chilling at the hotel. They were just about to crack a bottle of Moët that he'd copped from the after-hours spot over on Linwood.

"Slow ya roll, killer. They broke camp just before I got here." Joey laughed. "Karen's shady ass told me."

"Oh, I was about to say."

"Yeah, I know, but dig what else she told me."

"What's that?"

"Man, them cats is dumber than I thought. They hanging with Monique's clip-n-dip ass."

"Ahhh . . . hell, naw." Trevon motioned for the female to go ahead and open the champagne. "If I didn't wanna put some hot lead up in they grimy asses, I'd kinda feel sorry for them. Monique and her peoples don't fuck around when it come to getting that shit how they live!"

"Dawg, I feel you, 'cause that bitch be on some other type of shit," Joey stated as he walked up to the carryout counter. "If Monique has her way, we ain't gotta do shit but sit back and let that bitch and her crew risk catching that case."

"Well, call me if you need me. I'm about to get off into this right here." Trevon rubbed on the girl's thigh.

"All right then, peace." Joey slipped his cell back on his hip and placed his order, making sure to get a slice of the sweet potato pie that Li'l T loved so much. As he sat patiently on the stool, spinning around, he kept wondering exactly why the dude with the gold fronts seemed so familiar. *I can't remember for shit where I seen that coward from.*

Ten more minutes, Joey's number was called, indicating that his food was ready. He paid the cashier, double-checked his order was correct, and strolled out the door, heading toward his car.

As he started his engine, Karen made sure she made her presence known by waving her hands around like she was in a freaking parade. He blew the horn twice at her and handed a grateful Willy Dale some spare change before speeding out of the parking lot and into traffic.

"Stay up, old-timer!"

"Thank you, youngblood," Willy Dale yelled out into the wind at Joey. "I appreciate ya."

Jazz music softly playing on the radio eased Joey's trouble-filled mind. The night was about to come to an end just the way he liked it to, in the presence of his firstborn, Li'l T. Seeing his perfect sleeping face made Joey forget any foul shit going on in the outside world. Not drug deals, drive-bys, bitches, hoes, or anything other than Elmo and Big Bird mattered when it came to his seed.

So, with Li'l T's pie, Simone's beef and broccoli soup, and fresh, warm pita bread in tow, Joey's next stop would shortly be her front door. It was time to relax. Time for family. His family.

Chapter Eleven

Simone was in a deep, coma-like sleep. All her worries and fears of what was to come were temporarily put to rest. With her subconscious mind taking over, Simone was visiting a place she hadn't been in years. The setting was all too familiar. Her mother was in the kitchen with an apron on. The small one-bedroom project apartment was bursting at the seams. Simone's mother, as always, had the crowd going by singing old Motown songs while she deep-fried catfish and puffed on a joint. You could tell it was the first of the month because all the normally depressed low-income tenants had just received their food stamp benefits and were in the party mood. It was nothing like getting your check or some stamps to get someone's quiet ass to get the Holy Ghost. The secondhand, half-price stereo blasted sounds of Stevie Wonder, Diana Ross, Smokey Robinson, and The Temptations. With two card games going on and plenty of food and drink, it would be damn near daybreak before the monthly get-together would let up.

Simone, Chari, and some of the other project children danced around, showing off their best moves. The spur-of-the-moment contest winners would receive anything from a dollar bill to a sip of beer. The grownups would do just about anything to keep their kids quiet so they could keep the party going as long as possible. Everyone loved everyone, and that made the atmosphere perfect.

Ms. Harris had Simone trained. She was pulling double duty serving plates, emptying ashtrays, and bossing around the other children. The fact that Simone was a few years younger than some of them didn't matter one bit. Her mother made sure that Simone knew everything that went on in the world so nothing would come as a shock. When the evil lady that lived on the second floor got even more malicious, Simone was the first one to point out the fact that she must've been going through menopause.

The fact that her mother treated her like an equal made Simone feel on top of the world. To her, there was no better feeling than to get respect from her mom. It was her and Simone against the world. It seemed as if they lived in a fancy castle up on a hilltop above everyone else in town. The nights the pair would spend watching old spooky movies and grubbing on food that one of Ms. Harris's many admirers would bring by were the best times in Simone's young life.

Now that Simone's mother had done a 180, turning her life over to the Lord, cutting all ties with anything that her church deemed unholy, Simone and her bastard son Li'l T were left on the outside looking in. But she still had her memories, and it was those memories that Simone kept with her that caused her justifiably paranoid self to sleep like a baby, even though shit was about to get ugly.

Joey pulled up in front of Simone's house and reached in the back seat, grabbing the food. With a huge smile of contentment on his face, he made his way up the walkway and onto the front porch. Every step he took had him feeling as if he was being watched. He glanced back over his shoulder. His hands were filled, but he started wishing that he'd remembered to get his pistol out of his stash box underneath the passenger's seat.

Realizing that the always-populated block was deserted gave him an eerie chill as he knocked on Simone's door repeatedly. Even at three o'clock in the morning, her block was usually jumping, so seeing it take the form of a ghost town was strange as hell to Joey. He had no way of knowing that just about an hour ago, his son's mother had shut the entire motherfucker down. Not getting a response, Joey set the bags on the lawn chair and took his cell phone off his hip, dialing Simone's number.

What's taking her silly ass so long?

After the fifth ring, a sleepy-voiced Simone answered. Joey could hear her turning the locks on the huge, solid steel door. After the last lock turned, the door seemed to have been opened by the wind as Simone walked away, not even greeting him. She threw her body back on the couch and balled up like an infant trying to get back to sleep where she left off at.

Her dreams always seemed so real. It was the only time that the hard-core, bitter Simone would be able to visit her mother and feel truly loved and cared for unconditionally, and she wasn't in the mood for Joey to stop that emotion. Simone missed her mother and would do almost anything to make things right again.

The fact that part one of her dangerous equation had just come into her home didn't seem to faze her one bit. Simone had unfinished business with her mother. Li'l T's two fathers controlled most of her days, but her dreams belonged to her, and her alone.

"What took you so long, baby? I told you I was coming, sleepyhead. How you feeling?" Joey went into the kitchen, placing the bags on the counter. "I'll fix your food for you. That way, you don't have to get back up."

He opened up the cupboard, taking out a bowl and a small saucer. Joey then poured his son's mother a warm cup of tea and put her meal on a tray. When he got back in the living room, Simone was once again knocked out.

Joey smiled as he watched the slobber form in the corner of her mouth. *This is the only time your annoying pretty ass ain't begging,* he reflected to himself while caressing her soft cheek.

Placing Simone's food tray on the coffee table in front of her, Joey quietly went back into the kitchen getting Li'l T's pie. It was in a plastic container, looking too perfect to be touched. He held it in his hands as he tiptoed to his son's room. Slightly pushing the door open, he noticed that Li'l T wasn't in his bed. Joey's face filled with disappointment. His first thought was to wake Simone up to march her behind across the street to Yvette's to get his son, but then he remembered that she was claiming to be sick.

Turning around to go back in the front of the house, Joey heard tiny snoring sounds from Simone's bedroom. Peeking inside, he found his firstborn curled up in the same position as his mother. He stood there watching him sleep as he'd just done with Simone. Joey couldn't wait until Li'l T got old enough to go shoot hoops at the park with him or toss a football around. He was Joey's pride and joy. His number one priority in life was providing for his son and making sure he stayed safe. Being careful not to make any noise to disturb him, Joey proudly displayed the huge piece of pie on the nightstand and softly kissed his son good night.

"Sleep good, Daddy's little man," he whispered. "Daddy loves you more than life."

Closing the door behind him, Joey came back into the living room where he found Simone sitting up, wiping her eyes, trying to focus on the light in the room.

"Oh my God! What time is it?" She leaped to her feet, mistakenly knocking the food on the floor. Reality set in when she realized that her other baby daddy, Kamal, was probably minutes—if not seconds—away.

"What the fuck is the matter with your crazy ass?" Joey threw his hands up in the air, demanding an answer.

Kamal was less than ten minutes away from reaching Big Ace's truck. They'd run into an accident on the way, making a twenty-minute trip turn into double that. After they had endured plenty of gawkers, several police cars, and a few ambulances, the exit was finally coming into view. Kamal looked over to his right and noticed that his boy, Big Ace, had his head tilted back and was knocked the fuck out. After a survey of the back seat via the rearview mirror, Kamal saw the complete opposite with Monique.

"Damn, your good-sac-chasin' ass is hanging, ain't you?"

"Chill on all that madness, Kamal. Why you all on a bitch back so fucking hard and shit?"

"My bad." He made eye contact with her in the mirror. "I thought a ho like you liked a guy on ya back hard!"

Monique was sick and tired of Kamal's mouth and was overjoyed when he came up top and off the freeway. Big Ace was asleep, so there was no one to referee the two.

"The way you talking makes me think you jealous."

"Jealous of what?" Kamal laughed.

"You act like you want some of this."

"Some of what? I don't like fat meat."

"Oh, so you like them bony, like Ms. Thang you fuck with, huh?"

"What's it to ya ass what the fuck I like?"

"I'm just saying, that's all."

"Well, say some other shit."

"Like what?"

"Like whatever, crazy ho."

Monique knew that Kamal was watching her, so she pulled out her two secret weapons that always worked on a man. She grabbed both of her breasts, squeezing them together firmly. When she made sure that Kamal was good and mesmerized by the sight, she stuck out her wet tongue, revealing a diamond stud piercing. Monique then started to lick across her nipples while still caressing them tight.

"Do your girl Simone got it like this?" she teased, flicking her tongue around.

Kamal made sure that Big Ace was still asleep before he responded. "Damn, bitch! I ain't gonna front. That's some freaky shit, and you got a nigga's dick hard as a motherfucker, but you about to get with my manz here."

"See, that's where you wrong. We can all party. I can handle both of y'all at the same time." Monique did the same thing that Kamal had just done, checking to see if Big Ace was asleep. "I like it like that!" She continued trying to convince him, knowing that she'd get double pleasure and double pay.

The huge F-150 hit a pothole, causing Big Ace to open his eyes and cut the sexually charged conversation short. Monique slipped her breasts back into her dress before Big Ace got a chance to look at her.

"What's taking so long?" He stretched out his arms and cracked the window to get some fresh air to wake him all the way up.

"Damn, dude, you was knocked out." Kamal sneakily stumbled over his words. "It was an accident blocking that motherfucker!"

"Yeah, sweetie, you slept through all of it." For the first time all night, Monique cosigned with Kamal. "It was stop-and-go traffic for about three or four miles."

"Oh, dig that. Shit, I'm just glad we here. I done rested up. Now a nigga ready to hang for the rest of the night."

Kamal made a left turn into the Crestwood apartment complex and pulled next to Big Ace's truck.

"All right, then, dude, go do you." Kamal gave his boy some love as he watched Monique squeeze her breasts once more behind Big Ace's back. "Fuck this bitch extra hard for me. Maybe in the mouth or something. That way, you can shut her the fuck up forthe first time all night."

"Why don't you come do it yourself?" Monique hissed back, blowing a kiss. "Or are you man enough to handle all of *this?*"

"Damn, is y'all still talking fucking shit?" Big Ace interjected.

Kamal watched Monique's wide ass climb down out of his truck and into Big Ace's. *Her backside is hot,* he thought. Even though she was far from being the type of female he usually found attractive, he would still fuck the dog shit out of the tramp from the back. Kamal's manhood started to throb at the thought of what his boy Big Ace was about to experience.

He blew the horn twice at them as they drove off, headed toward a hotel to get their freak on. With a hard dick in his pants, Kamal sped off, anxious to get over to Simone's house. *I'm gonna really give her something to be sick about!* He bent a few corners and jumped down on the expressway, hit 80, and put the F-150 on cruise control.

Chapter Twelve

Joey stood stone-faced, waiting for Simone to answer his question. Watching her act frantic and showing no form of concern for her precious new carpet that now had big chunks of beef and broccoli on it caused him to ask her the same thing. "I said what in the hell is your problem?"

"I just had a nightmare, that's all." Simone tried her best to calm down. "It was kinda scary."

"Oh, is that all?" Joey bent over, picking up the bowl, spoon, and a few pieces of the meat. "And you knock over all the dang-gone food I bought for you?"

Simone agonized, staring at the digital clock that was flashing brightly on her DVD Player.

3:31 . . . 3:31 . . . 3:31.

The light was blinking repeatedly as if it were calling out to her.

3:32 . . . 3:32 . . . 3:32.

Her heart seemed to be beating in perfect rhythm with constant glow.

3:33 . . . 3:33 . . . 3:33.

Kamal is probably on his way. Naw, maybe he changed his mind. Damn, what am I gonna do? Oh, shit!

"Do you hear me talking to you?" Joey looked up at a quiet Simone. "Are you deaf or something, crazy girl?"

"Yeah, I heard you. I was just thinking about my dream."

"Don't you mean nightmare?"

"Whatever, Joey." Simone rolled her eyes.

"Whatever, my ass," Joey screamed back, shocking Simone into reality. "Is your deranged-looking behind gonna help me clean this mess up or what?"

"It can wait for a minute, can't it?"

"All right, then, but don't be bitching later when this crap leave a stain, 'cause I ain't buying your ass no new carpet, so you can just forget about it."

Simone had bigger things about to jump off at any fucking moment. A couple years' worth of scheming, manipulating, and careful planning were all about to fall apart. She had to get prepared for the inevitable. The vein in her neck was bulging, and the room started to spin.

Joey took notice of Simone's demeanor and stopped what he was doing to show her some attention. Taking his time to hold both of her hands with affection, he pulled her close to him.

"Was it that bad?"

"Yeah, it was," she lied.

Joey ran his fingers through her long hair, trying to get her to relax. For a brief second, Simone wanted to blurt out the truth and confess. Joey didn't deserve to be ambushed by all the madness that was coming, but what else could she do? It was against the Player's Code of Ethics to actually drop your hand and expose your own secrets. No matter how tight shit was, that damn sure wasn't an option.

"I think it was all that liquor I drank." She tried to shake the uneasiness, putting back on her game face. "Maybe I should go to bed and just get some rest."

"Yeah, you right," Joey agreed, taking some of the mess to the kitchen. "In the morning you'll feel better."

Oh, shit! This nigga about to jet! Hell yeah! Simone's mind took control. *3:40 . . . 3:40 . . . Damn, hurry up!*

When Joey came out of the kitchen, he had his shirt thrown over his shoulder. Simone took her eyes off the clock, doing a double take at Joey.

"What's up, baby? I thought you was about to go home."

He gave Simone a strange look and laughed at her off-the-wall, crazy, middle-of-the-night comment. "Girl, it's late as hell. I'm tired as shit. A nigga like me about to lie down next to my son and fall the fuck out!"

"What?" she objected loudly.

"I said I'm about to crash with Li'l T."

Almost on cue, after the last word came out of Joey's mouth, Simone's stomach bubbled, and she threw up everywhere. Joey instantly jumped back just in time to avoid getting soiled. "Your ass don't need to drink shit ever again in life."

"I'm sorry." Simone's hand was full of a clear, slimy discharge. She trembled as she ran toward the bathroom, trying not to gag again.

Joey paced the floor outside the door, watching his woman once again on her knees, blessing the porcelain god. It had been a long night, and he'd had about enough of Simone's overdramatic behavior.

"I'm out. I'll be in the bedroom asleep when you get yourself together."

Simone got off the cold floor, trying to stall him, when a musical sound rang out, scaring the shit out of her. Simone bumped her head on the sink.

Oh, dang! It was Joey's cell phone that was on the kitchen counter. She suspiciously peeked around the corner, listening closely as he answered the late-night call.

"You bullshitting! Oh, yeah! Where you at? I got you! Sit tight. What room? I'm on my way!"

Simone ran back into the bathroom, turning the water on in the sink, trying to act nonchalant and uninterested.

Joey set his phone back on the counter as he wrote down the room number the person had given him on a piece of paper. He then went back into the living room, grabbing his car keys.

"Simone, I gotta go handle this situation. I'll holler at you tomorrow some time."

Simone was happy that he was about to leave but still had the nerve and audacity to be nosy and jealous. "Who the fuck was that?" With her hands on her hips, she demanded a response. "And don't say your momma."

"I ain't got no time to get into it with you." Joey turned the doorknob, heading outside. "I'll put you up on the shit tomorrow."

As Joey sped off in a rush to who knows where, Simone felt her blood pressure go back down to normal. She shut the door and went to clean herself up, hoping that Kamal was somewhere passed the fuck out.

After a long look in the mirror, Simone said out loud, "Son of a bitch, that was close as a motherfucker! I gotta get my shit together. I'm slipping on my pimping, and I'm way too pretty for all this stress these mark busters is causing me! That's probably why a ho gaining all this extra weight! I need to cut one of them tricks loose!"

Simone got a hot pail of water and a few rags. She then got down on her hands and knees so that she could scrub the spot where the spilled food and vomit had started to soak in. As she squirted a small amount of all-purpose cleaner, her eyes started to water, and the smell made her feel nauseated.

"This is some foul shit! Who told Joey's always-trying-to-do-something ass to bring this garbage in my house any-fucking-way?"

Big Ace and Monique drove in the parking lot and checked in at the Red Roof Inn on Dequindre and I-696. It wasn't the Ritz Carlton, but it wasn't a hole-in-the-wall either. It would be 100 percent different if Monique was a straight-up dime piece. Then Big Ace would've served the bitch up wifey style instead of low budget.

The night was quiet and hushed until the pair got there. After making a gang of noise on the way to their room, Monique took the room key, opening up the door. She held Big Ace's hand, practically dragging him to the bed. Pushing him backward, climbing on top, the top-heavy female shoved her breasts in his face. Big Ace then took it upon himself to suck on each one simultaneously. Monique ran her tongue across his neck, licking and sucking like there was no tomorrow. When she worked her way down to his muscular chest and stomach, she suddenly stopped and started massaging his manhood.

"Hey, baby. Why don't you go take a hot shower and clean him up good so I can sing him a lullaby?"

"Yeah, I feel you." Big Ace happily leaped up. "Just be ready and naked for daddy when he gets back."

"Ummm . . . I can hardly wait." Monique moistened her lips while hiking up her dress to reveal her red panties.

Big Ace quickly disappeared into the bathroom, shutting the door behind him. He was too geeked. *Hell yeah!* he thought, unfastening his belt. *I'm about to bang that bitch's lights out!*

Hearing his pants hit the floor and making sure that the water in the shower was turned on, Monique grabbed her cell phone, placing an important call.

"Hey, it's me. . . . Yeah. . . . We at the Red Roof. . . . He's in the shower. . . . I know the routine. . . . I got you. Just hurry!" She put her phone on silent ring, then back in her purse, tossing it on the nightstand. With a huge smile, Monique undressed, then lay spread-eagle, butt-asshole naked on the king-size bed, awaiting Big Ace's return.

Trevon was just getting good and relaxed. The female he was with was giving him the royal king treatment. She had filled the hotel's ice bucket with warm, soapy water and was washing his feet and sucking them dry. With a blunt hanging in the corner of his mouth and a XXX porno playing on the television, Trevon was in true pimp player heaven.

"Why don't you crawl up here and bless me with some of them brains?"

"Yesss . . . daddy." She blushed while obeying. Quickly obliging to serve her king for the night, the sex-driven chick really made her presence felt and blessed his mic.

With every deep-throating gulp of his dick, his toes curled. Switching back from the movie to reality was causing him to be on the verge of a supernut. The only thing that was stopping that wonderful feeling was the distracting noises of two loud voices that were outside in the courtyard. Frustrated, Trevon pushed the female off his hard dick and slipped on his pants. He cracked the door and leaned over the balcony.

It can't be! Hell, naw! Ain't this some shit! Watching the loud, obnoxious pair enter room 117, Trevon ran back in, calling his boy to inform him.

"Hey, Joey, I know it's late, but you ain't gonna believe this! Red Roof. . . . Just now. . . . Room 117. I'll be waiting."

Trevon gave the confused girl cab fare, plus a little extra, and sent her on her way. Even though she wanted to have her turn being treated like royalty, the unexpected money definitely made things all good in the hood for her.

After the girl left, Trevon watched room 117 like a hawk. Fifteen minutes later, he peeped a car with its headlights turned off pulling in and parking on the far side of the lot. Three dudes got out, putting on Halloween masks.

"What the fuck!" he mumbled under his breath, watching the drama unfold. "This is nuts." Trevon was stunned as the trio systematically inched toward room 117. He wanted to scream across the lot to the late-night creepers and tell them that Big Ace's ho ass belonged to him and his boy, but he chilled. *Let me see how all this madness is about to play out.*

He dialed Joey's number again to put him up on the latest developments, but unfortunately got his voice mail. *I hope ol' boy ain't close to this joint yet.*

Trevon didn't want his boy driving in on the middle of whatever was going down, possibly a shootout, so he continued to watch the seemingly well executed plan jump off. He would try hitting Joey back again in a few, and hopefully next time, he'd pick up.

Chapter Thirteen

Kamal saw Linwood Avenue and bent the corner. Crossing the railroad tracks around the curb, his mind drifted back to his childhood and how fucked up shit was for him and his sister back in the day. . . .

"Hey, Kamal, why don't you go down to the gas station and see if you can pump some gas for a few dollars?" His drug addict old dude was taking his last sip of Wild Irish Rose and would soon need another and a rock of crack.

"Yeah, that's a good idea," his mom agreed quickly when realizing that they were out of "Get High Funds." *"Matter of fact, take your little sister there with you and let her ask all the dudes. She's developing now, so I know them old men will throw her some change or a few bottles."*

"Why do I have to go do that?" a younger teen Kamal argued. *"All my friends be laughing at me."*

"Me too." La Tonya pouted. *"They be making fun of us."*

Kamal grew heated. *"Yeah, and I'm tired of that."*

"So fucking what? Get y'all ungrateful asses up and do what the hell I told y'all to do!"

"What we got to be grateful for?" Kamal said.

"What you just say?"

"You heard me." Kamal's voice raised in volume and deepened in bass.

His drunken father got up from the torn, musty chair, backhanding his son against the empty china cabinet.

Kamal's lip started to bleed as he tried to protect himself from his father's wrath.

Several closed fists later, Kamal decided he'd had enough and swung back with all his might. The emotional force behind the blow knocked his father unconscious. These impromptu beatdowns had gone on long enough. Kamal had suffered through black eyes, broken bones, and busted lips. His days of being a coward against his unstable sperm donor were done. He felt he had to do something this time. He'd reached his boiling point.

La Tonya, his sister, had tears of joy flowing down her face that her big brother had finally found the courage to stand up for himself and her. But at the same time, she shed tears of uncertainty, knowing that when their boozed sperm donor woke up and got his bearings, Kamal would really be in for it.

To make matters worse, the children's mother never lifted a hand or opened her mouth to stop what was going on in front of her eyes, which were already stretched open from being on a crack attack. Any real mother in her right mind would try to protect her kids from that type of drama, but not theirs.

"Well, Kamal, just don't stand there looking all stupid and shit! He ain't dead or nothing!" she yelled out. "Now, go on up there and see if you can get your momma some money real quick before he wakes up and tries to drink it all up."

"But, Momma—"

"But, Momma, what? Now go," she insisted.

The pain of that day still haunted Kamal after all these years. He remembered refusing his mother's demands and instead, packing his belongings, which amounted to little or nothing, saying good-bye to La Tonya, and going out into the world to try to survive on his own. At that very moment, Kamal became a man and made due. Any place was better than how he was forced to live at home.

Leaving his young sister home alone with two alcoholic junkies as parents hadn't felt right to him, so Kamal made a decision in her best interest, placing a call to Protective Services to come out and investigate the living conditions. If he had thought for one minute he could take care of them both, he would have. He'd found out weeks later from one of the guys in the hood that the agency had swiftly stepped in, doing their job, removing a suffering La Tonya from the household and placing her in foster care. When they showed up to rescue her, she practically ran, jumping up in their arms.

Kamal often wondered exactly where she was and if she was being properly taken care of, but considering the fact that he was still himself just a minor, contacting the people down at Protective Services would only cause him to get caught up and become a part of the system, and that wasn't an option for him. Kamal would rather tough things out and take his chances roaming the murderous, crime-filled streets of Detroit than be bounced from home to home in search of acceptance from strangers.

As Kamal's truck approached the Davison intersection, he saw the blinding high-beam headlights flashing from a car, which, coincidentally, was Joey's, going in the opposite direction. A couple of loud horns blowing brought him out of his grief-packed flashback trance. Reminiscing about his treacherous upbringing had almost caused him to veer over into the oncoming traffic and crash.

"Shit! That was close." He rubbed his chin, ignoring the other late-night drivers giving him the finger, and turned on Simone's block and up to her house. Pulling in the driveway and jumping down out of his vehicle, he went on the porch, banging loudly twice on her front door. *I need to piss. This tramp better hurry the fuck up!*

When it took Simone longer than he wanted it to, Kamal unzipped his pants, spraying her front lawn like he was a wild dog off his leash. Before he could finish behaving so rudely, Simone flung open the door to let him in and witnessed, firsthand, once again, how low and unpolished Kamal really was.

"What's wrong with you? Why would you do some old stupid shit like that?" she argued. "Why didn't you go around to the backyard at least?"

"Bitch, who the fuck you talking to like that?" Kamal took his hand, mashing Simone's weary face, backing her out of his way as he came inside the house. "I done told you about that smart-ass mouthpiece of yours."

Simone had already been catching hot fire hell all day and chose not to stretch the no-win disagreement out. She pushed the door shut, not even bothering to lock it, and sat on the couch. Considering the fact that she'd played sick earlier on the phone with him, she had to keep the game going.

"I still don't feel good, Kamal," she whined, grabbing for her blanket, wrapping it around her as if she were an Indian. "I think I have the flu or something like that."

"Oh, yeah?" Kamal marched through the house suspiciously, inspecting every inch. "Why is this big-ass wet spot here?"

"I threw up some food, that's all."

"I thought your lying ass was so sick. Where the hell did you get some food from?" Kamal got a glance of some carryout bags thrown on the kitchen counter. It was his time to catch her up in her lies and beat that ass proper.

"Prayer brought it over for me on her way home from work and dropped it off." Simone passed the ball back over to Kamal. Mentioning Prayer always got him heated and off his square. "She knew I was sick and thought about a sista's health." Simone rolled her eyes at Kamal.

"What the fuck that's supposed to mean?"

"What you mean, what it mean?"

"Just what I said, bitch!"

"Nothing! Just that she cared!" Simone stood her ground with the lie, knowing that on the for-real side of the game, Prayer, at this point, didn't care if she coughed up a lung.

Kamal was tired of hearing Prayer's name and quickly changed the subject. "My dick been rock hard as a motherfucker all night. Go get in the bed so I can get some of that pussy, or did ya girl Prayer take care of that too?"

"Why you gotta act so dumb all the time?" Simone leered at him with disgust. "Didn't ya momma teach ya any better?"

Kamal froze in his tracks. "Simone, I'm not playing with ya ass. I done told ya more than once to keep my people's names outta ya mouth." He yanked her off the couch. "Now come on and give me some."

"I told you I was sick. Plus, Li'l T is in my bed."

"So throw his crybaby ass in his own damn bedroom."

"Kamal, why don't you be quiet? It's late, and I don't wanna wake him up." Simone put her finger up to his lips in an effort to shut him up.

Kamal snatched her wrist, squeezing it tight. "Well, okay, then, we can do it right here."

Simone smelled the liquor on his breath and tasted it on his tongue that he shoved in her mouth. She tried her best to talk Kamal out of having sex. After all the throwing up she'd done, she really wasn't in the mood. Turning her head to the side to avoid any more of his sloppy kisses, Simone soon felt his street-conditioned hands open up her blanket and rip her panties off.

"Please, Kamal. I don't feel good."

"Shut that shit up," he replied, using his body weight to cause her to fall back onto the couch.

Kamal then dropped his pants, exposing all six-and-a-half inches of his hard dick. Normally, Simone enjoyed the thuglike loving he'd put on her, but this time, Kamal seemed to be vindictive and extra gangsta with it. "Who pussy is this?" he slobbered, growling in her ear. "This here belongs to me!"

Simone felt like an old rag doll as Kamal took all his aggressions out on her body. He worked her off the couch and onto the floor, where he really got rough. Blank expressions of nothingness filled her face with each movement of in-and-out thrusting violation Kamal gave to her. It didn't matter to Simone; she wasn't even there. An unwilling participant, Simone daydreamed herself to a different world, leaving Kamal to go for it and get his own nuts off, pants down to his ankles, Tims still on. Thirteen long minutes of twisting Simone's hair between his fingers, snatching back her head, one leg lifted over his shoulder, a purple, unwanted passion mark on her neck, and a carpet burn on her ass, Kamal finally was done screaming out in triumph as he climaxed.

"Damn, that was good." He collapsed onto Simone, who didn't mutter a word. "Round two in a minute. But first, go get ya manz some cold water."

Simone got up, going into the kitchen. Opening the refrigerator door, she saw the light inside shining on a butcher knife that was in the sink. *I'm starting to hate his ass! I wish he was dead, or at least back in prison.* Simone's mind kicked into overdrive as she imagined stabbing Kamal to death. *Fuck that. I'm too pretty to be jailing it!* It would be hard, but for the time being, her only choice was to deal with him. He was a damned good paymaster, but playing the game was getting old.

Feeling the bottled water sweat in her hand gave her chills of deceit. As she shut the door, she was startled by the sounds of "Slum Village" coming from behind the bags on the counter. *Oh, shit! No, he didn't leave that motherfucker!* Simone tried to grab a dish towel to muffle the ring tone blasting from Joey's cell phone. *Out of all the times a bitch be trying to get a hold of his shit, now he decides to forget it!* Simone held the towel down, covering the phone until it stopped ringing. But before she could get a chance to turn it off, Kamal came into the kitchen fastening his pants.

"Where was that music coming from?"

"What music?"

"I thought I just heard some damn music coming from somewhere. You didn't hear that shit?"

"Maybe it was a car or something." Simone had to get Kamal out of the kitchen quick. "Come on back in the living room so we can watch some videos."

"Naw, I'm tight on all that. Now, stop playing with me. I wanna know what the fuck was that I heard."

"Boy, I don't know. You bugging."

"Don't try to play me, Simone. I ain't slow."

"I ain't, daddy." Simone knew that Kamal was like a dog with a bone and wasn't gonna stop till he searched and found what he was looking for. She had to go into survival mode, unzip his pants, and bring her famous A-game to the table. *When all else fails, drop down and suck a nigga's dick!*

Kamal was mesmerized and drifting in the zone. Simone was showing out, sucking like her life depended on it and there was no tomorrow in sight. He'd forgotten all about the mystery music he'd just heard and was now totally preoccupied with the slurping sounds that a naked Simone was generating with her lips.

Things were going perfect, and bloodthirsty Kamal was well on his way to coming for the second time, and then hopefully, to sleep when once again—wouldn't you know—"Slum Village" kicked in.

Simone stopped in mid slurp, still down, posted on her knees with a mouth full of dick, looking up at crazed-face Kamal as he leaned over, moving the dish towel, revealing the source of the noise. Opening the strange phone, Kamal saw the letters *NFL* flashing on the screen. Everyone in Detroit, especially Kamal, knew it stood for *Niggas from Linwood*—his sworn enemies.

Chapter Fourteen

"You know that feels sooooo . . . good." Big Ace buried his face into the pillow, letting Monique's hands rub and massage almost every inch of his huge body. After fifteen minutes of steaming hot shower water pouring down on him, he was feeling nice, and this kingpin massage was like the icing on the cake to top off the night.

"Just close your eyes and let Monique take care of you."

"I hear you talking, girl," Big Ace cooed like a baby. "Go ahead and handle your business."

Monique started at the back of his neck, applying soft but firm squeezes, getting him to totally relax to the fullest. *Oh, yeah.* Then on to his strong shoulders, where she paid extra-special attention. Using her palms, she kneaded the still-damp skin of his upper back.

"Oh, shit, you good." He let the words barely escape his lips as he drifted off slowly. By the time Monique reached his lower torso with the touch of her magic hands, Big Ace was chilling in la-la land, snoring his big ass off.

"Hey, baby," Monique whispered, "are you asleep?" Big Ace didn't open his mouth or even make any sort of motion to indicate he'd heard her question. "Hey, baby, did you hear me?" She posed the same question to him once again, waiting to see what, if anything, he'd say. The only sound that she was met with was long, drawn-out snoring.

All that Big Willie talk and this mark buster asleep. Niggas kill me with all that bragging, then punk out.

Monique was on a mission but was still disappointed that she didn't get a chance to get some of that thick dick that Big Ace had between his legs. *I should cut the motherfucker off and take the bitch home for later!* Monique had to cover her mouth from laughing out loud at her own thoughts.

Slowly, she reached over for her purse and retrieved her cell phone. The text message she was expecting was there. When she read it, the project-bred female went into full action. Carefully easing her body off the bed was a task because of all the weight she possessed. With every movement, Big Ace's snores took on a different tone. Monique wasn't sure if he'd wake up at any moment, so that made the mission all the more difficult.

Successfully placing both feet on the floor, Monique rose up instantly, pausing as Big Ace lifted his head, turning it to the other side. His clean-shaven face was now facing her, and he appeared to be waking up. His eyes were wide open and seemed to be staring right at her and her every move.

"Hey, baby." She tried seeing if she got a response, but all he had to offer was a lot of gibberish. Monique stood there trembling, decked out in her birthday suit, trying to figure out what to do next. Big Ace was mumbling something about some dudes or a park and some guns. She frowned and sighed with relief when she realized that Big Ace was still fast asleep, but he was one of those weird sons of bitches that sleep with their eyes open.

Ain't this some crazy shit! Monique couldn't quite make out for certain what he was saying, and taking into consideration that he was talking in his sleep, she couldn't give a fuck less. As long as Big Ace didn't catch her creeping toward the door, throwing a monkey wrench in the gameplan, she'd be fine.

The sneaky, conniving con artist tiptoed her naked body to the door, putting her fire-engine red polished fingernails on the chain, sliding it off. Glancing back at Big Ace once more to ensure he wasn't awake yet, she then twisted the bolt, unlocking the door.

Yes! she thought as she watched Big Ace appear to watch her walk around to the other side of the bed. Monique stopped momentarily, looking at Big Ace's perfect muscular frame and licking her lips. *Just stay asleep, boo boo. I swear to God, it'd be such a waste to lullaby a motherfucker as fine as your black ass is.*

She then disappeared into the bathroom, leaving the door slightly cracked so she could hear clearly. Monique sat down on the toilet and played with herself with Big Ace in mind to waste time as she waited for part three of her well-crafted gameplan to jump off.

Joey was on the freeway traveling to the hotel where Trevon was waiting. He reached under the seat, getting his pistol, setting it on his lap as he drove. He tried to drive the speed limit, knowing good and damn well that he was in Oakland County, Michigan, and out there, the white man didn't play games with your ass. A Negro could easily get ninety days for coughing too loud in the middle of the night. With that in mind, Joey slowed down even more.

It seemed as if destiny kept causing them to cross paths with Kamal and his crew, so ten or fifteen minutes wouldn't matter that much. Joey usually wasn't into all that gangbang madness, but he felt he had no choice this go-around. It's one thing to blow a lot of smoke out ya mouth with idle threats, but it's a different ball game on a whole different level when a nigga starts actually busting. That's when and where true players draw the line and chaos kicks in.

While gripping the steering wheel, trying his best to seem inconspicuous to the State boys, Joey thought about Simone and how strange and jumpy she was acting. As long as he'd known her, she never, ever would let him get out of her sight without getting some dough, especially some that he'd already promised her. Until he finished with the business at hand, Simone would have to be on the back burner. But that still didn't stop him from thinking, *This the second time tonight she done let me slide on the money tip. I wonder what her slick ass is up to now.*

Monique removed her hand from between her legs and peeked out the door. She took a deep breath as the knob slowly turned. The sounds of Big Ace's snoring filled the room as the three masked men crept inside with their guns pointed directly at the bed. The first man to enter was immediately thrown off by the fact that Big Ace was lying in the bed, looking dead at them, without saying a single, solitary word.

"What the fuck?" the man yelled.

Big Ace blinked his eyes twice and squinted, trying to get a grip on what was happening. Before he could get a chance to mutter a word, the second guy rushed over, slamming the side of his gun into the side of his head. The force of the blow caused a gash to open wide and blood to flow down the side of Big Ace's face.

With the third man shutting the door, the real reason for the invasion became apparent, and Big Ace was beaten almost unconscious. He was gangsta to the nth degree as he took punch after punch without so much as one word of protest.

After being stomped several good old-fashioned times and then kicked twice in the mouth, Big Ace watched

helplessly as one of the masked men ran into the bathroom, where Monique pretended to be hiding, and
snatched her out. Her nude body was hard to cover as
she screamed, trying to act as if she was fighting off the
robbers.

After a brief struggle, the masked man backhanded her
once hard and covered her mouth with his hand. With
the other hand, he probed every inch of her nude body
while she let the fake tears flow. As he was feeling on her
huge breasts then sticking his fingers one by one inside
her already wet pussy, she tried to yank away and resist.

"Bring the tramp over here so her man can see her,"
one of the men ordered.

"Lay her big butt on the floor near this sucker," the
next said, pushing a seemingly hysterical Monique to
the ground.

"Please don't! Please," she sobbed and pleaded.

Monique was good at this part of the routine. This was
her specialty. She always had to make things look good
because if she didn't, one of her many victims might get
suspicious about the setup scam, catch her fat ass on the
streets, and kill the bitch. So, the game continued, and
after twenty long, dragged-out minutes of Big Ace being
forced to watch all three masked men taking turns having
sex with Monique, even violating her anally, he saw
each spit in her face, leaving her unbeknownst-to-him
nymphomaniac ass balled up in a corner, happy about
the different dicks that were just inside of her.

Damn, that was the shit, she thought.

Big Ace was now facedown, naked on the dirty carpet,
with a drenched combination of blood and perspiration
dripping off of him. As bad as he wanted to come to the
female's rescue and his own, he had three guns pointed
directly at him and his hands duct taped behind his
bruised back. The street warrior couldn't do anything but
wait and see what else the gunmen had in store.

Injured and suffering, he tried his best to at least recognize the voices that were coming from behind the masks, but he couldn't. Lying there in a growing pool of blood, Big Ace thought back to the shootout at the park and came to the conclusion that this whole fucked-up situation must be somehow connected. *If I get out of this alive, them motherfuckers gonna pay!*

"Should we let this punk live or what?"

"Naw, let's do his ass!"

"Yeah, let's kill both they asses!"

After a short discussion that had already been pre-planned, the three intruders went through Big Ace's pockets, taking all his money, his wallet, jewelry, and Monique's purse. The trio neared the door and turned around to double-check, making sure they hadn't left anything.

The first two were outside the room as the third reached on the floor by the bed and grabbed the last take for the night before making his exit. "Thanks, player. Good looking out! I need a new pair of these!"

Big Ace and Monique watched the dude deliver the final kick in the balls for the night by taking the brand-new fresh pair of Tims that Big Ace had just bought earlier.

With the couple now alone, both bloody and sore, a still-naked Monique was relentless in playing the scenario all the way out. Her whimpers of pain were of soap opera category. The way she crawled over to Big Ace's body, wrapping her arms around him, was sheer genius. Her hands shook with fake-ass fear as she tore the duct tape off with her razor-sharp teeth. Monique might have been born and raised in Detroit's grimiest projects, was a hundred or so pounds overweight, had different baby daddies, a head full of weave, and couldn't dress like shit—sure, the tramp had the unsophisticated grace of a wild llama in heat and the educational level of a kindergartener—but there wasn't a person that walked the face of the earth or moon that could deny the chick could act her ass off.

"Oh my God, baby! Are you okay?" She closely held a dazed Big Ace.

"Naw, I think you better get some help," he managed to say through the pain. "Call my boy Kamal. Tell him them dudes from the park must've followed us or something."

Monique knew calling Kamal would be a bad idea. Even though Big Ace didn't immediately suspect her involvement in the robbery, her crew needed time to get out of Dodge and back safely across town. Instead, the actress stalled for time by pulling the phone down off the nightstand by its cord and slowly dragging it over toward her. With a deep breath of desperation, Monique dialed the operator.

"Hello, front desk. . . . We need an ambulance in room 117!"

Chapter Fifteen

Trevon watched as the men, one by one, entered room 117. His adrenalin was rising as his heart rate increased. It was eating him up inside with every passing moment that he focused his mind on the goings-on behind the closed door. *Damn, what the fuck is they doing in that bitch?*

Paying attention to the burgundy curtains just in case they moved, revealing a quick peek, or maybe hearing a gunshot or two was all that Trevon was waiting for. A couple of cars turned into the lot, parking in front of their rooms. Happy couples, walking hand and hand, who had no idea what was probably going on in the room right next to theirs, laughed and joked. Those few late-night stragglers reminded a hawk-eyed Trevon to try once again to get in touch with Joey to warn him. Glancing downward long enough to see the redial button and push it, he listened to four long rings.

Pick up, nigga! Come on, pick up! On the fifth ring, as soon as he was about to hang up, a strange voice answered.

"Yeah, who this?"

"Hello?" Trevon paused with uncertainty, not recognizing the voice on the other end of the line.

"I said who this?" the person demanded once more.

Trevon took his eyes off room 117 so he could check to make sure that he'd pushed the right button. When he read Joey's number out one by one to himself, he knew that something was wrong. "Man, who the fuck is this playing on my people's phone?"

The stranger yelled into the cell phone at Trevon, "Bitch-ass nigga! Don't be getting loud with me! *I'm* the one asking the questions. Now, like I said, *who* the fuck is *this?*"

Trevon pushed END, hanging up on the mystery man, believing that Nextel must've been slipping and got its wires crossed. "Let me do this dumb shit again." As he took his time scrolling down his list of contacts, he came to Joey's name and hit CALL.

Simone tried to get up and run out of the kitchen but was stopped by Kamal's huge hands snatching her back.

"Whose goddamn shit is this?" Kamal wrapped his hand firmly around her hair, twisting it until his knuckles were pressed into her scalp. "And matter of fact, fuck that! Why you got one of them Linwood niggas calling this motherfucker?"

"Wait, Kamal!"

"Wait for *what,* bitch?" He tossed the phone back on the counter. "What lie you about to tell me?"

Simone had to come up with something quick. "I'm trying to tell you if you just give me a chance."

He smacked her as hard as he possibly could. "There goes your chance, ho! Now, answer me!"

"That must be Prayer's phone. She must've left it when she was fixing my food."

"Don't lie to me, Simone!" He smacked her once more.

"I'm not! I swear on Li'l T's life that's Prayer's phone!"

"Don't make me sock you next, ho." He stiffened up his grip.

"Please, Kamal, you're hurting me."

"Like that shit matter any to me!"

With her face beet red and an imprint of Kamal's hand plastered across it, Simone started to hyperventilate from fear. She'd seen Kamal pissed off before, having had plenty of ass kickings administered by him, but this time was different. He had the undeniably cold, callous persona of a psychotic killer on a late-night horror movie. Before Simone could concoct a way to weasel her way out of what could easily turn out to be the worst beating she ever experienced, Kamal struck her twice more in her face, only this time with a closed fist. One blow grazed her jaw, while the other found its way to her ear. As he let go of her hair, Simone flew into the side of the stainless steel refrigerator, seeing stars as she made contact.

Kamal cracked his knuckles, walking over to an already-wounded Simone with more brutal thoughts in store as she was trying her best to regain her senses. Dazed and confused by the hit she'd just taken, his son's mother was too weak to move. Just as he raised his boot to stomp her, "Slum Village" distracted him.

"Oh, I see your punk-ass boyfriend is calling back."

Simone had no comment, remaining quiet as a mouse as Kamal went over to the counter once again, answering Joey's ringing cell phone. She knew that this time was much different than the others when she'd fucked up. This time was the mother of all mothers.

"*NFL*. Yeah, that's his ho ass," he grunted, pushing TALK. "Yeah, nigga! Why you keep calling my mother-fucking girl?"

Trevon was speechless in responding to whoever had his boy's phone. Less than a half hour ago, Joey was just talking on the shit, and now this clown had it. He had a bad feeling about the whole thing, knowing that it couldn't be anything nice behind it.

"Listen, playa! Where dude at whose phone you hold-ing?"

"And what dude is that?"

"Come on, playa, and stop bullshittin'. You know who cell you got! NFL, nigga!"

Trevon heard the person slam his hand on something and scream, "Damn, Simone, I thought this was that ho Prayer's phone."

"I-I-I-thought—" She tried to speak but couldn't get the words out without stuttering.

"Man, shut the fuck up."

Trevon heard him say Simone's name and shit started to click. This had to be one of her trick busters that done got a hold of Joey's phone. "Put Simone on!"

"She busy about to get an ass kicking," the guy fired back.

"Oh, yeah? Well, that's between you and her. All I wanna know is where is my peoples at?"

"Dig dis, Linwood! Ya some real ho-ass motherfuckers, and next time I see any one of y'all, it's *on!*"

"You coward bitch." Trevon snickered smugly.

"Whoever this is, you don't want none!"

As he and the dude exchanged insults and promises, Trevon wondered exactly who this buster was that was going for hard.

"Whatever, guy. Just tell your peoples to stay the fuck away from my pussy."

Kamal got a glimpse of Simone trying to crawl out of the kitchen unnoticed and snapped. "Did I tell your bitch ass to move?"

"Wait, hold up. I think I hear Li'l T crying," she whined, breathing hard.

"So what?"

"He needs me!"

"So fucking what, Simone?"

"But—"

"But *what?* I told you not the hell to move, Simone. Now, I'm not fucking around wit' ya ass no more. If you even blink an eye, I'm beating ya ass *and* Li'l T! Now, *try* me!"

"Please don't," Simone begged, sounding sincere.

"I warned you, bitch. Now I'm about to *show* you!"

Trevon was still on the line, ear hustling. Simone deserved and needed to get mashed for playing both ends against the middle and getting caught up, but this fool was talking about putting his hands on Joey's son. "Damn, dude! Why you threatening a kid? You's a ho!"

"Stay outta my business!" Kamal ended his conversation by major-league pitching the cell phone into Simone's leg, causing an almost immediate dark red bruise to form on her light skin, matching the ones on her face.

Trevon tried calling back but only got the voice mail. *Damn, Joey. Where you at?* He looked back out the hotel room window, anxious for his boy's arrival, just in time to witness the three masked gunmen exit room 117 as quietly as they had entered, commotion free. Five minutes later, he heard police sirens.

Joey was a few minutes away from touching base with Trevon when a gang of cop cars roared by. Their obvious unmistakably white suburban asses had their hats on tight and their guns polished, ready to burn a nigga down. Joey held his breath as each one passed him, not even looking in his direction.

"Whew, that was close." He cut his eyes over at his gun, which was still riding shotgun. When he turned onto Dequindre Road, he was faced with the police vehicles again. They were swarming in and around the entire perimeter of the hotel where Trevon was at. *What this fool done did? I told his ass to chill!*

Turning into a nearby gas station so he could get his thoughts together and call Trevon, Joey searched the car for his cell phone, realizing that he'd left it back at Simone's house on the kitchen counter. *Shit, I know her jealous ass calling every number on that motherfucker!*

Luckily for Joey, he was in the white man's territory, and there was a payphone conveniently located on the far side of the gas station. He walked over and lifted up the receiver and actually heard a dial tone. Back in the hood, a Negro could search until the soles of his Tims wore out and still couldn't find a payphone, at least one that worked. Depositing the correct amount of change the recorded voice had requested, Joey dialed Trevon's cell.

"Hey, dude! What up?"

"Damn, Joey! Boost Mobile! Where the fuck your ass at?"

"I'm down at the corner. I seen a bunch of them boys and thought your ass did something drastic."

"Naw, I didn't have to." Trevon rushed through his explanation. "Some other cats with Halloween masks on crept they asses. I'm still in my room chilling."

"Damn, they straight holding you hostage, huh?"

"Joey, man, later for all that. I just called your cell phone, and—"

"I know. I left that bad boy back at Simone's. What she doing . . . answering the motherfucker or what?" Joey laughed at his son's moms.

"Naw, guy! Some lame wannabe gangsta answered that bitch!"

"What!"

"Yeah, nigga. Just now!"

"All right, then, Tre, is you tight? I'm about to go catch this trick Simone in the act!"

"I'm tight, dawg. Do you! And chin check that buster for me! It's one thing to slap around a broad, but I heard that fool talking about whooping up on your seed!"

"Li'l T?"

"Yeah, dude, Li'l T! That's what he said while he was smacking ol' girl around."

"You bullshittin'?"

"Naw, cuz, I heard her screaming. Ain't no telling what that buster over there doing right about now."

"I'm out! I'll holler!"

Joey slammed the receiver down, jumping back in his car and heading back to Simone's. Fuck the police. Fuck the speed limit, and fuck any stray-ass sissy fool that thought he could get away with putting they hands on his son. He loved Li'l T. That was his little man, and he'd walk through a blazing hot barn fire with gasoline underwear for him. Any motherfucker putting they hands on him was out of the question.

Chapter Sixteen

It's now a little after four o'clock in the morning in Detroit, and you're listening to 105.9 FM. The temperature is a balmy 75 degrees, which is unusual for this time of year. You've got ya main man, DJ Smooth-N-Groove waking some of you early shift factory workers up so you can punch that clock, and helping those late-night, party-hopping, casino-going, can't-seem-to-go-to-sleep folks chill out. Whatever applies to you, grab a hold, Motown, and reminisce on a little bit of this. . . .

Chari was in the bed with the darkness surrounding her. She was lonely, with no one to keep her company except the sounds of the radio. The rhythmic beat of the song caused her to reexamine her life.

Damn, I'm tired of living alone. I wish I had someone to love me like Drake loves Prayer or even that love Simone's crazy self gets. It was at that very moment in time Chari decided that as soon as she got off from work and got home, she was gonna stop fronting and ask Trevon over to dinner. Who knows, maybe he was her knight in shining armor. It was worth taking the chance and giving it a shot if it meant love. Chari knew that if there was one guy on the entire earth that had no designs on trying to get with her friend, Simone, it was Trevon. And with Simone, the feeling was mutual.

***

Prayer stayed on the telephone with Drake as he drove down the interstate, heading back from Baltimore. The couple was ecstatic that he'd concluded all his business dealings early and would be home shortly after daybreak. Listening to her radio in the background took the pair on a heartfelt trip down memory lane to the time when they were young teenagers. Taking the bus downtown to Hart Plaza for the summer festivals, walking hand in hand at Northland, going skating at Wheels, and even their first real kiss on the side of Drake's grandmother's house on Glendale were the main topics of the night. After all the turmoil and dangerous crap Simone had taken her and Chari through at the club, Prayer was more than ready for Drake to enroll back in school to finish getting his degree and leave the game alone altogether. He was already headed in that direction, but she intended on giving him that extra nudge she felt he needed.

Trevon watched out the hotel window as the EMTs rolled their gurney out with a body on it. After careful inspection from afar, he realized that it was the dude from the park. They had an oxygen mask over his face and were moving at a fast rate of speed. The female that he recognized as Monique was following closely behind with a blanket wrapped around her. The police seemed to be taking notes as crime scene cameras started to flash. Everyone from the hotel managers to the guests and nosy passersby wanted to see what crime had taken place. Even when the ambulance pulled off en route to the local hospital, the crowd still stayed, gossiping as the police investigated, trying to make heads or tails of the true story, since Monique was acting like she was in shock.

Trevon was trapped inside his room and lay across the bed with only his gun to keep him company. He turned the radio on his favorite station to pass the time away as he waited for Joey to call him and fill him in on how he ended up beating the piss out of the big-mouthed wanksta who answered the phone and Simone's no-good behind.

Yvette's headphones were turned up to the highest volume. She had grown accustomed to sleeping like that every night to avoid hearing the thunderous-like sounds of Ms. Holmes's snores. It was four o'clock in the morning, and she still couldn't sleep. With the combination of Simone smacking her foster mother, who, in turn, called the authorities, and the thought of Simone totally cutting her off, which meant no more cute outfits or purses, Yvette was up and down all night.

Watching the stars twinkle and the bright full moon shine over the row of vacant houses near the corner, the young girl couldn't help but notice all the after-hours traffic that was opening and closing doors over at Simone's house. Even though Simone often had company, this much in and out was not ordinary.

As Yvette bopped her head from side to side to the old-school jams that DJ Smooth-N-Groove was playing, she first saw Joey come over carrying some bags. *He's so nice. He's always bringing Simone or Li'l T something.* A little bit after that and four songs later, she observed Joey running off the porch with his feet barely touching the stairs, jumping in his car, and racing off down the block. *Where's he going so fast? He just got there!* Before the commercial about the Summer Jam Concert and the after-party at The Marriott on East Jefferson could go off and the music start again, Yvette saw Kamal pull up in the driveway behind Simone's Lexus and bang on her front door. *Dang gee, Simone! That was close!* With contempt for Kamal in her heart for the way she'd witnessed him talk to her idol, Simone, not to mention the way he mistreated Li'l T, Yvette turned her lip up with disgust as she watched him pee in the grass. *Ughh . . . He so nasty! I hate him!*

When Simone finally opened the door and Yvette saw him push his way in the house, she lay back down in her bed and tried to get some rest. *Hey, this my song!*

Chapter Seventeen

"Simone, trust I'm not fucking around with ya bitch ass no more." Kamal used her ears as handles, grabbing her up off the floor, throwing her into the living room.

"I'm sorry." Simone gasped for air as Kamal harshly stomped his Tims down on her stomach. "Please, I can't breathe!"

Simone turning pale as a ghost was not a deterrent for Kamal as he applied more pressure. Simone's once beautiful eyes were now bloodshot and rolling toward the back of her throbbing head. With snot and mucus filling her face, she was well on her way to passing out completely. Any strength that she had left in her body was fading rapidly.

"Tramp, it ain't that easy." Kamal removed his boot out of her abdomen, backhanding her twice to bring her out of it. "Now get the fuck up and take this ass whooping like a woman."

She shook, glaring at him with disbelief as he got her back up on her feet, only to give a massive body blow to her side, causing her to crumble once more, falling on the carpet.

"You wanna lie and creep around behind a nigga's back and shit?" Kamal hawked a huge glob of spit down on her. "I be out here putting my motherfucking freedom on the line for your slut ass, and you giving away my pussy to the next cat."

Simone's cracked, dry lips quivered as she tried repeatedly, unsuccessfully to speak.

"Don't even try it, Simone. All them games you be playing is the hell over. Where is my fucking car keys?" he fumed with anger. "You ain't about to be driving no other man around in the Lexus I got you pushing."

When Kamal saw no movement or reaction, he realized that his son's mother was now unconscious. That was his cue, and he went throughout Simone's house like Hurricane Katrina, destroying everything he came in contact with. He ripped the fabric off her new furniture, cut the cord on her flat screen television before snatching it down off the wall mount and smashing every DVD he could lay his hands on. Whether he had purchased the items for Simone didn't matter to him as he caused irreparable damage to her property.

In the midst of the noise and commotion he was making, Kamal heard sounds coming from the hallway and turned around to see Li'l T emerge out of the darkness, crying for his mother.

"Go back to bed," Kamal loudly ordered.

"Mommy . . . Mommy," Li'l T whined with a constant flow of tears streaming while wiping his eyes. "Mommy—"

"Shut the fuck up with all that sissy shit and take your ass back to bed!"

"I want my mommy . . . Mommy . . . Mommy—"

"What the hell did I just say?" Kamal approached the tiny, innocent little boy. "Now get the fuck on!"

The loud tone of Kamal's voice only made matters worse. A scared Li'l T began to sob more. He held his hands up toward Kamal to pick him up and take him to his mommy like he'd done in the past. Sadly, he got no response but fury as one of the men he was taught to call Da-Da knocked his arms down to his side. Kamal cupped the small child's head in his hands, turning him around, then shoving him toward bedroom. Li'l T was thrown off balance and confused about what was taking place.

"Go get in that bed! Now! Before I beat your little crybaby momma boy's ass." Kamal yanked Li'l T's arm damn near out of the sockets as he tossed him into his room and onto the bed, yelling out one more final demand before closing the door tightly shut. "Stay the fuck in here and lie the hell down!"

As Kamal returned to the living room to finish his tirade of physical assault on Simone, he could still hear their son's piercing screams. *What the fuck?* With his eyes darting from the space on the carpet where he'd left Simone lying to every corner of the room, Kamal searched for where she'd disappeared to. *Oh, this bitch think I'm playing with her ass.* Not saying a word, he went over to the front door, putting the double lock on. Then he went into the kitchen to slide the chain on the back entrance. "All right, whore. You only making the beatdown worse when I find that ass!" Kamal knew Simone was hiding somewhere in the front of the house because there was no way she could've snuck by him in the back. "You only pissing me off more and more, you slut bag, dick-sucking tramp!"

After a quick check behind the couch and love seat, he spotted a foot sticking from under the dining-room table. Kamal took his time heading in that direction, making Simone sweat it out. "Do you really think I'm gonna let you get away with playing me for a sucker? Especially with one of them Linwood motherfuckers?" He grinned wickedly, running his tongue across his teeth. "You got the game and me all fucked up!"

Simone's heart pounded with fear as she watched the soles of Kamal's boots submerge into the thick, padded carpet and come closer to her. *Damn, I messed up for real this time.* Her life seemed to flash before her eyes as one of her son's fathers dug his strong fingers into her ankle and tried dragging her out into the open.

"Stop! Stop!" She kicked at him in an attempt to break loose. "I ain't do shit! I swear! I ain't do shit!"

"Shut up, bitch."

"Please, Kamal."

"Hell, naw."

"Let me go! Pleeeease!"

"Fuck you, Simone. I ain't done with your ass yet."

For what seemed like an eternity, the two of them struggled back and forth. Simone was already injured and at a disadvantage by being a woman. She was exhausted, not being able to fight and hold him off any longer. Her body gave out, going completely limp as he climbed on top of her.

"You two-timing project rat." His fist came down by her face into the carpet. "You can't beat a grown-ass man."

Simone panted repeatedly, trying to catch her breath as Kamal pressed his sweaty body down, smothering hers. She couldn't move one inch as they were now nose to nose.

Kamal was furious as he continued to talk shit. "Your ass wanna give the pussy away?" He momentarily waited, knowing that he wouldn't get an answer. "Well, after tonight, that crab faggot nigga can have your tainted, broke ass!"

Kamal reached one hand up to his mouth, removing his fronts. He saw the look of panic on Simone's face as he rammed the curved gold mouth ornament deep inside her pussy. Simone was speechless as Kamal's continuous, heinous movements tried to ruin her for life.

"Please don't," she muttered in distress and pain.

"Now let's see you give this worthless, stankin' mother-fucker away," he said, laughing wickedly.

Simone's arms were stretched out and lying above her head. The strong, traumatic scraping force that Kamal was applying pushed her fingertips close to a small plastic crate that she kept cleaning supplies in. With her skin numb and tingling from the misery of the torture she was enduring, Simone grabbed a bottle of Windex Glass Cleaner and squirted the preoccupied, crazed Kamal in his eyes, causing an almost immediate halt to his unthinkable act.

"Get off me!" screamed Simone at the top of her lungs as she managed to squirm away and crawl to the other room.

"All right, bitch. You gonna die for that." Kamal got off the floor, blinded by the chemicals in both eyes, feeling his way to the kitchen sink. "I'm gonna kill you!"

As he stumbled, passing by a still-naked Simone, she smashed a hand-carved imported vase across the back of his head. Candy-apple-colored, thick blood started to ooze through his perfectly parted braids and drip down. Simone paused, waiting to see if he would fall. He slowly reached up, touching the open gash, and got a handful of wetness. Kamal was dazed but still on his feet in search of water to rinse and relieve the burning sensation in his stinging eyes.

Now was Simone's time to make a getaway. Running to the front door and unlocking it in an attempt to escape, she looked down, realizing that she didn't have any clothes on. *Oh my God! Oh my God!* She pondered as she heard the water in the kitchen running. *What I'm gonna do now? Oh, shit! Oh, shit!* Simone snatched her cell phone off the table and ran toward the bathroom to lock herself in and call for help. She was less than ten feet away from the door when she heard Li'l T calling out for her from the hallway.

"Mommy! Mommy," he whined, getting closer.

Simone saw her small son on the other side of the living room, coming toward her. Out of the corner of her eye, she saw an infuriated Kamal also heading in her direction. *Oh, shit! Damn!* she thought as she made the selfish decision to leave her baby to fend for himself on the other side of the bathroom door. Turning the lock, leaning her weary body against the thin wooden door, Simone pushed 911 on her cell twice before realizing that the battery was completely dead.

Kamal's fist hit the door, causing the frame to shake. His boots were soon kicking the splitting wood. Time was ticking!

Joey raced down the freeway with one thought in mind: Li'l T. He loved his woman, but she was a big girl and could take care of herself. The anticipation of getting to Simone's house to find out what the hell was taking place made the veins in his neck bulge. If his small son needed him, he was gonna be there even if it meant breaking every law that the state of Michigan had on its books. *Damn, this traffic is crazy for this time of night. Where all these motherfuckers going?* He swerved around a huge semi-truck and pushed the gas pedal close to the floor. Flying by an old-school Monte Carlo and one broken-down Checker cab, Joey made good time. Less than ten minutes later, he saw his exit in sight: LINWOOD AVENUE 1/4 MILE.

Joey took the same exact path that only a short time earlier Kamal had taken. Flying around the deep curve past Fenkel, he never let up on the speed. He went down Oakman Boulevard, Davison Avenue, and finally, Glendale Street, where the red light and crossing traffic stopped him. *Awwww . . . Shit!* His first mind told him to fuck all the cars and make his move, but seeing a carload of "Detroit's Finest" harassing some late-night creepers shut that idea down. After all, he did have his gun sitting on the seat next to him in plain view. When the light turned green, he slowly drove the speed limit past the police, glancing back in his rearview mirror to make sure they weren't on him. *Five more blocks to Simone's.* Joey tapped on the steering wheel with his palms sweating.

"Get out of my house before I call the police." Simone tried bluffing the already-agitated Kamal.

"Call the sons of bitches." He kicked once more. "By the time they slow asses get here, the only thing they gonna find is your dead body."

"I'm not playing!" she screamed through the closed door.

"I ain't either, bitch!"

In the midst of their back-and-forth threats, Li'l T's cries were louder and much more heartwrenching. He was now right underfoot of Kamal, who only had one thing on his devious agenda at this point: vengeance. The sounds of Li'l T's voice were like a powerful echo to Simone, who felt she had no choice but to try to remain barricaded.

"You better come out here and get this little motherfucker before I kick his little ass up on the mantle." Kamal collared his son up, shaking him wildly.

"Mommy! I want my mommy!" Li'l T begged, snottynosed, face full of tears.

"You listening to this soft faggot you done raised?" Kamal used Li'l T's tiny body, ramming it against the door for Simone to hear. "He wants you, bitch!"

Li'l T whimpered with pain as he was being used as a pawn in his parents' tragic game. "Mommy!"

"Please stop, Kamal, please! What in the hell is wrong with you?" Simone was trembling from fear as she searched the bathroom with her eyes for any sort of a weapon. "How can you do that bullshit to your own child?"

"I'm counting to three, ho, and if you don't come out, I'm gonna give his little ass another taste of the beat down you got coming," he warned.

"Don't, Kamal!"

"One . . ."

"I swear I'm gonna call the police!"

"Two . . ."

"Please! Please! Don't hurt my baby!"

"Three . . ."

"Wait! Wait! Wait! I'm begging you!"

"Hell, naw! Fuck you and him!"

As if on cue, a stone-faced Kamal grabbed a defense-less Li'l T by his long braids and tightened his grip. His own son, his own supposed-to-be flesh and blood, Kamal swung him around twice. Recklessly, he finally let go, flinging the child's wilted body across the living room, resulting in him crashing into the wall. Li'l T appeared lifeless as he lay near the front door beside the couch with a small trickle of blood coming out of the corner of his mouth. Kamal wasted no time as he got his gun and put one up top.

"Okay, Simone! You up next, trick." He turned the radio on loud to muffle the sounds of his plans.

Simone knew that her firstborn was hurt and now it was really life or death. As sounds of rap filled the air, she leaped to her feet, opening up the medicine cabinet, pulling out a straight razor. "I'm gonna kill him!"

***

Joey turned the corner out of view of the police and flew down Simone's block. When he got in front of her house, he slammed on his brakes, threw the car in PARK, and jumped out, gun in hand.

What the fuck is this bullshit about? He couldn't believe that the same F-150 from earlier was all up in his baby momma's driveway. *I know this coward ain't in there with my family!* He placed his hand on the hood to see if it was still warm, but it wasn't. That let him know that Mr. Shoot-Up-the-Park-in-Broad-Daylight had been there for some time. *Damn! I just left this motherfucker! That bitch work quick!*

Joey cautiously walked up on the porch. Within five seconds of standing there, he heard Li'l T cry, a thud, silence, then loud music. The loyal father wasted no time kicking the door almost off the hinges, confronting the unknown.

Chapter Eighteen

"What the fuck!" Kamal turned, facing the door as the loud noise and vibration shook the entire house.

"Oh, hell naw! Shit!" As soon as it flew open, Joey immediately spotted an injured Li'l T, lying on the floor spread-eagle, facing the ceiling. "What the fuck your ass do to my motherfucking son?" He wasted no time waiting for his response, opening fire on a shocked Kamal, who immediately dove behind a chair, taking cover.

Letting off round after round, Joey was sure that he'd hit Kamal at least once or twice in the lower body. *Who the fuck is this punk?* Joey thought while never letting up on the trigger. *And where the hell is Simone?* He could only hope and pray at this point that her fate wasn't as bad as Li'l T's appeared to be. *And how the fuck he know her sneaky ass?* That Scooby-Doo mystery only added more heat to his already-boiling adrenaline.

Shit! I think I'm hit! Kamal looked down at his hip, realizing that he had a gaping tear in his pants and dark blood starting to soak through. *And what that nigga mean his son?* If he lived past daylight, he would have to deal with that bullshit then, but for now, ol' boy was on a crucial, straight, high-alert soldier detail. Kamal was 100 percent true to the game and the streets that helped raise him. He indeed had caught a few hot ones but had no worldly intentions of going out like a pussy. He lifted up, all Scarface style and shit, returning fire, ripping Joey a nice-size hole in his left shoulder as well as his chest.

"Now what, motherfucker?" Kamal hissed with anger.

"NFL, nigga! We don't die, we multiply," Joey shouted back as he let off one more round into a demented Kamal before dropping to the ground near Li'l T's still motionless, tiny body.

"Fuck Linwood," Kamal howled as a boiling hot sensation tore through his upper groin area then raced to his stomach, throwing him back against a bookshelf, knocking the loud stereo and its speakers to the ground.

"Naw, fuck you," Joey managed to get out as he turned his head toward his young son and reached out for his small hand.

Both of Li'l T's potential fathers were severely wounded. At this point, it was uncertain who'd gotten the best of the other as they both bled and moaned.

Simone was still in the bathroom, straight razor in hand, but she was smart enough to lie down in the bathtub to shield herself from a stray bullet. *Please, God, let my son be okay. I swear I'm done playing games*, she prayed as the sound of a door getting kicked, not to mention the rapid gunshots, gave her chills. Jumping with every passing echo, she shivered. *Damn, what the fuck is happening? What is his crazy ass out there doing?*

She had no idea that Joey had doubled back to save the day, so to speak, and was now in her living room, taking part in destroying her already-twisted world. Simone was under the impression that a jealous, immature Kamal was just showing his natural black ass, that he was shooting holes in her furniture and walls to teach her a lesson. He'd torn up her house on several prior occasions when shit didn't go his way. He'd spattered bleach on half of her wardrobe, including two full-length fur coats, pissed in and on every shoe in her closet, and worst of all, the satanic asshole killed Li'l T's puppy by snapping its neck. So, nothing Simone thought Kamal was doing tonight surprised her one bit. She just hoped her son was safe.

After another big, deafening sound, Simone carefully peeked her head up from the tub. Two long, grueling minutes dragged by before she made the hesitant decision to go back to the door and listen for any movement. She hoped that Kamal had finally given in, done enough damage, and left.

"It's quiet out there." It was the loudest silence she'd ever heard as she whispered to herself, feeling the light tan handle of the razor. "I need to go check on my son and stop thinking about myself." It was as if someone up above had clicked on the light switch in Simone's head, informing her that she wasn't only responsible for her own well-being, but also Li'l T's. She wrapped a fluffy white bath towel around her naked body and took a deep breath.

As the frightened mother gradually turned the lock, cracking the bathroom door just enough to see, Simone smelled the strange mixture of gunpowder and blood. Stepping out a few short feet, she saw the bottom of Kamal's boots and heard him sigh in pain. *What the fuck is he trying to pull? And where is my motherfucking son?*

Yvette leaped from her bed, running to the window. The sound of Joey's screeching tires could more than likely be heard blocks over. As she watched him rush, gun in hand, over to Kamal's F-150 that was parked in the driveway and touch the hood, she knew that her hero and mentor, Simone, was seconds away from being busted. *Damn!*

Joey was at the door a few seconds before, all of a sudden, Yvette saw him kick the son of a bitch in and loud, crazy gunshots jump off. *Oh my God!* She panicked as she flew out of her room, grabbing the telephone, calling 911. Ms. Holmes, as well as the entire neighborhood, made their way onto their front porches to see the outcome.

Chapter Nineteen

Thinking that Kamal was running game on her, Simone took her time in approaching him as she saw the condition of her once-perfect home and became infuriated. *Look at my front door! He gonna die for this crap! I'm just gonna be with Joey from now on out! Period!*

Simone got close and couldn't believe her eyes. There was big, bad Kamal, lying helpless on her new carpet, semi-conscious, drenched in blood, moaning for help. *What the hell! This shit is crazy as a fuck!*

She was confused. Before she could process what had really taken place, she turned her head, hearing another noise of agony, and came face-to-face with her worst nightmare yet. Joey was stretched out near the front door, gasping for air as he coughed up dark globs of blood. There, to his right side, also sprawled stationary, Simone was horrified to see Li'l T, her only child.

"Oh my God! Oh, no! Oh my God!"

Forgetting all about Kamal, a towel-clad Simone ran to her son and Joey. One look at her other baby's daddy made her feel instant queasiness. She focused her attention on Li'l T, dropping the razor from her hand and leaning protectively over her child's body, rubbing his cheeks, asking him repeatedly if he was all right and if he could hear her.

"Mommy loves you, baby," she reassured him as her maternal instinct kicked in. "Are you okay? Talk to me!"

"Yes, Mommy." Li'l T finally cried out a soft reply.

"Don't worry, baby. Mommy's gonna get help!" She was getting up to call 911 when she was stopped.

"Simone." Joey somehow managed to lift his arm out toward her, still coughing up blood. "Is my son okay? Are you okay?" He had a massive hole in his chest big enough for Simone to stick her fist in. His shirt was soaked in perspiration as his stomach heaved up and down. "I'm sorry it took me so long to get here." Joey struggled with every word he spoke. "I let you and my son down." The devoted father's breathing was getting fainter and raspier with each second that ticked by. "I tried. I tried."

"No, you didn't let us down, Joey," Simone confessed hysterically in tears. "This is all my fault! I'm so sorry, sweetheart! I'm so sorry!" Relentlessly pleading while realizing that her constant knight in shining armor was slipping away from her, she shouldered the blame. "If it wasn't for me and all my scheming, shit would've been so different for us. Can you forgive me, Joey?"

Simone, not caring about the awful state that he was in, pressed her face close to his and apologized one last time. "I'm so sorry! I'm gonna call 911. Just hold on, baby!" She wanted to own up about all the awful games she'd been playing with him, Kamal, and Li'l T, but she knew at this point the shit really didn't matter. The only thing that truly mattered was him getting medical attention.

Joey didn't answer, so Simone raised her head to look in his eyes in an attempt to beg for forgiveness once again. A weary Joey seemed to be staring straight through her as he started shaking violently, going into convulsions. Within a brief snap of the fingers, the young man who was a son, a possible father, and a loyal friend to the bitter end, Mr. Joey Ladon Carter—born March 17, 1981—was gone.

Frantically in denial about the events that were quickly unfolding, Simone was still praying to God that this was just one of her terrible nightmares. Some old *Twilight Zone* bullshit. It had to be. Maybe she drank too much at the club and was hallucinating.

"This ain't happening! This shit ain't happening!" she insistently mumbled, holding Joey's bullet-riddled body, rocking him in her arms like a newborn. "Joey is still alive! I'm only dreaming! I'm gonna wake up at any time!"

Off in the distance, Simone heard police sirens that brought her back to reality as she laid Joey gently down. "I'm sorry, Joey." She kissed his lips in spite of all the blood and mucous. "Even though I always knew deep down inside that Li'l T wasn't yours, I was still out for self."

The once pure-white towel she was wearing was now completely soiled, saturated with his blood along with hers from the beating and brutal rape she'd suffered at the hands of Kamal. With the sirens getting closer, she knew she'd had enough of Kamal. It was more than the average person could take. He stood for everything evil in her life. In Simone's now-deranged mind, Joey was gone because of him and not the deadly game of Baby Daddy Russian Roulette she had been playing every second since Li'l T's conception.

Coldly picking up her straight razor off the floor, Simone walked toward a still-suffering Kamal, the man she was certain was truly her son's no-good daddy. As her bruised, battered body got closer and the sirens got louder, her palms began to sweat.

"Get over here and help me, trick," Kamal yelled out as he saw her come in view. "Or else!"

Simone's bare feet tiptoed closer and closer to him.

"Hurry the fuck up! I need help." He barked another order out. "Ya little faggot boyfriend got a good hit off."

She was now towering over him, not saying a word.

"Don't just stand there, dumb bitch! Get me some help!"

Simone stood still, fuming with rage, straight razor down at her side.

Kamal reached his bloody hand out, grabbing her leg with the last bit of strength he could muster up, bringing her down to his level. "You gonna make me stomp that ass again. Yours and Li'l T. Now, keep playing with me."

Looking directly in Kamal's hate-filled eyes, Simone knew that she had to avenge Joey's death. "I hate you and everything about you," she finally blurted out, raising the razor up to his throat.

"Bitch, I wish you would." Kamal wasn't fazed. He taunted death, keeping his front up, street-hood style to the end.

"You ain't shit, Kamal! You deserve to die! Everything you ever touched in life was fucked up!"

"Come on, Simone." He groaned in pain. "You's a weak-ass little project tramp. Now, get that motherfucker away from my throat before I make you eat that shit!"

Simone, for the first time ever, saw the heavy paternal resemblance of Kamal and Li'l T. Their eyes were just alike, the thick braids, the barely noticeable mole that was on the left side of each one's lower jaw, and the small dimple in their chin. Realizing those similarities made her hand tremble as she held the razor tight. "I hate you."

Kamal got a last, sudden burst of energy, putting one hand around Simone's neck, making her drop her weapon as she snatched back from his weak grip. "I knew you ain't have that shit in you," he teased, pointing over at Joey's dead, crumpled body. "You's a ho like ol' boy laying over there."

An infuriated Simone crawled over in the corner of the living room, grabbing Li'l T's huge Sesame Street throw pillow. Aware of the screeching sounds of the police sirens closing in on her block and house, she rushed back over to a heartless, cruel-spirited Kamal, who was fighting to live. Losing the bath towel along the way, a completely nude Simone closed her eyes shut and climbed on him, forcing a colorful collage of Big Bird, Elmo, and the Cookie Monster down on his face.

"I'll see your ass in hell, motherfucker." Her unorthodox retaliation was short but sweet. "Oh, yeah. By the way, for your information, back in the day, I fucked ya boy Big Ace twice! And trust, his dick was way bigger than yours!"

Kamal's arms flung wildly, struggling as Simone Harris continued to maliciously cut off all means of his oxygen. Soon, the demented, ruthless street warrior's body gave in as his legs shook and his bowels totally released, signaling that the devil would soon have company. That much was destined.

"Talk that bullshit now, motherfucker." Simone couldn't resist ridiculing Kamal, who, of course, couldn't hear a word that was being said as she bounced her weight on top of the pillow to make sure that she'd finished the job. "You ain't so big and bad now, is you? I thought not, asshole," she answered her own question. "I hate ya yellow ass! I hate you with all my heart!"

Simone felt that she'd now settled the deadly score and vindicated herself on Joey's behalf. When she was 100 percent sure that Kamal had taken his last breath on the planet Earth that she was made to occupy with him, she removed the sweat-stained, blood-soaked pillow and looked once again into Kamal's face. Just like Joey, Kamal's eyes were wide open, seeming to be watching her every move. After hawking the hugest, nastiest, mucus-filled glob of spit she could muster, she spit dead into his eyes and felt a slight bit of contentment watching it slide down the side of his face.

Hearing the sirens only houses away, the self-appointed Death Angel tossed the pillow to the other side of the room and wasted no time in going back to her injured son's side. He didn't move or make a sound as both of his fathers took their last breaths. He was innocent of everything that he was going through. He was just a pawn in his mother's deadly game. Now the shit had hit the fan. There wasn't any comeback from death, no turn around, and no "dang, my bad."

Simone was still naked but felt no disgrace. At this point, none of that mattered. She held Li'l T in her arms and rocked him back and forth, praying to God for strength. "I'm sorry," she repeated with remorse.

Within seconds, a gang of police stormed inside of Simone's house, pistols in hand. The invasion of uniformed and plainclothes officers in her front room didn't make her blink an eye. Her battered, still perfectly shaped nude body seemed to capture their attention, but she didn't care. Normally, Simone would be full of wisecracks and insults for the police. This time was different, as she was glad to see them coming.

"What happened in here, miss?" one cop swiftly inquired.

"Can you tell us who did this to you?" The next took his turn at trying to get an answer from a nonresponsive Simone.

"Who are these two men?" a female officer asked while kindly grabbing the blanket off the couch, wrapping it around Li'l T and Simone in hopes of getting her fellow officers to show some respect.

Simone was in a horror movie, and she was the star.

Chapter Twenty

"We got two males fatal and two wounded, including a small child." The sergeant on duty called his shift commander, informing him of the state of the crime scene as he waited on the ambulance to transport the victims.

Simone's house was swarming with cops parading in and out of every room, removing bullets out of walls, trying to investigate what went on, as homicide detectives started to arrive and ask questions. As Simone, the local hood hero, and Li'l T were being brought out of the house alive, Yvette and even fake-ass Ms. Holmes shed tears of relief.

Simone refused to let Li'l T out of her arms, despite pleas from the EMS techs who needed to check his vitals. "No, don't touch my son!" she instructed en route to the same hospital she'd given birth at. Looking down at a weary Li'l T, she kissed his forehead, whispering almost the same exact thing she had the day he was born into the game she forcefully manipulated him to become a part of.

Simone was remorseful with her words. "Don't worry. We don't need no man! I got us this time around, and we still ain't gonna want for shit. I promise you that. I'm gonna step up and be your mother and father. I'ma be that boss bitch!"

When the EMS finally arrived at Detroit Receiving Hospital's Emergency Trauma entrance, Simone was forced to loosen the tight grip on her son. His body was limp, and he was unconscious, unaware of his surroundings. The medics carefully placed Li'l T on a stretcher, transporting him into a triage evaluation room. Doctors and nurses swarmed around the young patient, trying to determine the full extent of his injuries. With as much confusing information as they could gather from a distraught Simone, they quickly realized that the small boy had no doubt suffered some sort of spinal injury.

Yvette and all the neighbors stayed posted in the same street that they'd just hours earlier vacated in shame. It seemed to be some sort of a Detroit hood tradition to count how many body bags were brought out of a crime scene, like they thought a bloody hand would unzip the bag from the inside and jump out of that bitch. Better yet, they would try their best to be the all-star, VIP, ghetto-fabulous motherfucker the local news cameras chose to put on Breaking News that, for real for real, really ain't know jack shit about what had happened.

"That's what that uppity bitch get," one person coldly commented.

"Yeah. You right." A dopefiend put in his two cents.

"I wonder what the hell went on inside that house."

"Who is in them bags?"

"Did she shoot they asses?"

"Why wasn't the baby moving?"

"Her tramp ass finally got caught in her shit!"

"Did y'all hear all those gunshots?"

"I know Simone looked messy as hell!"

Person after person had their own speculation about the version of events and the way they could've unfolded.

As the police made their rounds through the crowd, trying to find any witnesses, Yvette was the only one who truly had something to say that could make a difference. Despite the disapproving frowns and whispers of folks who generally hated the police and considered helping them out class-A snitching, even when it had to do with a neighbor, Yvette told them everything she'd seen from her bedroom window. Her information made it simple for the detectives to easily establish a timeline of the deadly bloodbath and heinous events of the night. Now they knew exactly who Joey and Kamal were and what their affiliation was with Simone and Li'l T.

With two smoking guns near each deceased body, the investigation was sure to go smoothly. Besides, when Simone, a victim herself and a live witness, calmed down and dealt with Li'l T's emergency situation, she could answer and clear up the entire homicide mystery.

Chapter Twenty-one

It was almost the break of dawn, and the sun was on its way to emerge out of the darkness. Richton Street was emptied of all the police, medical examiners, and various news reporters that had been camped out for hours, trying to make heads or tails out of the bloodbath inside of Simone's house. Yvette sat on the edge of her bed, watching out the window, praying that Simone and Li'l T were okay. None of the fancy cars, trucks, or high-priced clothes she admired Simone for possessing really mattered at this point. After all, let's face facts. What good would any of that materialistic bullshit truly do if your ass was dead?

Yvette wanted to call Simone's cell to check on them, but as usual, Ms. Holmes was on the phone, bad-mouthing everyone she knew. Of course, the main topic of discussion was Simone and the double homicide.

"Yes, sirree. I couldn't believe it. That no-good child done messed around and probably killed them boys," Ms. Holmes said into the phone.

"How do you know what truly happened?" the person responded. "They didn't arrest her, did they?"

"Naw, but you know that don't mean nothing much these days and times. Don't you watch *Cops* or Court TV?" Ms. Holmes objected. "They probably gonna do it later, at the hospital."

"Let's stand in agreement and pray they don't," the caller requested. "Was the baby looking okay?"

Ms. Holmes raised her beige-and-red coffee mug to her old lips, taking a small sip before answering. "Oh my God," the gossip queen yelled out, testifying as if she were in the front pew of a down-home country Baptist church service. "Now, you know I love me some Li'l T, but I can't lie. He wasn't moving a single solitary muscle, the poor little thang."

"Oh, no. Please don't say that."

"Yeah, but if he dies, it ain't nobody's fault but that low-life slut Simone. Matter of fact, it would serve her right, especially after she put her dirty hands on me last night."

"What did you just say?" The listener grew increasingly enraged.

"You heard me. Honey, you know good and damn well yourself she ain't worth two wooden nickels and never has been."

"Regardless of what Simone is or isn't, it's certainly not your place to judge her, let alone speak out the side of your neck about the baby."

"Wait one minute!" Ms. Holmes acted as if she had the nerve to be offended by being checked.

"Hell, no! You wait one minute. I let you continuously talk about my flesh and blood last night and didn't stop you, but enough is enough. You're going too far!"

Simone's estranged, now religiously devout mother periodically stayed in touch with her old running buddy to get updates on her daughter and grandson. But lately, the last few times she and Ms. Holmes spoke, there seemed to be an air of bitterness and contempt toward Simone. Even though there was bad blood, so to speak, between them, she would be less than a woman, Christian or not, if she let anyone say the type of foolishness that Ms. Holmes was trying to get away with.

"Oh . . . so now you want to play the mother role, huh?"

"I don't have to *try* to do anything of the sort. I *am* that child's mother, and Terrell is indeed my grandson whether I speak to her today, tomorrow, or never."

"Whatever." Ms. Holmes took another sip of her warm coffee. "Then instead of sitting on this phone throwing insults around, why isn't your self-righteous behind down at the hospital?"

Her sarcasm cut deep like a sharp, double-edged knife.

"Maybe I should be, because it's painfully apparent that your only purpose in life is to be the devil's co-conspirator." With that being said, Simone's mother angrily slammed down the receiver, leaving a stunned Ms. Holmes looking completely dumbfounded. Whether Simone's mom actually went to the hospital still remained to be seen, but at least hearing the wagging tongue of a human form of venomous snake was over

Meanwhile, across town, Chari, who was feeling guilty about the way she and Prayer had treated Simone the night before, woke up and made it her first priority to go over to take breakfast to her homegirl as a peace offering. When she pulled up in front of the house, Chari was beyond shocked. Yellow tape was everywhere, and the picture window was shot out. The front door had a piece of plywood leaning up against it, and the porch railing was dangling. A police cruiser was slowly driving by, keeping a watchful eye on the house.

Chari frantically flagged the police car down but got limited information from the rookie cop and his partner. Her head was spinning from disbelief. With cell phone in hand, she immediately called Prayer, who, together with Drake, who'd just made it in from his trip, rushed over.

After talking to the next-door neighbor, Mister McNab, the trio found out some of what was supposed to have happened. The girls then quickly called a few hospitals, finding out exactly where they'd taken Simone and Li'l T.

Prayer and Chari left to be by their friend's side, while Drake got in touch with some of his folks so they could secure the house and the perimeter. Mister McNab was an elderly man, and there was only so much he could do in the way of security. If Drake and his crew didn't damn near put steel boards, three pit bulls, and an around-the-clock, in-house Negro to watch that motherfucker, the crackheads and dopefiends would run havoc in Simone's crib. After a long, tiring, action-packed night, the old man excused himself to lie down and take stock of exactly what his once calm, quiet, respectful, and crime-free block had been reduced to through the passing years.

As he waited for his boys to pull up, Drake grew infuriated by what had taken place. Looking at Joey's car and Kamal's truck, he shook his head. They were still sitting in the same place where the two deceased had left them. That reality made him make the final decision that Prayer was right. It was time to get out of the dope game for good and do something different and productive with his life.

In Detroit, there were only two ways that a guy in the streets could expect to go: either in a casket, or in the back of a squad car headed to jail. When both young men, who Drake knew in passing, had woken up yesterday morning, neither had any clue that it would be their last day on earth. Each went to the park, hung out with friends, talked shit, partied, got they drink on, and got some ass. But okay, now what? Now nothing! Ghost! Game over! Flatline! See you later, bye! Peace!

This shit is definitely for the birds. Niggas killing their own over dope and pussy! Drake thought, cracking his knuckles, taking a deep breath of the polluted city air. *After this bullshit, my girl ain't never hanging out with that foul bitch Simone again! I just hope Li'l T is all right. Li'l man done lost both his old dudes in one night!*

Yvette was still looking out of the window and saw Chari pull up. By the time she finished throwing on some clothes and packing a bag, Prayer and Drake had arrived. This was the time to prove her point, stand her ground, and make a statement. She'd listened to Ms. Holmes run her mouth and talk shit for the last time. Finally realizing it was Simone's mother that her foster provider was talking to was the straw that snapped the camel's back. She was out of that bitch! She'd make it on her own! After hearing Ms. Holmes hang up the phone, Yvette made her presence known and felt. Shaking her head in disgust, she gave Ms. Holmes a swift smack to the face, leaving her with some words of wisdom: "Grow the fuck up!"

Chapter Twenty-two

Prayer and Chari burst through the emergency doors of the hospital, causing the security guards on post to become alerted. As the pair quickly approached the front desk, they practically knocked over a woman who was pushing a baby stroller.

Without waiting in line for the nurse on duty to call next, Chari blurted out her question. "Excuse me, excuse me, but we're looking for Simone Harris!" Receiving stern glances from the people behind her didn't seem to bother Chari one bit. "She and her son were brought in here sometime late last night."

Before getting a chance to respond, the heavyset Caucasian nurse was startled by the clanking sound of Prayer's keys slamming down on the counter. "Can you ladies please wait a moment?" the nurse pleaded as she shuffled through a stack of papers.

"This is an emergency," Prayer insisted.

"Yeah, this is an emergency," Chari vouched.

"We all got emergencies," a chick with a bad weave and no visible edges yelled out. She was patiently standing in line, coughing.

Chari turned around, giving the female a look that could have set the bitch on fire. In order to put a stop to any drama jumping off, the nurse once again got Simone's first and last name. Pushing the information into the computer revealed the exact whereabouts of the girls' injured friend and her son.

With visitors' passes and directions, Chari and Prayer hurried to Trauma Care. Upon exiting the elevator, they came face-to-face to a frazzled Simone with her black-and-blue bruised face pressed up against the window. She appeared done in as she held onto the frame to keep from falling to the ground. Her hair was all over her head, and the side of her lip was busted.

"Simone! Simone!" Chari darted over to her friend's side. "We just found out!"

Simone made eye contact with Chari and Prayer, then passed out. Them being in the hospital waiting room, her baby boy rushed into surgery, devoted Joey and criminal-minded Kamal both dead on her living-room floor was a combination that was powerful enough to knock a grown man on his ass.

"Quick, get her some water." Prayer caught Simone in her arms and placed her in a chair. "There's a cooler over there." She pointed across the room.

"Okay, okay." Chari filled two paper cones from the dispenser and carefully walked them over so as not to spill any. "Here you go."

Prayer took the water and splashed a little in Simone's face, then shook her. A few moments later, Simone came around and burst out sobbing.

"We here, girl. It's gonna be all right. Don't cry." Chari held her hand. "Where's Li'l T? What did the doctors say?"

"Yeah, have they said something yet?" Prayer added while handing Simone one of the cones of water.

After taking a small sip, wetting her cracked lips, Simone finally spoke. "I don't know nothing yet. They ain't telling a bitch shit. They just got me out here." She leaned over in the chair from sharp, excruciating pains that kept racing through her body. When she had come in with Li'l T, the nurses strongly suggested that she get checked out, but Simone refused medical treatment until she found out about her son's status.

"What's wrong?" Chari felt Simone's grip on her hand tighten. "Are you hurt bad?"

"I just can't believe it. Joey is dead," she announced like Prayer and Chari didn't know. "Kamal killed him at my house. He gone, y'all! He gone!"

"We know, girl." Prayer reached for Simone's other hand. "We know."

The friends, who just hours earlier had been partying, sat in the room, agonizing over Li'l T's fate and mourning Joey for what seemed like hours before they got company from three people all at one time: the surgeon, a homicide detective, and a woman from Child Protective Services. From the grim expressions on all of their faces, the girls could only assume that what was about to come next would be nothing nice. Prayer, Chari, and especially the out-for-self Simone, on whom it would have the worst effect, braced up.

Chapter Twenty-three

A week to the day after both of Li'l T's possible fathers last walked the notorious streets of Detroit, they were simultaneously laid to rest.

He was loved!

On the far west side of the city once known for Motown musical stars; a lucrative, booming, and stable automotive industry; and, of course, the world-famous Detroit Pistons, a.k.a. the "Bad Boys," Joey's double-breasted Armani-suit-clad body was lying peaceful in a burgundy-and-silver, top-of-the-line casket. A solid 24-karat gold chain with a cross was placed in one hand, while his childhood Bible graced the other. Drug dealer or not, Joey, along with his parents, never missed Sunday services, where they were loyal and devoted members.

Florists from as far away as Texas, North Carolina, and Alaska had sent multiple deliveries to the funeral home that was handling the arrangements and to the church where the service would soon be held. Local youth groups, various organizations, and the head pastor were scheduled to speak and offer their heartfelt condolences.

As one o'clock neared, the tear-filled, impatient crowd continuously grew. Joey's parents, per request of the church deacons, had to hire extra security to ensure calm inside and outside of the sacred sanctuary. Even though Joey wasn't a player when it came to the females, he was still loved and admired. There were more women in line than anyone else. Trevon and more than twenty of Joey's close friends argued for days concerning who'd have the sorrowful but distinguished honor of serving as pallbearers.

Even though Mr. and Mrs. Carter needed no financial assistance in the burial costs associated with their son, Trevon felt that, considering their age and failing health, he'd assume the organizing portion and all the running around that came with that. The Carters, who were devastated to lose their child, welcomed the help. The one and only thing they demanded be enforced was each and every security guard on post had a picture of Simone and would refuse her entry into the funeral services, even if it meant physically restraining her.

Joey's parents, as well as the entire town of Detroit that had seen the story on the news or read about it in the paper, felt that Simone Harris was at fault for the tragic double murder at her house. Most newscasters and just plain ol' folk used her as a prime example of the age-old adage that "playing both ends against the middle" or "burning the candle at both ends" can only lead to getting ya ass caught up in some serious bullshit—in this case, death. If teenagers, confused females, and so-called grown-ass women using their babies as human weapons to get back at the motherfucking men who refused to step up to the plate and be fathers didn't learn a lesson from Simone, then so be it! That was on they dumb asses!

Longtime residents of the Motor City who'd lived through and witnessed the combination of the rise and fall of The Young Boys Incorporated, The Chambers Brothers, Pony Down, and countless other high-profile, so-called outlaws of their era, now ranked Simone up there when it came to coldness in the game of getting that dough. The fact that many believed she stood silently by, watching Joey and Kamal shoot it out in front of her small, innocent son, didn't sit well with them. Ms. Simone Harris, single mother, gold digger, backstabber, and all 100 percent bitch, was now labeled the new Public Enemy Number One in Detroit.

Simone had already been made aware that her presence at Joey's funeral would be blocked by armed guards his parents vowed to have. So for once, out of respect for someone other than herself and to avoid any type of disturbance or risk arrest, she didn't even try to show her still-bruised face. Chari and Prayer promised her that as soon as it was over, they'd bring her an obituary to the hospital where she was still posted with Li'l T.

He was feared!

The East Side of Detroit was always known as straight gully. It was the side of town that most west-siders dreaded venturing to. Smack-dab in the middle of all the chaotic wildness that took place on Mack Avenue stood a small, dinky, unattractive building. Bricks were missing from the front pillar. The paint was starting to peel, and the awning across the doorway was damn near rusted out. That was the home to McMatterson's Funeral Chapel. They were the cheapest route that a Detroiter could take to bury a supposed loved one. It also served as the facility that handled most state-paid services. Any unclaimed corpse, unidentifiable deceased individual, or person with no family or responsible party were their specialty.

Unfortunately for Kamal, he met one of those criterias. Even though his boy, Big Ace, wanted to do right by him and lay him out in style, the police were still buzzing around, asking a ton of questions pertaining to the gun they'd found by Kamal's body that deadly night. Big Ace and the typically unloyal crew weren't fools and opted not to put their freedom on the line by too much involvement.

It seemed a few days after ballistics tests were performed on the weapons found at the crime scene, Kamal's was proven to have several bodies on it.

Fuck that! Let the state bury that motherfucker! was the combined consensus of the entire crew, who couldn't really care less if their reckless, self-appointed leader was dead. *That stupid nigga brought that on his damn self, beefing with that west side dude over a piece of rotten pussy!*

After getting turned down flat trying to get the fellas to get Kamal some flowers, Big Ace sent the only floral arrangement that would be set next to the cheap, low-budget casket. As Big Ace cautiously drove up to the front door, he looked into the rearview mirror for any signs of the police. Believing that it was safe, he parked and raised his still sore body out of the driver's seat, tucking his gun in his waistband. He then pulled his shirt down to conceal it.

Making his way to the front door, he noticed that the handle was welded back as he yanked on it. There was no one else in sight or waiting to pay their respects to Kamal, just him. Stepping inside, Big Ace's nostrils took in the smell of stale mildew. You could tell there must have been some sort of a leak in the roof at one time or another, and the owners never removed the musty carpet. Glancing up at the 1960s velvet paintings on the wall made Big Ace think that Shaft was running the place.

Suddenly, out of nowhere came a little old lady, who appeared to be intoxicated. With a broom in her hands she used to balance herself and shoes on her feet that had definitely seen better days, she spoke. "Yeah, you need some help?"

"I'm looking for my boy." Big Ace suspiciously sized the old broad up. "Y'all supposed to have his body up in here somewhere."

"Ohh . . ." she slurred. "By the looks of you, you're probably talking about the youngster with all the holes in him. He's in there." Her bony finger directed him.

Big Ace slowly walked into the dimly lit room and saw the lone flower on a pedestal next to Kamal, just as promised. His blood started to boil as he saw how cheap the box was that these motherfuckers had the audacity to call a casket. Kamal's body was dressed in some old-fashioned Salvation Army throwback suit, and his face was done up like a crackhead clown at a welfare kid's party. Big Ace wanted to go smack the cow shit outta whoever was in charge, but at this point, what good would it do?

Damn, dude! They fucked you all around! was the only thing he could think of as he stood, assumingly alone. After no more than five minutes of Big Ace somberly giving his road dawg a final face-to-face update on the crazy events that followed his untimely demise, including the robbery out at the hotel, the devoted comrade heard a raspy cough come from the back corner of the dark room.

"Who dat?" Big Ace turned around, placing his hand on his pistol. "Who back there?"

The shabbily dressed man almost immediately emerged out of the shadow and into the light. Big Ace did a double take as dude came closer and his identity became apparent.

Confused by his presence at the funeral home, especially considering the way Kamal always disrespected and mistreated him, Big Ace started in on the questions. "What the hell is you doing here, old-Ttmer?" He eased up the grip on his gun. "You the last cat I'd expect to see."

"I thought it was the least I could do." The guy coughed again, this time trying to cover his mouth.

"What you mean? What you talking about?"

"I mean, I know I wasn't shit in the way of a father figure, but Kamal was my son, my firstborn."

"Your son?" Big Ace yelled. "You Kamal's pops?"

"Yeah." Willy Dale lowered his head in shame, rubbing his unshaven face. "I thought you knew."

"Damn, is that why he used to be tripping on you?"

"I guess I had it coming." Willy Dale reached inside the casket, touching Kamal's chilly, stiff hands that were peacefully folded. It was the last physical contact that he'd initiated since the day his young son knocked him out cold and struck out to make it on his own. "Me and his mother was into some heavy shit back then when drugs were drugs, uncut."

Big Ace, still puzzled and overwhelmed by what he was hearing, let a remorseful Willy Dale continue without interruption.

"I'm just an old drunk now, but back in the day before Kamal's mother passed away, me and her got high off of everything we'd get our hands on. We was getting high the night he was born in the back room of a crack house." He paused, pondering the distant past. "It's a wonder he even lived a normal life with all the hard-core drugs she had flowing through her system."

Big Ace, for the first time since meeting Kamal, now fully understood what made his boy tick. There was now some sort of rhyme and reason to his bizarre behavior toward others, especially his cruel treatment of women.

Damn, dude, you really did have it rough, Big Ace thought as he and Willy Dale stood side by side, paying their final respects. *All you needed was some help.*

Chapter Twenty-four

It was shortly after four in the afternoon when Chari and Prayer showed up at the hospital. They were still dressed in black. There they found Simone slumped over in a chair, dead-tired from exhaustion. The doctors had just wheeled Li'l T out of the room for some more tests from a specialist that was called in to further evaluate his condition. In the week that had flown by, Li'l T had yet to regain consciousness. Nevertheless, Simone was being a soldier, doing her best to stick by her son's side.

Barely closing her eyes, she had worn the same outfit for two days at a time. The once-young, carefree mother was catching pure, 198-degree hell. Whenever she thought the bad luck shit streak was ending, it was thrown back in her face. Simone was suffering through grueling, countless interrogations from police authorities and an insulting and rude inquiry from Child Protective Services. Each challenged her parenting skills. She was withstanding jeers of disgust and judgment from nurses and just about every individual she came in contact with who knew the story behind her son's injuries. Simone was at her wit's end and about to go fucking nuts. Stressed, Simone had become a nervous wreck.

If that wasn't enough turmoil for her to deal with after being thoroughly checked out by an emergency physician on staff, she found out the reason for her slight weight gain and constant vomiting. It seemed that Simone was pregnant and had suffered a miscarriage. Even though the mental stress could've played a factor in her losing the baby, the doctor's examination proved that blunt force trauma to her body's midsection and extensive damage to her internal female organs were the culprit. Kamal's brutal act of rape with his grill was the final determination. Even though, once again, Simone had no idea which one, Joey or Kamal, was the father, it was still a trying situation and circumstance to lose a baby. And even worse than that, it was stated that Simone, who was just beginning the prime of her life, could probably never have children again.

"Hey, girl. How ya holding up?" Chari whispered with pity in her tone.

"I'm good." Simone tried perking up. "Just worn all out."

"What's the latest with Li'l T?" Prayer inquired eagerly, hopeful that the situation had changed for the better.

"The doctors should be back any time now with an update from some uppity-ass Negro they done flew in," Simone ungratefully spewed, switching the subject like she was always famous for doing. "Now, tell me about Joey. How did he look? Was it crowded? Did y'all bring me an obituary?"

Chari knew her friend needed to be treated for some sort of bipolar disorder as she listened to Simone go into an impromptu rant. Reluctantly, she dug in her purse to give Simone a few copies of thick, picture-filled, expensively custom-designed tributes to Joey Carter, one of her supposed-to-be baby daddies. What came next didn't surprise Prayer or Chari one bit. They knew the shit storm was coming and about to touch down as the two watched Simone look at and read the booklet cover to cover.

Five, four, three, two, one—Bam!

"Son of a stankin'-faced bitch!" Simone unjustifiably hit the roof. "Oh, hell to the double naw! Joey's old-ass parents got a lot of nerve not putting Li'l T's name on this shit. He's their only grandchild, and they gonna just say fuck him! I knew I shoulda came to that bitch and turned the whole motherfucker out!" Simone was on a rampage, screaming at the top of her lungs. "How they gonna play Joey's son? His ancient, wrinkled-skin momma probably had that ugly-ass, broke-down, churchgoing tramp Belinda he used to mess around with all up in the mix. I'm gonna stomp that ho. Please tell me that trick wasn't there. I swear to God if she was there, it's gonna be some real shit." Simone was out of control as she paced the floor. "I mean, for real, doe. How they gonna carry it? My baby should've been the first fucking name printed on this overpriced piece of shit."

Simone threw the obituaries against the wall as she stomped her feet and balled up her fists in anger. Prayer and Chari couldn't get a word in as their girl acted a straight fool. They stared at each other with amazement because despite the fact that it was totally the fault of Simone's deceptive ass that their son's life was cut short, she still expected the Carters to list that child's name as an heir to their bloodline. As far as they were concerned, if a DNA test revealed Terrell to be Joey's son, then by all means he'd be entitled and would receive everything that was coming to him.

"Calm down, chick. Stop tripping on that. It ain't that important." Prayer intervened.

"Just tell me what other bitches were there," Simone demanded. "Who was crying and shit, acting like Joey was they man?"

"What's wrong with you?" Prayer leaped to her feet, shaking her head. "That boy is dead and gone, and all you care about is who did what. You're petty and pathetic."

"Fuck you, Prayer! Matter of fact, what ya snake ass doing here anyway?" Simone ran up on Prayer like she was about to swing. "Didn't you just throw me outta your punk-ass truck and run over my damn shoe?"

"Bitch, please." Prayer smirked. "I wish you would. You think Kamal kicked that ass?"

"Come on, y'all. Don't start that mess up again." Luckily, Chari was there to mediate. "Besides, Simone, you can't behave like this in a hospital of all places!"

"Yes, miss." The team of doctors returned with several charts in their hands. "I agree with your friend." One spoke up. "The level of your voice very much needs to be lowered, and we'd greatly appreciate you not using profanity."

With no shame in her game at all, Simone rolled her eyes to the ceiling and poked out her lips. "Yeah, all right then, whatever." She was back to her old self.

Well, that didn't take long, Chari thought, laughing inside. *I knew the loving parent role was too good to be true.*

"Excuse me, sir. How is Terrell?" Prayer asked the million-dollar question. "What did your tests reveal? Is he getting any better?"

The doctor, with chart in hand, looked at Simone for her approval to discuss her son's condition and the test results. When the defiant, arrogant mother nonchalantly shrugged her shoulders, indicating that she couldn't care less what he said or who he said it in front of, the physician delivered the final blow to end the game Simone had started at the moment of Li'l T's conception.

"I'm sorry, Ms. Harris, but your son Terrell . . ." When he finished giving the present prognosis, the room grew momentarily silent. It was as if you could hear the buzz of electricity passing through the air.

"What in the fuck did you just say?" Simone went berserk.

"I'm sorry, miss. We tried everything we could and still got no response from your son. . . ." After that, everything else just sounded like, *blah blah blah.*

Chari and Prayer tried to get Simone to hear the doctor out and listen to what he suggested she do in the weeks to come to aid Terrell in his long, impending road to recovery. However, Simone was not in the mood for hearing shit else anyone was saying. She'd heard enough. Karma had finally bit that ass. The once cocky, fast-talking gold digger who lived life on top of the world fell to the ground, crying and mumbling the same word repeatedly.

"Cripple, cripple, cripple."

What had seemed like a moment of terror soon turned into a lifetime. The day that Joey and Kamal were buried was indeed awful. Both her free rides of getting easy money were over. But more than that, the worst pill to swallow out of all her recent bad luck was her baby boy not being able to walk on his own ever again. Days, weeks, and months of Simone trying to remain strong for her son started to dwindle. She wanted to be a good, kind, loving mother and support system for Li'l T, but she was failing. The streets were calling her almost on a nightly basis. The once-self-proclaimed queen of the club could not resist answering. Simone soon put Li'l T's needs to the side, leaving others to pick up the slack. Surprisingly, her constant verbal foe, Prayer, stepped up to the plate. Drake joined her in the effort to be a great backbone for the disabled child to lean on. At times, Simone would show up and try to take over her son's overall care, but the couple was wise enough to go to the courts and make their presence in Li'l T's life permanent and legal.

Chapter Twenty-five

"Time flies; lives change, but somehow stay the same"

Please, please, please, make no goddamn mistake about the bullshit! You can't hold a true bad bitch down! Especially one cut like me! You best believe, trust, and recognize we Detroit hustlin' hoes always land on our feet. That's a sho' 'nuff given on any day of the fuckin' year!

The main floor auditorium of Detroit's illustrious Cobo Hall was packed beyond regulation capacity. The special occasion was the senior graduation ceremony for Shrine High School, where her one and only child, Terrell, was unanimously voted Most Popular, Most Likely to Succeed, in addition to Class Valedictorian.

"These other out-of-shape mothers in here wish they looked half as good as my pretty ass." Simone Harris complimented herself out loud, not giving a hot damn who in the crowd was listening to her gloat. "I'm the shit. Always was and always will be! It don't matter what age a man is, he'll want me, even these pimple-faced, rude teenagers." As usual, the overly conceited female desired and selfishly sought the spotlight to shine directly on her. Flossing in a handheld mirror, checking on her still-flawlessly applied makeup, Simone was convinced wholeheartedly that she was the center of attention for the day and all eyes should rightly be focused on her.

Suddenly interrupting her private praise party over the left shoulder of her expensive dress, Simone caught a quick glimpse of Drake and Prayer walking past her. Full of envy for the love they shared, she watched them finding their way to their front-row reserved seats. Simone's vindictive claws instinctively came out as she exhaled.

Here comes these cornball wannabe-all-something-they-ain't motherfuckers. Damn, a bitch hate they asses. I mean, seriously, I hate them. Immediately, Simone twisted her neck ghetto style to mean mug the pair and make her presence felt with a piercing cold, callous stare, sucking of the teeth, and rolling of the eyes.

Mrs. Prayer Martin, who was once, back in the day, considered Simone's friend, snickered at the ridiculous, childish display as she proudly held on to her husband's strong arm, ignoring the obvious dis. The couple was truly there for Li'l T and nothing really else. In a matter of moments, the young man they'd stepped up and raised as their own would deliver a speech that he'd nervously practiced for weeks. He was about to obtain a diploma signifying his passage from childhood to manhood.

Despite all the obstacles in Terrell's young life, none being his fault, he was determined to be just like everyone else. Not physically able to play sports, he showed up at every game, posted in the stands, supporting his peers. Li'l T was a team player in life—where it really mattered. Nothing slowed him down. He was always laughing, and like his estranged mother Simone, he mesmerized all his friends.

As the excited multitude of parents, siblings, and special invited guests chatted festively among themselves, waiting for the ceremony to start, Simone, irritated and full of melancholy about being there without a husband on her arm like Prayer, reminisced, thinking back almost fifteen years to the dreadful night that changed Terrell's and her life forever. It only seemed like yesterday when Li'l T, her only child, was helplessly lain out on her Westside home living-room floor, barely clinging to life. She got chills in the crowded venue as she hesitantly closed her eyes, reliving the eerie events of her jaded past. Simone shivered as she remembered collapsing on the floor when she heard the doctor's heartwrenching words. The nightmare flashback was, thank God, interrupted by the school's vice principal beginning the ceremony.

Countless awards and special certificates of recognition were given out to several retiring instructors, and then Li'l T made his speech.

"Ladies, gentlemen, honored guests, teachers, and students," the vice principal, Mr. Griggs, proudly announced, "I present to you Shrine High School's Valedictorian of this year's graduating class, Mr. Terrell Harris."

Everyone jumped to their feet, cheering and clapping with admiration as Terrell made his way across the stage. With his royal-blue cap and gown on, gold tassel to the side, he looked just like the rest of the young men. The only thing that made him stand out was the black-and- silver steel wheelchair. He'd been forced to make it a daily part of his young life ever since his supposed-to-be-but-never-DNA-proven biological father, Kamal, crippled him a little over fifteen years ago. Surprisingly, Terrell wasn't the least bit bitter about the hand that was dealt to him. He had just learned to adapt, or so everyone thought.

His mom, Simone, had damn near had some sort of a nervous breakdown when she found out that he couldn't walk, so he was told, but Auntie Prayer and Uncle Drake had stepped up to the plate after getting married. They petitioned the court for temporary custody, which, luckily for Terrell, turned out to be a permanent situation after a while.

Prayer and Drake, as bad as Simone hated to admit it, were excellent parents to her son. Although Simone was granted liberal visitation rights for years and years, she never came around to see a small, confused Terrell, who missed his mother terribly. She claimed that she hated seeing her child "like that," when the truth was she was busy running behind different men, chasing that almighty dollar she worshiped so dearly.

After all the bicoastal trips to various specialists, late-night fevers, expensive medications, and tear-filled nights Prayer and Drake spent, an arrogant, self-absorbed Simone finally resurfaced, coming back into Li'l T's life.Full of animosity and resentment toward her used-to-be homegirl, Simone complained about each and every aspect of the way her paraplegic son was being reared. From the color of his bedroom carpet and his Batman pajamas to the type of toilet paper that was used to wipe his yellow ass, there was a constant problem.

Out of love for Li'l T, Drake and Prayer had put up with Simone's outrageous bullshit. Nevertheless, now the once-helpless child was a grown-ass man about to step out into the world and make his own mark on it. What Kamal and Simone's bastard child did from this point on and how he did it was gonna be solely on him, and he'd eventually have to pay the debt in full on his own consequences.

As Terrell rolled to the microphone, the room grew respectfully silent. His speech was short and humble as he acknowledged everyone in his life that had somehow helped him along the way. He gave special praise to his favorite teachers and mentors. Then, he pointed out just how much he appreciated Prayer and Drake's sacrifices, which made the audience teary-eyed—with the exception of a wide-eyed, livid Simone, who was barely mentioned.

As she moved around in her seat, squirming from side to side with bitterness and contempt rushing through her system, Simone's head pounded with intense pain as she listened to her son speak at the podium.

This little punk got some nerve. I swear to God he got me all the way fucked up! I could've been somewhere else spending the next nigga's dough instead of hearing this fake shit! And look at that ho Prayer all hugged up! Drake's fine butt could do so much better for his bottom bitch! Had it not been for the three heavyset people sitting on her right-hand side and the pregnant woman to her left, once again, Simone would've bolted. Instead, she was forced to suck the shit up and be content with burning a hole in the back of Drake and Prayer's heads.

At the end of the commencement ceremony, the jubilant graduates gathered in front of the pavilion to take group pictures and say their good-byes. Terrell, of course, was front and center of every snapshot that was taken, surrounded by all his peers. When he finally found the time to break free, making his way to his family, he rolled up, smiling from ear to ear.

"Hey, fam, did y'all like my speech or what? Was a brotha looking good? Was the females on me?"

"Yes, Terrell, you looked your usual handsome self." Prayer waved her hand, trying to create a breeze.

"Slow down, young man." Drake was swollen with pride, leaning down, grabbing his surrogate son, hugging him close.

"Dang gee, Auntie Prayer, why you over there crying?" Li'l T questioned, sympathetically gazing up at her.

"You know you made us all very proud up there on that stage, don't you?" Overcome with pride, she took a crumpled tissue out of her purse, wiping away her tears. "Your speech was perfect. And you know you really surprised me today with that mushy stuff you said about us."

"It sho' in hell surprised the shit outta me too." A tight-faced Simone busted in on their special moment, twisting her hand in Terrell's face, then placed both hands on the steel handles of his wheelchair, leaning down directly in his dental. "You could've said more about me. I *am* the damned bitch that brought ya rotten, miserable ass in this world. You *do* remember that much, don't you? Or has a certain person you live with brainwashed you?"

"I know, Ma." Li'l T frowned. "I said your name too, didn't I? So why you out here bugging?"

"Yeah! Near the damn end of that crap when nobody was listening to ya behind no more!" She sulked.

Prayer had enough of Simone's antics and intervened, cutting her pity party short. "Why don't you grow up and start acting your age? He mentioned you, so be quiet. You haven't changed in years. Always out for self."

"Whoa, bitch, slow ya roll. Was I talking to you?" Simone fired back, making Prayer talk to the hand. "You best stay outta mines. I ain't gonna keep telling you that bullshit time and time again, year after year."

The humid day seemed to cause the temperature, as well as attitudes, to flare. Other students and their parents tried to ignore the impromptu display, yet couldn't seem to not pay attention to the uncalled for disruption to the festive occasion.

"Come on, ladies. Not now!" Drake, a self-made private investor in select neighborhood humanitarian projects, tried defusing the situation, playing the role of a mutual peacemaker. "Lower your damn voices out here."

"Yeah, y'all," Li'l T agreed, embarrassed as his friends' parents glanced over at them. "Chill!"

"Well, ain't this about nothing." Simone seemed to get louder with each passing word she rattled off, pissed, taking two steps backward. "Why is all y'all looking all at me, blowing that garbage out y'all's grills? *I'm* the one that just got practically shitted on up on that motherfucking stage."

"Probably because you're the main one standing here being totally unreasonable," Prayer swiftly answered Simone's selfish and ridiculous question, hoping to avoid a scene in front of the women of the PTA. "That's why."

"Whatever, trick. Don't get smacked out here."

"Yeah. You right. It is whatever." Prayer, who was now a good twenty pounds or so heavier than Simone, stood her ground. She was letting Terrell's mother get under her skin and resorted to name-calling. "So now what, you common sac-chaser? Huh? Now what?"

"You tell me now what," Simone screamed back, ready to come to blows. "Ain't shit changed from back in the day. I'll still bust that ass proper style. You got shit bent because this is my baby, not yours. So, don't get mad with me 'cause your fat, bloated behind can't have kids of your own. Now, bitch, what you know about *that?*"

"Ho, I should—" Prayer, who'd come all out of her uppity act, raised her hand but was thankfully stopped by her husband.

Li'l T was now considered a man, and one of his first duties was staring him dead in the face, checking the dog shit outta his momma. "Listen, Ma, I said what I said. Now, the mess is over, so please be quiet. People are watching us."

"What you just say?" Simone hissed at her son.

"Okay! Okay! Fuck!" Drake, after years of separating his wife and Simone, put extra bass in his voice, showing Li'l T how to handle the two women as he put an end to the verbal disagreement and confrontation that was on the verge of turning physical. "This ain't the time or place for y'all's clown show. This is Terrell's day. Point-blank period. Y'all both know better. Now, today, both of y'all gonna shut the fuck up or else. Ya feel me?"

"You right, baby." Prayer regained her senses and backed down, knowing her husband was correct and was tired of being the ringmaster to their constant circus. "I'm sorry for acting like this, sweetheart." Throwing shade on Simone, she kissed Li'l T on his cheek.

"Well, I'm out of this tired, played-out event," Simone hissed at the three, displaying her vicious attitude, and in true Detroit diva fashion, slammed her souvenir program onto the ground. "This was a waste of my time anyhow, and as for *you*"—she pointed at Prayer—"me and you got unfinished business. Trust in that." Infuriated, Simone then turned around, disappearing into the thick crowd, not even taking the time to at least say congratulations to her only child.

How that non-being-able-to-breed bitch gonna turn my son against me? She lucky I don't really tell her ass what's good. Then let's see who's laughing, she thought. *Her proper act will really be cut short then. Most of these Detroit tricks don't think fat meat is greasy, and Prayer is one of them.*

"Good riddance," Prayer mumbled under her breath, avoiding direct eye contact with the other parents. *Look at her in them tight clothes. She needs to grow up, that old, still-dressing-like-a-hoochie skank.*

"Don't worry, guy. She'll calm down and be back around soon." Drake placed his hand down on Li'l T's shoulder, reassuring him as he, like every other hard-dick man in the crowd, stared lustfully at the curves of Simone's hips shifting from side to side as she made her grand-style, flamboyant exit. "You know how your mom is when she feels like shit ain't going her way."

"Yeah, unfortunately for me, I do." Li'l T curled his upper lip, watching the back of his mother's head. *But at some point that shit gets old.*

Drake caught himself before Prayer noticed his extra interest in her sworn enemy. *Damn, look at Simone. Umm-umm-umm. She still doing her thang after all these years. I ain't mad at her.*

Chapter Twenty-six

The abnormally spacious living room was packed with all Terrell's friends and his surrogate parents' relatives. Prayer and Drake had really, if truth be told, outdone themselves with the enormous spread that they'd laid out for his guests. Soft-shell crab, huge lobster tails, jumbo shrimp, and grilled porterhouse steaks topped the menu of the celebratory open house.

"Man . . . your uncle and fine-ass, thick aunt done hooked you all the way up." Stuff sat back on the couch, full of admiration for his boy's luck. "My moms and them didn't do anything except pat me on the back."

"Come on, dude," Terrell insisted. "Ya pops and step-mom gave you a gang of savings bonds and some loot. Besides, stop complaining." He bit into the last shrimp on his plate. "Your trust fund about to be all yours in a few damn months. Then you really gonna be sky balling."

"Yeah, true that, but they ain't cool like your people are. My father barely speaks to me unless it's to give my moms an important message or to give me his credit card."

"At least you got a damn old dude around that you can talk to." Li'l T momentary got sad, looking down, rubbing his legs that didn't move on their own. Staring at the dark material of his slacks, Terrell got caught up in a trance, remembering the night Drake found him passed out in the cemetery. . . .

"Damn, dude! Why'd you fuck me over like this? Why? I ain't deserve this bullshit. Look at my legs. You's a

ho-ass coward." Li'l T's hands were bright fire-engine red, and his fingertips were raw, exposing the pink-and-white flesh as he screamed out repeatedly in an agonizing tone, looking down toward the earth. "Answer me, nigga. I know you hear me talking. Why you do me like this?"

It was an almost impossible attempt to dig up the hardened, snow-covered grave of Kamal, but Terrell kept at it with tears flowing down his face. He was demanding total satisfaction with every inch of dirt he removed and each drop of blood that spilled from his trembling hands. "I was just a little-ass motherfucking kid!" he bravely slurred as the bone-chilling winter hawk ruled the night. "Your own son. You rotten son of a bitch."

Exhausted, overcome with emotion and resentment, the young paraplegic teenager wanted answers as to how a man, who people constantly alleged he looked so much like, could deliberately cripple him the way he had.

"I'm a grown-ass man around this motherfucker. Now try putting your hands on me. Now do that dumb shit." Terrell's knuckles were swollen. With each chaotic, heart-pounding movement, he made it grow worse. Small rocks and the sharp edges of broken, discarded beer bottles that littered the unkempt city burial ground hidden underneath the still falling fresh blanket of snow cut deep gashes into his light tan skin. "I'd never do nothing that rotten and foul to my own seed. You ain't about shit, ya faggot. I wish you was here in my face so I could kill your bitch ass all over again my damn self."

Despite the bitter, frigid cold Detroit temperatures and the intense pain he was suffering, Li'l T fought being out of breath. Panting, he continued clawing away on his mission to uncover his father's final resting spot in a desperate effort to bring some closure to his tormented soul.

"My momma was scared of your ass, but I ain't." He
spit on Kamal's grave site as he dug, delusional in the
belief that he could actually see his sperm donor face-to-
face and at least get an apology out of him.
After hours of Prayer placing back-to-back phone
calls to Li'l T that went unanswered, she convinced
Drake to do something. He'd just flown back in town
from one of his all-too-famous mysterious business
trips. However, Prayer had him search using the van's
GPS system to pinpoint exactly where Li'l T was. When
Drake finally located the unusually inebriated teenager,
the unthinkable had occurred. Terrell's underdeveloped
legs were inflicted with severe frostbite, and he was
unconscious, sprawled out facedown on top of Kamal's
grave, lips blue-and-black with a life-threatening case
of hypothermia that ultimately had him hospitalized for
over a month.

From time to time after that, Terrell still had sweat-
drenched nightmares. Kamal's face would creep into his
peaceful sleep and somehow transform into a heinous
monster trying to murder him. Unexplained shortness of
breath and flash spells of darkness had become regular.

Fighting with his demons constantly, Li'l T wanted
nothing more than to search for his father's immediate
family. He wanted to at least find out the moment-by-
moment, blow-by-blow details of that terrible night
he was injured. Knowing Simone would bug the hell
out each time he mentioned the subject, Terrell wisely
decided it was best to keep all his many questions on the
DL. He'd seen the many old, dated newspaper articles
and overheard the whispers from different people over
the passing years.

Usually, Simone and Prayer were on opposite sides of
the fence when it came to Terrell, yet Kamal and anyone

affiliated with Kamal were subjects that were off limits in the Martin household also. So for now, Li'l T, a graduate of several anger management classes as a youth, stayed in the dark.

Stuff understood the fury that his longtime best friend was feeling but reminded him what was really good. "Come on now, Terrell, these are your folks here. Look around. That's all that matters."

"You know what? You right. Auntie Prayer and Uncle Drake are tight. I'm just tripping, that's all."

"Yeah, who wants a punk-ass credit card, especially one with a limit? Be thankful, dude. They in your corner."

Kenneth Ian Spencer III was Li'l T's right-hand man. That name was always a mouthful, so his family nicknamed him Stuff. His parents were both in their early fifties when he was born. Having three grown sisters made him the youngest, as well as the only boy. Stuff was one of those "last chance to give birth" babies. His father went through some off-the-wall, crazy midlife crisis bullshit a few years shortly after he was born and broke camp on him, the girls, and his moms, and ended up marrying his skank-ass twenty-four-year-old secretary. Of course, like most men, he used money as a substitute for spending time with his only son.

"Dude, fuck that. I guess I'd rather have that money."

"Man, money isn't everything," Stuff said.

"Shut ya rich ass up." Li'l T swung a pillow off the couch across the room, hitting Stuff in the face. "You can pass that loot my way. I'll show you how to spend it."

"Stop playing, guy." Stuff straightened up, trying to look tough. "Here come some girls."

Li'l T grinned when the giggling females entered the room. He and Stuff wasted no time whatsoever running their best mack lines on the females, making the inexperienced young women blush.

After twenty minutes or so of them playing the Big Willie role, Drake came over and got the fellas, ushering them to the backyard deck area so Li'l T could say good-bye to all of his guests and thank them for attending.

One thing Prayer stressed in her household was perfect manners and keeping up appearances, no matter what the case would be. Over the years of living the suburban lifestyle, she'd transformed all the way into a white woman trapped in a black body and had lost her ghetto soul edge, which had originally attracted Drake to her years ago when they'd first met. Gaining several pounds here and there and running her own home-based business, Prayer was more interested in what other people thought of her and her family than pleasing her man.

It was close to eight o'clock in the evening, and everyone had left the Martin household full of food and spirit.

"Today was definitely off the chain." Li'l T got out of his wheelchair and slid over to his favorite spot on the couch.

"Yes, it was," Prayer happily agreed. "You received a lot of fabulous gifts from a lot of good friends."

"I know. I was clocking dough all evening."

"Oh, yeah. That reminds me. I almost forgot." Prayer walked over to the solid oak mantle, reaching her hand behind a 10 X 13 framed family portrait. "Chari and Trevon sent you this card." She handed him the envelope, already knowing the contents.

When Li'l T tore it open, five crisp hundred-dollar bills fell out on his lap, as well as a first-class plane ticket to Phoenix, Arizona. Years ago, after learning about Joey's sudden death—or murder, depending on whom you asked—Chari and Trevon found comfort in each other as they mourned his passing. Now the couple had four kids and were living the perfect so-called All-American

Dream—a big crib with a white picket fence, three-car
garage, and a housebroken dog that looked just like
Lassie. The graduation card read that any time Terrell
felt like getting away before starting college, he was more
than welcome to fly out for a visit. As a small child, he
and Prayer would make the trip every six months or so,
despite grief from Simone. With the year-round warm
climate out West, Terrell's young body never ached

"That's good. Maybe you can go check them out and
relax," Drake hinted. "I'm gonna be in and out of town all
summer myself, but on business."

"Yeah, sweetie, that way you can clear your head and
spend your birthday there," Prayer tossed out while
giving her husband a suspicious glance.

"Naw, I'm tight on all that. Besides, remember," he
reminded them both, "I promised my mother I'd spend
most of the summer basically with her."

Drake and Prayer tried slyly to give each other a firm,
disapproving expression, but it was apparent to Li'l T
that they weren't feeling that idea at all. Every time he'd
gone to spend any amount of time with Simone in the
past, Terrell would get into it with one of her part-time
boyfriends or some fake-ass, hood-wannabe gangsta that
didn't know who he was and called himself trying him
because he was in a wheelchair.

"Are you sure, Terrell?" Prayer quizzed. "Chari and
Trevon haven't seen you in a good while."

"Come on, Auntie Prayer. I know you and my moms be
beefing at each other's throats, but she's my family too.
She needs me."

"He's right, Prayer." Drake went over to the bar cart,
pouring himself a shot of Hennessy before trying to
use reverse psychology and hopefully change his mind.
"He ain't a little kid anymore. You gotta stop babying
him. Give him some air to make his own mistakes."

"Yeah, Auntie. I got this." Terrell ignored his uncle's slick remarks.

"All right, you guys can stop the double-teaming-me routine. I get the point, okay?" Prayer, feeling outnumbered and not wanting to make her adopted son angry, gave up the battle she was now single-handedly waging. "So just go ahead and go."

The rest of the evening at the Martins was spent the way they always spent their evenings: laid-back talking, chilling, and watching old-school movies as a family. From time to time, Li'l T would text his friends, and Drake would take a couple of after-hours calls, some business and some personal. But not another single, solitary word was mentioned all night on the subject of Li'l T's impending summer plans with the infamous Simone.

Chapter Twenty-seven

It was already a sweltering 89 degrees in the shade and barely eleven o'clock in the morning. Because it was unseasonably warm for a week this early in June, every air conditioner in Detroit had to be turned on high and working overtime. Terrell was all packed for his "visit to the hood" as Prayer had arrogantly named it ever since coming to terms with the fact she'd not been able to change his mind. Yet, truth be told, even if he were going to lay his head down nightly at T. D. Jakes's summer mansion in the middle of the Hamptons or at a weeklong convention of strict Baptist ministers, if slimy, ill-mannered Simone Harris was gonna be there in attendance, Prayer considered it "H-double-O-D" hood and trouble waiting to happen.

The last time Terrell spent any amount of time with his biological mother, it was nothing but turmoil and bullshit. Simone, who hadn't changed much over the years, still had the bad habit of sleeping around to get what she needed in life, even if it meant with someone else's man or husband. After a late night of sexing with a married man, Simone had brazenly taken it upon herself to answer his constantly vibrating cell phone while he was in the shower washing her trademark scent off him. Of course, all holy hell erupted, and the man ended up trying to halfway kill Simone for her blatant disrespect of his wife.

204 Ms. Michel Moore

Hearing the muffled screams from his mother, without hesitating, Li'l T managed to use his arms and get up the stairs and into her room. Before the enraged married man knew what was happening, the cock-strong teenager had snatched him down to the carpet and pressed his massive biceps downward on his throat, cutting off his circulation. When the man tried swinging back to defend himself against Terrell's attack, it somehow made matters worse and fueled Li'l T's devoted, protective wrath. The teenager started choking him while making the sounds of some sort of an animal. Simone couldn't believe her eyes as the tip of the man's nose was being savagely bitten off by her son and spit across the room at her bare feet.

Using the heel of a six-inch patent leather stiletto to beat her son's hands off the man's neck before he killed him, Simone pleaded with a bloody mouth for Li'l T to stop. She appreciated Terrell for sticking up for her and her honor, even though she was as wrong as two left shoes for fucking the next bitch's husband from the gitty-up, but at the rate he was going, Li'l T was gonna catch a murder case.

After the smoke had cleared, Drake and Prayer finally picked Terrell up from the hospital Emergency Room, where Simone was receiving treatment for the black-and-blue swollen eye she'd suffered in the attack, and the weary, cheating married man was trying to get the tip of his broken nose reattached while his distraught wife looked on in disbelief.

"Be safe, sweetie," Prayer said, thinking back on that crazy visit as she prepared to send Terell off to spend time with Simone again. She leaned inside the window of Terrell's specially equipped minivan, kissing him on his forehead. "You know we love you. So be safe, and please stay out of trouble!"

"I will. I promise." Terrell started the engine.

"Call me when you get there."

"What did Unc tell you about letting me fly?"

"I don't give two hot shits about you or him with all that macho crap," Prayer huffed with a grin. "I said call me." She pushed his head. "Do you hear me?"

"All right, Auntie, I'm out." Putting the chrome-rimmed customized van in reverse, making his way out of the long driveway and cautiously into traffic, Li'l T blew the horn twice as he drove away.

Damn, she be on some other type of new wave shit! he thought as the sounds of his bootleg mix CD filled the air. *I'm a grown-ass man!*

Terrell merged onto the crowded 696 freeway, then took I-75 heading toward downtown Detroit to Simone's house. She'd moved from the old Dexter Linwood neighborhood a few months shortly after all the shit had jumped fifteen years ago, and into Joey's place that he'd left to her and Li'l T in his will.

Joey's parents had unsuccessfully tried going through the court system to get a legal injunction to fight Simone tooth and nail every step of the way, considering the circumstances of their only son's untimely demise. However, they were elderly, sickly, and too God-fearing to sink to the level that Simone Harris was willing to drag them through to take control over what she felt was rightfully coming to her and her disabled son.

The house, tucked away in the small, elite, upscale gated community, sat directly on the banks of the murky Detroit River. You could see clear across the water to Windsor, Ontario from her living-room window and watch the parade of cars head over the bridge to Belle Isle from the bedroom's balcony. It was somewhat of a getaway from the rest of Detroit. The only downside to the dream location was that directly rooted across

Jefferson Avenue, living in absolute poverty and squa-
lor, were a lot of folks that weren't as privileged as
Simone's immediate next-door neighbors. Most of
Detroit's infamous throwaway citizens who resided
there had no other alternative but to turn to a life of
crime, mischief, and mayhem to support their families
or their long-standing drug habits.

Whatever the case, the condescending occupants of
Simone's well-to-do, uppity development were callous,
never making eye contact or showing the slightest bit
of sympathy toward the misfortunate people they were
forced to encounter daily. The occupants of "The Gates,"
as they were called, kept to themselves, just as Simone
liked people to do when she couldn't use or manipulate
them.

"Naw, Yankee. Terrell is not here yet, so stop calling
this motherfucker and try his cell phone."

"Sorry about bugging you, Miss Harris." Yankee was
overly apologetic as he flirted on the sly with his boy's
mother. "But he ain't picking up."

"Well, try ya ass again and leave me the hell alone! I'm
attempting to get some rest if you don't fucking mind,"
Simone furiously shrieked into the receiver.

"Oh, late night, huh?" Yankee laughed, trying his best
to prolong the one-sided conversation. "I feel you."

"Listen, you little punk, stay outta grown folks' business,
okay? Now, get off my line."

Simone turned the ringer low on the cordless phone,
slamming it down on her nightstand next to the digital
clock, which flashed 11:27 a.m. She irately grunted,
yanking the caramel-colored satin sheet over her head
to block the bright rays of sunshine that were fighting
unsuccessfully to break through the curtains.

Goddamn, I hope this shit don't be going on the entire fucking summer. And if Terrell know like I know, he better use his own keys. Five minutes later, Simone was almost back out like a light.

The Jefferson Avenue Exit was next, and Li'l T's adrenalin started to rise at the thought of what the summer days with his ol' girl would hold. It was now almost noon, and the temperature had jumped another three degrees and was climbing. As he came up topside, Terrell spotted the gas station, which was already on packed with cars getting last-minute fuel before hitting the island, which was the spot to be in Detroit on a hot summer's day. The red light, fortunately, caught him, giving him a long chance to gawk at all the sights the inner-city hood had to offer.

"Damn, she looks good as hell," Terrell mumbled out loud as a bright-skinned, half-dressed sista seductively bent over, tying her fresh winter-white sneaker. Two seconds later, he saw a familiar face come up behind the ghetto face-painted princess, smacking her on the ass.

Ain't this some shit? Terrell made his way across traffic, pulling up to the brazen dude, who, by this time, was kissing the giggling girl on her neck. He turned the music down, lowering the van's window.

"Hey, guy. Get ya hands off my girl."

The young man looked up with complete elation, immediately running over to the van. "What's good, my dude? What it do?" Yankee greeted his boy with a smile, turning his baseball cap backward. "I just not too long ago hit your moms' crib looking for your pretty ass."

"Man, fuck you," Li'l T fired back. "I saw you called my cell, but I was in traffic, and I ain't have my Bluetooth switched on."

"Yeah, well, you know Mom Duke straight cussed a guy out and shit with her fine self."

"You know how that go." Li'l T shook his head, agreeing. "She be on the nut, and stop talking that slick shit about my mother!"

"Come on, dawg. Ya moms is hot."

"You want me to talk that mess about ya old bird?"

"Guy, if my moms was as fly as yours is, I'd be pimping her out on the regular. And that's my word."

Yankee then paused one second, signaling for the female that he'd abandoned to come over to the van. "Come here, Shauntae." He snatched at her arm playfully, pulling her close to him as he made the formal introductions. "This here is my boy Terrell."

"Hey, Terrell." The female winked, showing all thirty-two teeth as she admired his transportation. "Where you been hiding this one at?" Shauntae posed the question to Yankee, licking her lips at Terrell.

"Slow ya roll, girl," Yankee quickly instructed Shauntae, putting her in her place. "He one of them 'gated boys,' so you know your red-hot fire project butt ain't got shit coming in his direction!"

"Oh, yeah? Is that right?" She was determined to get on and not let Yankee's good cock-blocking ass throw salt in her game.

"Damn, dawg! It's like that?" Li'l T leaned back in the seat. "Why you wanna blaze on a dude like that?"

"Shit, is you crazy?" Yankee asked as he openly rubbed Shauntae's huge breasts through her thin, almost-two-sizes-too-small T-shirt. "Real talk! I wish my family did live on the other side of that gate."

"Me too," Shauntae spoke up, still on flirt patrol, wondering what it'd be like to have everything she ever wanted given to her on a silver platter without sucking a dick or dropping her panties. "You must be rich."

"Naw." Terrell, who at closer look could see that Shauntae was not his type at all, started to feel bad about being slightly well off and took a cop. "I ain't got jack. That's my family's dough. Me, myself, I'm broke."

"However it goes," Yankee snickered, pulling his sagging jeans up, "I just know you and your momma's high-post asses ain't missing no meals!"

"Anyway, later for all that." Terrell abruptly broke up the financial conversation, changing the subject to someone else. "Where Wahoo's at?"

"He'll be up this way in a minute." Yankee sighed, releasing the whorish girl to go back to her awaiting friends. "He had to make a run for his granny."

"Damn! That's fucked up." Terrell stared off toward Jefferson Avenue. "I know he's straight pissed."

"He used to that wild shit." Yankee frowned.

"I hear what you saying, dude." Li'l T grimaced, thinking about their running buddy, Wahoo.

"Yeah, I know thangs is pretty fucked up for ol' boy right about now." Yankee grabbed his crotch and spit through the gap in his teeth, acknowledging the obvious tension in the conversation. "It's one thang for your brother, sister, or even your moms to be strung out, but to have your grandmother on that shit gotta be a heavy load on a guy's back."

"Yeah, you ain't never lied." Terrell wiped the quickly forming beads of sweat off his forehead and informed Yankee that he'd get back up with him later. "Let me get over the way to my mother's and get situated. I'll holler."

"All right then. Peace."

"Peace."

Before Terrell could pull out of the gas station, a black SUV with double-dark tinted windows roared up, swerving in front of him. *What the hell?* With no regard for the traffic that he was temporarily blocking, the driver disrespectfully, with a fuck-who-didn't-like-it attitude, lowered his window, signaling for Shauntae, who instantly left her friends' sides, eagerly running over, and jumped up into the guy's vehicle. After a short greeting between him and her, the driver then arrogantly locked eyes with Terrell, almost daring him to complain.

"Nigga, what?" The SUV's driver mouthed the words. Then he pumped his brakes, making the truck appear to dance to the beat of his sounds before recklessly skidding back out onto Jefferson Avenue. Shauntae was riding shotgun as they disappeared into the sun-filled distance.

That faggot, whoever he is, got some serious god-damn problems! Terrell reasoned, zooming in on the personalized license plate on the truck that read: I GO HARD. He was trying not to get angry on his first day back in the hood.

He don't know who he fucking with. I'll put something hot up in that ass! After that unsettling exchange, Li'l T calmed down and was back en route to Simone's. Less than five minutes passed before he reached up onto the sun visor, pushing the button on his electronic remote, causing the huge black front security steel gates to slide open. Driving past the guard shack, a few short blocks down to the left and a couple of sharp turns later to the far right at the fork in the road, Terrell was pulling up in the gravel-filled driveway of his home away from home.

Chapter Twenty-eight

Terrell threw the van in PARK, then stretched his perfectly shaped upper body backward to get his wheelchair. He was built like a weight lifter from the waist up. Using his upper body ever since he was a small child made him quickly develop rock-hard muscles that most men never used their entire lives. Whenever a wife beater graced his body, women young and old stared with lust, thinking of what could sexually be if given enough time with the teenager.

Flinging the chair onto the ground, opening it up with the aid of his arms, he moved his legs outside the van, gripped the specially placed side bar, and lowered his frame into the chair. Reaching back inside, Terrell grabbed his duffle bag, setting it on his lap. Double checking that he had everything, the always upbeat young man rolled past his mother's front walkway and around to the rear entrance of the house.

It was damn near impossible, not to mention inconvenient at times, for Li'l T to cut across the huge grass area, especially in the snow, without extra effort. Simone, however, didn't seem to be the least bit concerned about her only child's obstacles. Selfishly, she felt that a wheelchair ramp in her front yard would look ultra-tacky and would definitely lower the property value of her precious home, which didn't cost her a dime from jump.

Fumbling with his keys, Terrell finally unlocked the several deadbolts and rolled inside. The climate of the house was ice cold and a pleasant, a much-needed change from the humidity that was ruling the Detroit day. Simone had the blinds still shut in the living room, and the interior was silent with the exception of the humming sound of the central air unit that was faithfully doing its job.

"Ma," he excitedly yelled out. "I'm down here. Hey, Ma, I'm home." Li'l T's room was located on the bottom level of the house right next to the den. As he cracked open his bedroom door, clicking on the light switch and seeing that it was as exactly as he'd last left it, he could hear his mother's angry voice echo as she marched down the thick-carpeted staircase.

"Don't 'Hey, Ma' me," Simone firmly demanded with a multicolored scarf wrapped tightly around her head, rubbing the sleep out of her eyes. "Why ya ass coming in this bitch making all that damn noise? Is you crazy?"

"Dang, I was just telling you I was here. Why you waking up bugging and acting all paranoid?" Li'l T had been there only thirty seconds, and it was on.

His mother, who wasn't in the mood for any type of noise, cut straight into him. "Boy, don't be rolling all up in here asking me a bunch of questions and carrying on." She walked past her son, heading toward the living room, tying the belt on her robe extra tight. "You act like you the goddamn FBI."

"If I was, ya ass would've been under the jail by now, don't you think?" Li'l T threw the sarcastic ball back into Simone's court. "All the sneaky thangs you do."

"Who you think you talking to with that smart mouth of yours?" She plopped down on the couch, bucking her eyes. "I ain't one of those nasty little funky chickenheads that be chasing behind your ass."

"Dang, Ma." Terrell grew frustrated by his mother's accusations. "I was just playing with you. Why's you tripping?"

"I know, boy." Simone tried softening up when she realized her overly spoiled son was pouting. "Come over here and give me a hug, you little crybaby. I was just bullshitting."

"Naw, I can tell from way over here you got that morning breath going on," he teased her.

"Oh, so now you got jokes, huh?" Simone joined in laughing as she blew into her hand to check.

"I missed you, Ma."

"I missed you too, with ya big-headed self." Simone got up and went into Terrell's room, unzipping his bag. After she helped her son put his clothes away, the mood quickly changed to more of a serious tone. Simone got to the business of breaking down her strict summer house rules to him.

"Okay, nigga, first of damn all."

"Dang, it's that many rules you have to count?"

"Shut up, boy, and listen."

"Okay, okay, I'm listening."

"Now, like I was saying." Simone put her hands on her hips in a critical-like fashion. "First of all, I don't want any of them hot-tailed sewer rats roaming around my house."

"I don't mess with any sewer rats," Li'l T protested, leaning forward in his wheelchair, clasping his hands together.

"Second," Simone said, overlooking his words, "them crazy fools from the other side of the gate you insist on running with . . ." She waited for her son to complain once again, but he didn't. "I don't even want them ill-mannered, petty thieves-in-training stepping foot on my motherfucking premises!"

"Come on, Ma, be for real." Terrell damn near jumped out of his chair and miraculously walked. "How am I gonna be here all summer long and not let Yankee or Wahoo in the crib? Them my boys."

"Easy, Negro. Just say no!"

"Ahh . . . Ma, stop fooling."

"I ain't playing around with you." Simone folded her arms, letting him know she was serious as four heart attacks. "They badasses be right outside these gates late at night, plotting on how to stick up a pretty bitch like me."

"Yeah, right." Li'l T rubbed his chin, knowing good and damn well he really didn't know what his hood buddies were up to 24/7. "That don't even sound like them." He downplayed his noticeable uncertainty.

"Terrell, you can't count on them idiots for much of shit but to help your soft ass catch a case." Simone deliberately taunted her handicapped son.

"Who you talking about?" He felt his anger reach the boiling point, arguing back. "I ain't fucking soft."

Simone made sure she faced him directly with her next words so he'd know she was serious. "Dig this here, Terrell. Just because your suburban-raised ass knows how to flip the script, throw together a few curse words, and act all tough, it don't make you the next Scarface!" She planted her hands firmly on her hips again. "So check yourself, little boy, and pay attention to my rules."

"You going way overboard with all this," Terrell huffed, listening to his moms chop it up. "You be straight bugging. And I ain't a boy."

"And last, pay the fuck attention, little *boy*." She stressed the last word. "I don't want you tripping on any of my friends." Simone fumed once again, insulting her son's manhood and character. "Now, do you fucking understand me? I don't want none of that Superman, Incredible Hulk shit jumping off this summer that you did to James."

"Whatever."

"Whatever, my perfectly shaped ass. Terrell, you need to stop acting like you my father and stay in your place. You ain't running nothing."

"Oh, I know you don't wanna bring up the word *father* considering all the chaos *you* caused."

"Guess what, Terrell? It's your luck day, and I'ma overlook that last comment because I know that slimeball bitch Prayer put that shit in your head. Now, you heard what I said. Stay in your place." Simone knew that her son was feeling major resentment toward what she'd done in the name of money and the coldhearted, selfish choices she'd made, even if it was years ago.

"Man, fuck them fake busters you be dealing with. All they want is some pussy anyhow," he announced, getting heated.

"Boy, I already done told you—watch your mouth. You done lost it."

"Let me get this straight. You can have company, and I can't? Is *that* how you feel?" Li'l T rolled his chair around, following Simone's every move.

"Boy, you don't pay no bills around here." Simone paused long enough to grab a cigarette out of her purse and light it. "So, shut the fuck up talking to me!"

"Oh, and *you* do?" Terrell snickered, making reference to his mother's various paymasters, which wasn't shit but another word for *trick*. "Since when did you get a damn job?"

"Terrell, this is *my* house." She inhaled deeply, then blew the smoke in a stream up in the air. "*I* make the rules around these parts, and if you don't like them, repack ya bags, crawl in that overpriced van, and take ya punk ass back to Whitey Land, where that backstabbing, uppity, I-think-I'm-the-shit bitch Prayer lives."

"Don't call Auntie Prayer a bitch no more. You need to be thanking her for doing *your* job," Terrell defensively flared up. "And besides, she ain't got nothing to do with what we discussing."

"Discussing? Did you say *discussing?*" Simone, acting offended by her child taking up for the next woman, went into the kitchen to get something to drink, followed closely by Li'l T. "Ain't no discussing shit. You heard what the hell I said, and in case you didn't get the memo, my word is law up in here." She poured a glass of cranberry juice and took a small sip.

"Well, check this out. I wanna hear you say that in about seventeen days from now."

Simone stopped, standing dumbfounded, with the refrigerator door still wide open. "And what exactly the hell is gonna happen in seventeen days?" she suspiciously asked, with her heart racing, taking another pull from her Newport, putting down the glass on the granite countertop.

"I'm gonna be eighteen, that's what!"

"And your point?"

"You already know my point."

"No, I don't. So stop playing your little overly educated word games and spit the bullshit out. What are you trying to say?"

"Come on, Ma, don't front." Terrell rolled closer to the kitchen counter. "You think I don't really know the deal? I ain't one of those dudes you got wrapped around your little finger. I'm not stupid."

Simone was getting chills, and they weren't from the still-open refrigerator. She slammed the door shut and tried to go back into the living room. "Listen, Terrell, I'm not in the mood for any of your fantasy mess today."

"Oh, yeah? Well, I seen the papers, okay?" He cut her path off with his wheelchair. "The lawyer sent a copy of the deed to the house last month, so you know I know."

"Ain't that a bitch," she ranted. "And ain't this about some rotten shit!" Simone screamed at the top of her lungs, putting the cigarette out in the oval-shaped ashtray on the counter. "After all this time, you got the nerve to throw that crap up in my damn face. You ungrateful-ass little bastard."

"I'm not trying to do anything like that." Li'l T tried reasoning with his hysterical mother. "But you need to stop trying to run over me. I got rights."

"Is that so?" Simone paced the floor, knowing that her free ride on Joey's dead back was about to come to an abrupt end.

"Yeah, it is." Terrell bossed up. "How you gonna tell me my friends ain't welcomed in here and in seventeen days, ninety percent of this house and the property it sits on will be turned over to me?"

"Who told you all those bald-faced lies? Prayer?" She stopped long enough to light another cigarette to calm her shaky nerves. "I pay these taxes."

"I said stop bringing up her name. And like I told you, the lawyer sent papers to the house, so don't try to deny it. My father, or should I say Joey, left this house to me! And I already know that the tax money comes out of the estate, so don't front."

"I already explained that controversy to you about your father a long time ago, so why you keep trying to bring it up? What's the point?"

"Oh, dang, my bad. Kamal, Joey, and whoever else you was sleeping with that might have been my damn daddy. That's the point." Terrell snatched the still full glass of his mother's juice off the kitchen counter, smashing it against the wall, breaking it into a million tiny pieces and leaving a gigantic red stain dripping down the cream-colored wall.

"Oh, so it's like that now, huh?" Simone was more angry than ashamed that her teenage son was calling her out on who his true sperm donor really was.

"Well, at this point, bet money it don't even matter to me. Real talk, Uncle Drake was, and still is, the only father I'll ever need."

"And Prayer? What about her?"

"Auntie Prayer is Auntie Prayer. Period!" After a long minute of silence, Terrell coldly stared into his mother's eyes.

Simone remained motionless as she watched her baby boy make her sweat it out. It seemed as if he was turning into someone else, someone evil. Terrell wasn't backing down and seemed to feed off of and enjoy his mother's nervousness.

Simone could barely breathe as she stumbled to speak. "So now what?" she questioned as tears started to flow, turning her face fire-engine red.

"Huh?" Li'l T stopped when he realized he had his mother at an obvious disadvantage, and he took mercy on her.

"You and them no-good, fake, can't-have-their-own-kids, wannabe parents of yours gonna get you to throw me out into the street now? Is *that* the fucking plan?" Simone's voice cracked with every word that passed across her quivering lips. "'Cause if *that's* the plan, don't forget, I *still* own ten percent."

"Ma, I would never ever do anything like that to you. Despite your crazy ways, I love you." He tried switching his attitude to reassure her. "It's always gonna be me and you against the world."

Putting the half-smoked cancer stick out, Simone once again tightened the belt on her robe. "Then why you call yourself set tripping, then?"

"Because I just want a little bit of freedom around here, that's all. So don't bug out."

"Oh, yeah." She wiped her eyes with hope, knowing the ball was now in her son's court.

"Yeah! We should both be able to have whoever we want over here. And don't worry, Ma, ain't no way in hell I would let a fool come in here and fuck over you or me!"

"Oh, yeah? Is that right?" she skeptically asked.

Terrell lifted his body over to one side, revealing the 9 mm Drake had given him for protection when he was out in the streets alone. "Hell, yeah, it is."

"Oh, so you gangsta now, right?" Simone wanted nothing more than to put her son in his place, but considering the circumstances, she remained quiet.

"Naw, but trust, Ma, this time around, I got you."

At that precise moment in time, squinting eyes, Simone took a few steps backward, looking at her son. Then it hit her like several tons of bricks exactly who Li'l T was behaving like. *Déjà vu!* The teary-eyed, confused mother was dealing with a younger version of Kamal. As her heart raced, Simone grew horrified by the sight, witnessing the inherited traits of his daddy unfolding firsthand.

Damn, why he have to be that nigga's seed? Out of both the niggas I fucked raw dog, why him? Simone reminisced, regretting not using a condom the night Terrell was conceived. *I should've got an abortion when I had the chance, or at least threw my black ass down the stairs.*

Chapter Twenty-nine

The next two weeks were filled with tension as a once-cocky Simone walked around the house on eggshells. Not only was she worried her son was gonna toss her out on that ass; she was also extremely terrified of the unthinkable, that a handicapped Terrell was becoming increasingly more sinister and Kamal-like. From his coldhearted words, his callous actions, and his arrogant mannerisms, her son was morphing into a perfect reincarnation of his father, down to a tee.

"Good morning, Ma." Terrell barely looked away from the screen of the television. "Or should I say afternoon?"

"Boy, don't start with me." Simone sucked her teeth, glancing down to see Yankee, who'd become somewhat of a permanent fixture since the "Great House Debate," lounged out ,snoring across her den floor. "And when did he get here, with his no-good, lazy behind?"

"We both came in late last night after everyone went roller skating."

"Skating?" Exhaling, Simone gave him a strange look.

"Yeah, a nigga can go hang out there and watch everybody, can't I?" The Kamal clone cut his eyes away from the video game he was so engulfed in. "Why you always dogging me on the sly?"

Simone, ignoring her son to avoid confrontation, opened the front door, grabbing the mail from the box. "Bills, bills, and more bills," she fumed at no one in particular.

"So stop complaining all the time and just pay the motherfuckers." Li'l T had straight lost all respect for his mom as he baited her on. He already knew she wasn't shit for not having his back growing up, so this was no different. "Or better yet, get one of them suckers you be chilling with to sponsor 'em. You know you do."

"Since you think you so grown, I got a bright idea. Why don't you step up to the plate and handle the shit your damn self?" She threw her hands up, showing him the collection of envelopes with "past due" stamped on them in bright red. "Matter of fact, I'm tired of all this crap. Here you go." After tossing the mail onto Terrell's lap, Simone stormed out of the room and back up the stairs.

Shortly thereafter, she returned fully dressed with several huge suitcases in tow. Li'l T was trying to be gangsta with her, so now she gonna show him what was really good on her behalf.

"Where you think you going?" A puzzle-faced Terrell put his PlayStation 7 controller down.

"My friend has been trying like hell to get me to go up North with him for the longest to check out some possible business ventures, and since you wanna be the *HNIC*, the Lord of the Manor so bad, go ahead and do you." Simone snatched her keys off the counter and proceeded to drag her bags out to the garage, throwing them into her car. "Good luck, big man. *You* hold us down for a change."

Lowering the window of her new 'Vette, she blew her son a kiss before driving off. "Oh, yeah. Since I won't be here tomorrow, happy motherfuckin' birthday."

Terrell was left looking stupid with a lap full of bills and no means to pay them. His first thought was to call his aunt and uncle to come to his rescue, but after he'd made such a big deal about being grown and taking up for Simone, it would be out of the question for him to fold like a pussy now. Li'l T had no choice but to put in some kind of work and maintain the home front.

Shit! Now what? After twenty minutes of sitting
dumbfounded by the stunt his mother had pulled, Terrell
shook it off, coming to terms with his reality. Simone
had the nerve to abandon him all over again like it wasn't
nothing to her.

*Let her dip! Fuck her! That bitch act like she the only
one that can get out in these Detroit streets and get that
bread!*

The first order of business for him was to wake Yankee
up, then get in touch with Wahoo, and finally text his
best friend, Stuff. He would need all hands on deck to
brainstorm on the situation if he wanted to succeed in
proving his point. He was grown as hell and ain't need no
female for him to survive, especially his always-out-for-
self mother! Owning ninety percent of a house was not
enough for him. Terrell was just like Kamal in the way
that he had to go overboard to prove a point—even if that
meant getting killed along the way.

"Hey, babe, it's me." Simone drove through the gates
with her cell phone pressed to her ear and the windows
down, feeling the humidity of the air. "Meet me at our
spot as soon as you can. I need to holler at you about
something."

"Is something wrong?"

"Naw, for once something is fucking right. Kamal's not-
good-for-shit son wants to be so damn mature, running
around thinking he a boss, so I'm gonna let him," Simone
informed the person on the other end of the line. "He'll
see life ain't all that easy."

"Yeah, sweetie, it be like that sometime. When boys get
a certain age, ya can't tell 'em shit. Ya just gotta let them
fall on they ass and take their hard knocks."

"Well, I pray he about to catch his fucking knocks."
Simone merged into the traffic and hit the highway.

"Come on, baby doll. Don't wish that life lesson on
Terrell by your hand. He's still ya son."

"Later for him." Simone put her designer sunglasses on
and ran her fingers through her hair. "I'm all packed, so
if you still want me to roll out with you, it's a definite go."

"All right. Give me about an hour or so to tie up some
loose ends with a couple of situations, and I'll meet you
around the way."

"Okay, daddy," Simone cooed, flipping her phone
closed.

There was no other way Li'l T could think of to get
things back on track with the creditors, avoid shutoffs,
and save face. "All right, y'all." Terrell was now surrounded by all his buddies. "Here's the deal. My moms
done broke camp, leaving me on my own, so now I got
bills to pay, and most of them, if not all, been due."

"Why don't you call your uncle Drake?" Stuff jumped
right in. "You know he got you."

"Because I want to make it on my own. I'm a fucking
man now. I can't be running to my people every time
something goes wrong." Li'l T rubbed his sweaty palms.
"I gotta get the money up. It's the point and the principle."

"Yeah, rich damn boy," Wahoo interrupted, passing
judgment. "Everybody just can't run to Mommy and
Daddy like ya soft ass probably do."

"Well, damn, excuse the fuck outta me." Stuff stood
up, straightening out his Polo shirt. "I didn't know that
being financially stable in America was considered such
a major crime."

"Yes, Wahoo. Don't be such a hating asshole." Yankee
jokingly mocked Stuff's condescending tone.

"Oh, my bad. You right. How dare I insult this man's money status! After all, he *is* better than us because he has more earning potential."

"Come on, y'all. Stop fucking around. We need to come up with a game plan," Li'l T demanded before the fellas started getting out of pocket and a full-fledged WWF SmackDown jumped off in Simone's living room. "Who in this room don't wanna make extra bread? Hell, we all got expenses. Times is hard."

"Yeah, dawg, you's right. In between my grandmother smoking every penny that welfare gives her and selling all the food benefits on the card, we about to be set out on the street again," a disgusted and disappointed Wahoo shamefully admitted. "I do need to make some serious loot to at least keep a roof over our heads and get ready for the fucking winter."

"See, *that's* what I'm talking about." Li'l T geeked up the urgency of Wahoo needing money by manipulating and preying on the weakness of his friends being some broke-ass, desperate motherfuckers trapped in the hood. "We gotsta get that shit how we live. You don't wanna be out in these streets without no cheese to fall back on. And, Yankee, come on, playa. Ya already know the deal."

"I already got us covered, T. We gonna be rolling in dough before you know it." Yankee turned his trademark baseball cap backward, knowing his situation wasn't much better than Wahoo's. "Let's holler at my peoples up in Harlem. They got the mix CDs and bootleg movies pumping on 125th. We just need some buy-in money."

"What we gonna do, sit around, listen to music, and watch flicks while we reflect?" Wahoo spoke out as he rolled a fat blunt. "Didn't you hear, nigga? We need to make some *real* dough."

"Naw, fool! Stop and use ya brains!" Yankee yelled across the den. "We can sling them bitches. It's good money in that game."

Stuff sat back on the couch with a huge, smug smile on his face. "Wow, Terrell, I see why you got in touch with me to help you figure out a solution to your problems. You've got Abbott and Costello sitting right here."

"Man, fuck you," Wahoo and Yankee blurted out at the same time, swelling up like they were ready to fight.

"Ahh . . . naw." Li'l T smiled, trying not to laugh, but he knew it was true. He didn't want to choose sides or make an obvious distinction between his friends, but it was definitely no secret that his hood buddies were slow-witted as a fuck.

Stuff gathered his thoughts, waiting for his two insulters to calm down as he tried to put another proposition on the table for them all to consider. "Are you guys blind or what?" he inquired as if he was gonna get a reply. "There's the answer right there." Stuff pointed to the marijuana that Wahoo was busy lighting up. "I got the connect on weed."

Li'l T was puzzled. "Dang, Stuff, everybody got trees."

"Yeah, what's so special about weed?" Yankee threw his two cents into the ring. "Everybody and they momma got weed."

"Not the kinda product I can get." Stuff proudly stuck his chest out. "Terrell, you know the type of people my old dude does business with."

"Oh, shit. You right."

"I know I'm right," Stuff gloated. "That should've been the first thing you thought of."

"Dang! Why didn't I think about that? But now, the only thing is how we gonna plug into that guy without your pops getting suspicious?"

"Yeah." Stuff scratched his head before smiling. "I think I'll just call ol' girl and ask her. Me and her are cool like that."

Yankee and Wahoo remained silent as the two recent high school graduates politicked. It was apparent to both of them that they were totally out of their league, financially and intellectually. And as far as this mystery connect who Terrell and Stuff, whose government names they were still yet to learn, were talking about, was of no immediate concern to them. They both realized the only thing that mattered was getting a hold of that top-notch product that was being discussed.

Stuff, determined to help his boy, reached inside his pocket, pulling out his BlackBerry. After finding Marie's number in his address book, he called her, setting up a lunch date for the next day.

Marie and her family lived up the block from him in a huge McMansion, but they were originally from Mexico. It was fairly well known in certain circles that her dad, back across the border, was some sort of narcotics kingpin. That's how Stuff's father, who was a high-powered criminal attorney, and Mr. Alverez originally met. Now on business-oriented occasions, their families would sporadically share meals. If Stuff could get Marie, who had a major crush on him ever since sixth grade, to speak to her older brother, who ran a small portion of the family business, then they'd be on and ready to set up camp. The next step would be ponying up on the possible front money they would need to start their enterprise.

Since Wahoo and Yankee's financial resources were limited, the majority of the weight fell upon Terrell and Stuff. It was therefore decided that their initial investment would be reimbursed to them first before any profits would be split. As the early afternoon turned into the late evening in Terrell's living room/new headquarters, all four of the young men came to a decision about what position they would soon play in their pending venture.

Terrell was the brains, the overseer. They'd weight up and keep the stash at his crib. It was one hundred percent safer when it came to possible police involvement or thieves because of the iron gates and electronic monitors. Stuff would be the pipeline to the connect and serve as the bank and sort of business manager. Yankee, by nature, was a hotheaded, crazed lunatic, making him the enforcer in control of their security and street team runners. For Wahoo, there was no doubt what role he'd play. He was a natural-born showboat and a true ladies' man to his playboy pumping heart. Bottom line, he'd be in charge of publicity and getting the word out that their newly formed crew had the greenest, strongest, and fattest bags in and around The D.

Chapter Thirty

The next afternoon came quickly, which was Terrell's eighteenth birthday. Any celebration would have to be put on hold until he and his boys successfully cemented their venture.

The sunshine was beaming down on the roof of the van as Stuff and Terrell headed down Fort Street toward Southwest Detroit. Marie and her much-older brother Juan, who she'd worked hard to convince to even show up, were going to break bread with the fellas at an out-of-the-way restaurant in Mexican Village. This was their one and only chance to get on, so they had to make the shit happen.

The aspiring, inexperienced drug dealers had a little over three thousand dollars in their possession, just in case Juan gave them the green light on the product. Stuff felt it best to let him know they were dead serious and about their business. As spokesman for the crew, he had to make a good impression, flat-out!

The meeting started off smoothly. Marie and Juan were already seated in a booth located in a dimly lit, secluded section of the restaurant. Enjoying a light meal before getting down to the main subject at hand, the conversation was filled with talk of family. When all the formalities were over, the real reason for the sit-down jumped off. Marie, winking her eye at Stuff while blowing him a kiss behind her brother's back, politely excused herself to go to the ladies' room so the men could talk.

"This surprise free lunch is nice and all, but what exactly do you fellas need from me?" Juan leaned in closer, directing his attention to Stuff. "I'm an extremely busy man."

"Then I'm gonna cut straight to the chase."

"Please do. I'm listening."

"Well," Stuff started, looking Juan eye to eye, "you know me and my boy here, Terrell."

"Yes . . . and?"

"We were figuring on starting us a little side hustle."

"Side hustle?" Juan rubbed his trimmed beard, surveying the restaurant's interior and the other patrons as he continued hearing his sister's former classmates out. "What kind of side hustle, and what exactly does it have to do with me?"

Terrell wanted to interrupt the cat-and-mouse game that was being played and just spit the shit out, but he had agreed, along with everyone else, that Stuff was the appointed mouthpiece. So, it was his duty to secure their connect.

Stuff took a small sip of water before breaking things down. "Listen, Juan, we're trying to get our hands on some potent-quality weed."

"Oh, I see." Juan reached for a nacho chip, dipping it into a bowl of fresh salsa. After crunching for a few brief seconds, he responded. "And just exactly why are you guys coming to me with this dilemma?"

"Juan, our families go way back." Stuff reminded him of both their fathers' original affiliation. "And I'm not going to try to play with your intelligence, and I sincerely hope that you won't play with mine."

"Yeah," Terrell butted in, running out of patience.

"Okay, youngsters." Juan got serious, real-talk serious, and his facial expression showed it. "You wanna play in the grown-up world, is that right?"

Stuff nodded as he stumbled to get the words out of his mouth. "Something like that."

"Well, tell me this: What about your daddy or your uncle?" The question was posed to both friends as Juan waited skeptically for their answer. "What you think they gonna say about your bright ideas and big talk?"

That was Terrell's cue. He'd been on the edge of his wheelchair, dying to add his take on things. Stuff was doing a good job being the go-between, but Li'l T felt he needed to be a bit more aggressive to get their point across and close the deal. If they couldn't get the trees from ol' boy, they'd have to go back to the drawing board and refigure the game plan. With a gang of past due bills, shutoff notices, Wahoo's impending eviction, and Yankee's expensive appetite for tricking with the females, that shit was definitely not an option.

"Look, Juan." His teeth were clenched as he spoke. "It's like this: We stand on our motherfucking own. Our people ain't got jack to do with this." Terrell gripped the arms of his chair, and his left eye started to twitch just as Kamal's used to back in the day. "Now, bottom line is, we're about to make some thangs happen in Detroit—with or without you." The birthday boy was truly feeling himself.

Terrell's brazen, boisterous outburst caused a business-minded Juan to take the young men more seriously. He pushed the chips and salsa to the far side of the table, giving them his full, undivided attention and some sound advice. "First off, lower your voice when you speak to me. Respect is earned in this game, not given just because you sat behind my little sister in some high school math class."

"Excuse him. He's just a little bit anxious." Stuff tried explaining his friend's irate demeanor to their guest, praying that Li'l T's mouth and firecracker temper hadn't fucked shit up for them. "We're just ready to go for ours."

"Okay, I tell you what. I might be able to hook you two wannabe big ballers up on a li'l something, but first, how much money are you working with?"

"Three grand." Terrell started to calm down when it seemed as if things were going his way. "And we can get our hands on some more if need be."

"Whoa." Juan appeared shocked. "I was under the impression that you guys just wanted to cop a half ounce or a whole—nothing semi-major."

"Naw, dude. That's what we been trying to tell you." Stuff opened the book bag sitting on the chair next to him, revealing the cash. "We need some weight."

"And not any of that garbage, either." Li'l T couldn't keep quiet.

With Juan seeing that cash, the game was on.

A good week had passed since Juan blessed them with the best weed that was available to him. After seeing that his sister Marie's friends were truly gonna be street soldiers, not just some rich kids trying to prove a point, Juan made it his personal mission to handpick each pound that was to be delivered. Now, normally, for anybody that has even copped a nickel bag, ya know it's the truth; the regular dude off the block trying to get on would have to go through damn near a hundred different connects in hopes to luck up and get one halfway righteous buster that wasn't selling garbage with a lot of shake and seeds or that wasn't seriously shorting a motherfucker big time on the weight.

Li'l T, Stuff, Wahoo, and Yankee, all not even old enough to legally buy a beer from the local corner store, were confident that their lives were about to drastically change as soon as any customer in Detroit, east or west, rolled up and blazed the weed they had blatantly spread out on Simone's precious marble dining-room table, breaking it apart and bagging it up. If she were to see them right about now, she'd freak, but even after that, she'd roll a joint.

"Damn, this bud is strong." Yankee pushed back from the table. "And fluffy as a son of a bitch."

"Hell, yeah," Wahoo cheerfully agreed as he twisted up a fat one then lit it. "It ain't nothing but red hairs all in this pound." He gagged. "We about to do the damn thang. Ain't nothing gonna slow our flow."

As the funky, thick aroma engulfed the entire room, Li'l T looked up at the clock, wondering where the time had gone. It was already 4:15 in the afternoon, and Stuff hadn't returned yet with the digital scales he went to buy from Office Depot, or Terrell's painkiller medication he'd volunteered to pick up from the pharmacy for him.

What's taking him so long? Li'l T contemplated momentarily before the trail of the weed smoke found its way to his nostrils. But instead of taking his turn hitting the blunt, getting a quick buzz, Terrell exhaustedly rolled out of the dining area and into his bedroom. Shutting the door behind him for privacy, he lifted his upper body over to the firm queen-size mattress. Using his strong hands to pull both legs up onto the bed, Terrell rested his head on the feather-filled pillow. Closing his eyes, he tried to calm his thoughts, focusing on something other than the moment.

Although Li'l T was, generally speaking, healthy as an ox, at times he would feel excruciating sharp pains in his nerve endings. To the doctors who'd treated him since his terrible accident, this didn't mean much. Their group diagnosis was that even though from time to time those nerve endings would inflict pain, discomfort, and involuntary twitching in one or both lower limbs, the young man would never stand on his own two feet again.

Before Terrell knew it, he was nodding off into never-never land. In his dreams, he'd be running up and down the basketball courts, shooting hoops, doing 360 dunks, going out for a long pass from one of the fellas, or even, at times, ballroom dancing with a female. Sleep was the only time he could accomplish his wishes.

Terrell's good times were soon halted by the sound of his cell phone ringing. As he sleepily reached on his hip, flipping it open, he saw that it was Prayer calling. It had been two whole days since he'd last spoken to her. Li'l T made it a point to stay in close touch with his auntie because he knew how she was subject to trip out on him at the drop of a dime.

He took a deep breath and pushed TALK.

"Hey, Auntie."

"Where you been?" She started right off, not even bothering to say hello first. "You too grown to call home now, or what?"

"No, Auntie Prayer, it ain't like that. I was going to call later. I was asleep."

"What you doing sleep during the middle of the day? Have you been hanging out late at night and overdoing things?"

"Naw, Auntie, nothing like that." Terrell felt a series of pains rush through his body and squeezed his eyes tightly shut, trying to fight off yelling into Prayer's ear. "It's just that . . ."

Prayer, who had raised Terrell since he was a small child, could tell when he was suffering. She could sense when he was happy or sad. "Boy, are you hurting? Have you been taking your medicine regularly since you've been at Simone's?"

"Yes and no." He was honest, feeling no good reason to lie to his surrogate mother.

"What does that mean?" she demanded.

"I ran out yesterday."

"And?" She wasn't letting him off the hook.

"And I'm waiting right now for Stuff to come back over and bring my prescription."

"Why didn't you just call me or Drake?" Prayer was leaping off into straight panic mode. "One of us would've gladly come and brought you some. And why Simone didn't go get your medicine? Where the hell is she at?" The questions kept flying.

Terrell couldn't keep up with Prayer's barrage and tried unsuccessfully to tune her out. *Damn. No dice!* Prayer wouldn't shut up for shit.

"I think I hear him at the door. You wanna hold on for a minute while I get back in my chair and go let him in?"

"No, baby. Go ahead and call me tonight, okay?"

Thank God the little white lie worked and Prayer hung up the phone. If she would've stayed running her mouth thirty more seconds, she would have heard Terrell shriek out in distress directly into her eardrum and broken every single law on the books getting to him. The young man then turned up his stereo system, buried his head in his pillow, and began to scream out in agony. The sounds of rap music drowned out his moans. Because Yankee and Wahoo were from the streets, Terrell knew they wouldn't understand what he was going through and would probably see it as a sign of weakness.

Less than half an hour later, Stuff returned with the scales tucked under his arm and, of course, the medicine. Dropping the much-needed digital instruments off in the living room with Wahoo and Yankee, who were still posted at the table, high as fuck, bagging up fat dime bags, he knocked on Terrell's closed door before opening it and finding his best friend sweating while clenching the bedsheet.

"Damn, dawg, you all right?" Stuff had witnessed Terrell go through this before and knew the drill.

"Yeah, just let me get those pills and some water, then a dude be back on his game and ready to hang tonight."

"Hold tight. I got you." Stuff loyally obliged.

"Good looking out." Terrell grabbed the bottle, swallowing almost double his normal dosage, and lay back, waiting for the pills to kick in. When the small, powerful pills did, he fell asleep and started dreaming, where he soon met up with Kamal.

Chapter Thirty-one

The line to get on the island was touch and go. It seemed as if every teenager that could borrow or steal a car was out stuntin', taking their turn to cross the bridge. Half-naked chicks, dudes rockin' oversized white tees, and even the police were bobbing their heads to the sounds of the summer. The state of Michigan was justifiably nicknamed the Winter Wonderland. The snow was always heavy, and the winds that whipped off the Great Lakes made the chill in the air sometimes unbearable. You'd be hard pressed to see foot traffic on the downtown streets of Detroit from early October to late April.

Now, fast-forward to the first warm weeks of the spring season. That shit was definitely on and freaking poppin'! Detroiters could, and easily would, turn a humid summer's day, afternoon, and night all the way the hell out. Getting their grill on or swimming in the river, they cut up.

With only a few months of fun in the sun to clown, Li'l T, Stuff, Wahoo, and Yankee were no different. Armed with a portion of their newly gained wealth and a trunk filled with dime bags to sling, it was time to let some folks outside of their own hood really feel them and the power they intended on building.

The billboard located on top of the corner liquor store read a humid 94 degrees. Stuff was driving his brand-new BMW with the air conditioner on high. With Terrell riding shotgun, Yankee and Wahoo holding the back seat down, there was no other way to describe them. The fellas were on point. Flirting with a carload of whorish females who were flashing them, with the hopes of being their companions for the day, Yankee and Wahoo played along, getting a full view of every breast and tongue ring that was exposed.

"Hell, yeah. Pull over and park near that royal-blue Toyota," Li'l T instructed. "That spot is right in the middle of the strip."

"Okay, bet." Stuff cut the steady flow of traffic off, backing into the spot.

With the sounds of car horns blowing teamed up with a hundred various stereo systems playing a thousand different CDs and at least a good three hundred or so people drunk, high, and just plain fucked the fuck up, the party was just beginning.

"This is what the hell I'm talking about."

"Yeah, these hoes out here is on us," Wahoo agreed with Yankee as they got out of the BMW, looking all high-profile, heading toward the traffic.

Terrell and Stuff were used to riding good, so the *ohhs* and *ahhs* the females were blowing out of their mouths were nothing. Stuff popped the trunk, getting out his boy's chair, and pushed it around to the passenger's side door. "Here you go." He nodded. "I got you."

"Good looking out." Terrell bit his lower lip. He glanced down at his new sneakers as he placed both feet on the footrest, wishing he could run at least once in his young life and get them bitches dirty. "You always got my back."

"We family, T. You know how we do," Stuff reassured Terrell as he watched Yankee and Wahoo stunt for hoes.

Stuff knew that Li'l T's friends from the other side of The Gates didn't know the meaning of teamwork or comradery. The only thing they were taught from an early age was the art of self-preservation; dog eat dog.

Watching them do their own thang made it painfully clear who Terrell could and could not rely on when times got real and shit got heated.

One positive thing about Yankee and Wahoo's character was they definitely had that hustle bone in them. No sooner than their sneakers hit the pavement, dimes and fat-ass twenty-five-dollar bags were getting sold. The usual, everyday garbage tree seller, no doubt, was gonna be shit outta luck this hot day. The boys had the entire strip on lock.

Terrell carefully scanned the crowd of park-goers every so often just in case the ho-ass po-po tried to ruin the flow of things and show their punk asses up. He wasn't worried one bit about somebody trying to get the balls to boss up and gangster their product or revenue. That shit was definitely out of the question. If anybody flexed or tried to go for bad, that would be like a gift from God for Li'l T, who every so often was showing signs of becoming like his deceased father, Kamal.

The huge pistol that was inconspicuously tucked under his wheelchair's cushion seemed to be calling out to its owner: *"Kill a motherfucker if they step to you!"* it repeated, sinisterly whispering into Terrell's subconscious. *"Let these people see that you ain't a joke and ain't for no type of foolishness!"*

Kamal's illegitimate, bastard-born son was innocently unaware that he was feeling the tainted bloodline of severe anger and borderline schizophrenic behavior that would soon rear its psychotic head. The murderous characteristics were rooted deep in his bones, and the ticking time bomb was undoubtedly destined to surface when Terrell was pushed into a corner.

"Shit is going good as hell out here," Wahoo, after hours of slinging, finally had time to acknowledge to Li'l T. "We gonna be out of bags way before the sun goes down."

"Yeah, he's right." Stuff placed his hand on Terrell's shoulder, agreeing with Wahoo's profound statement. "We should get ready to go put this money up in a safe place."

"Naw, we should lay back and mack on these dumb bitches," Yankee insisted, heading back toward the crowd of females.

Despite Yankee and Wahoo both wanting to stay until the entire island shut down for the night, Terrell made the final decision that it was time to rise up and break camp. Surveying the strip as they pulled off, he looked down at the stash of dough in his lap, coming to the realization that this was gonna be one helluva summer.

Chapter Thirty-two

It was slightly after four o'clock in the afternoon when half brothers Elon and Donté finished breaking down and bagging up the twenty pounds of weed they'd just brought back from Florida. Their drug-dealing fatherhad plugged the nineteen-year-old men in a long time ago, teaching them the hard-core unwritten laws of the street game. With two different baby mommas, he knew it was what it was. Each female could easily hold the joint title of official Motown rat-mouth bitches. Big Ace, being a true man and never pressing the issue of a blood test, took both boys from their mothers at the same time, raising them on his own. His sons were only weeks apart in birth and were mirror images of each other, with the exception of their hair.

Sure, Big Ace was well known and respected in and around Detroit and had been deeply rooted into the dope game for years. And, of course, he'd spoiled his sons rotten when they were kids, but now they were grown-ass men. Although he wanted them to go to school and take a different path than he had, the streets were calling, and the boys made the decision to answer. Disappointed, Big Ace didn't fight their choice but made it perfectly clear off rip that Elon and Donté had to grind hard to get that real longevity dough on their own. They could not depend on him and his hustle, which was exclusively heroin.

The initial setup was sweet as a motherfucker and handed to the boys on a silver platter. What they did with it from that point on was solely on them. All the pair had to do was maintain the operation. They'd drive down to Mobile, Alabama, where they would chill in a hotel near the coastline. When their people got the word they were in town and ready to do business, they'd shoot up from Pensacola, making the drop. From there, Eunice, their elderly great-aunt who was sixty-seven and still gangster about her business, sometimes recklessly drove back up the interstate with her car packed with weed. The brothers never had to take the risk of catching a transporting case. Now, you know *that's* what's really up!

"Y'all two made it back up top yet or what?"

"Yeah, Pops. We got back late last night."

"Did you have any problems?" Big Ace questioned his oldest and most-difficult-to-control son.

"Naw, Auntie E held it down for us." Elon lay back on the bed. "We could barely keep up with her lead-foot ass! She's an animal behind that wheel."

"Yeah, that ain't a good look at all. I done told Eunice time and time again about that driving of hers." Big Ace had to remember to chastise his mother's sister about being slow and safe instead of fast and furious. "I'm still out of town, so hold things down until I get back."

"Who ya with, Pops?"

"None of ya damn business, youngster! Just hold things down! You hear me?"

"You know it," Elon affirmed, cracking his knuckles, wanting nothing more than to impress his father and follow in his huge, infamous footsteps.

"Oh, and tell ya brother to call me later. Peace."

***

"What it do, bro? You about ready or what?" Donté was just getting out of the shower and ready to get dressed. "We need to hit the streets with this work!"

Laying out his brand-new linen shirt and freshly pressed plaid shorts, the chocolate-toned god removed the towel from his 38-inch solid waistline and dried off, admiring his own self in the mirror. Every inch of Donté's six-foot-two frame was bulging with muscles as his shoulder-length damp dreads dripped beads of water down his chest. Escaping even one scar or blemish on his torso from childhood to the present, Donté was flawless. Whether it was the fresh fruit, vegetables, and water that he'd practically lived off of for months at a time, or just a gift bestowed on him from above, Donté James was definitely blessed in the body department.

"Yeah, no doubt," a mean-spirited Elon grunted to his brother from his disorganized bedroom. "I'm almost ready my damn self."

Elon James was no different from his sibling in physical build, but the obvious, recognizable difference between them was that Elon kept an evil expression plastered on his face, favored a bald head, and didn't give a fast fart freaking fuck about shit but his money, his brother, and his old dude—and you can best believe exactly in that damn order. Unlike Donté, you wouldn't see Elon with a bottle of water or anything else remotely healthy. His drink of choice was Old E straight out of the bottle, and greasy pork would fill his belly.

"I'll meet you out front. And hurry ya ass up!" Elon instructed his brother as he massaged shea butter oil, of all things, into his clean scalp while heading toward the living room. *Damn, I'm fine,* he reflected, passing a mirror. Grabbing the dark red nylon bag containing nickels, dimes, and a few ounces and not forgetting an ice-cold beer out of the refrigerator, he was set to roll.

Stepping out onto the porch, Elon looked up directly into the sun as if he were trying to challenge it to stop shining and ruin their impending moneymaking evening. He and his brother had spent half the afternoon hooking up and only had those few short hours to grind before the sun went down.

"Come on, pretty boy. Let's be out."

Donté finally appeared on the front porch, joining Elon. Taking a deep breath of the fresh summer air with a huge jug of ice water posted at his side, he was now ready.

"We taking your whip or mine?"

"Mine, playboy," Elon eagerly replied, clicking the automatic starter on the midnight-black truck, causing the sound system to bump. "Now, let's go meet the rest of the team and put in this work!"

The truck then roared off toward its destination as the brothers leaned back in pimp mode, ready to make the rest of the day do what it do.

Chapter Thirty-three

The line to get off the island was almost as long and thick as the one to get on. Bumper-to-bumper cars, trucks, motorcycles, and even ten-speed bikes were fighting traffic. With the bridge as packed as it was, it was amazing and damn near a summer miracle in the hood Detroit's Finest hadn't shut that bitch down completely.

"Man, we should've stayed," Wahoo yelled up to the front seat. "It's some bad-ass females on the other side heading in."

"It sho' fucking is. Yankee enthusiastically licked his lips, cosigning with his boy. "You need to hook a U."

Stuff hurriedly glanced over at Li'l T with a stern, disapproving frown. He nodded his head back at the two wild rear seat passengers, sucking his teeth. "Damn! Where did you get them fools from?"

"Silly-ass niggas." Li'l T held tightly onto the money they'd accumulated as Stuff continued cautiously driving across the bridge.

"They just having some fun. Fuck 'em!"

"Yeah, okay," Stuff mumbled as he kept his eyes focused on the road to avoid slamming into the carload of much-younger teenagers who were obviously driving their parents' vehicles. "Call it what you want, but their asses are beyond ignorant!"

"It's all good." Li'l T laughed. "Let's just get off this bridge, grab something to drink, and head to the crib to count up this loot."

"Yeah, and get rid of them." Stuff pointed back, referring to Yankee and Wahoo, who were still busy hanging out the window, trying to get as many numbers as they could, not caring what was being said about their behavior or who the fuck was saying the bullshit.

"Hey, what it do?"
"You got the best hand!"
"Yeah, meet us at the liquor store on Jefferson."
"That'll work," the dude answered Elon.
"We'll grab some cold ones and a couple of hot hoes to chill with." Elon gripped the steering wheel as he talked into his Bluetooth.
"Me and the boys is about five minutes away."
"Dig that. Me and my brother is en route too."
Donté sat back in the seat, smiling at the prospect of making plenty of dough and recouping some of the funds they'd put up to cop. Most of their regular, good-spending customers were already out at the island, so he figured they'd be straight in a few hours. All they needed to do was touch down and the night would be perfect. They'd both have a few stacks by daylight.

"Turn into the store parking lot and pull up there."
"Okay, got you." Stuff sharply turned the Beamer into the debris-filled pavement, coming close to blocking the store's crowded front entrance. Yankee and Wahoo, still stuntin', proudly jumped from the backseat, making sure to speak to all the females that were within ear range. Running into the building to get a few bottles, they unexpectedly encountered Shauntae, Yankee's homegirl fuck buddy, and her crew.
"Damn, your ass is looking hot to death."

"Yankee, stop playing." Shauntae giggled playfully, pushing his shoulder. "You know you crazy."

"I ain't bullshittin'." Yankee grabbed her arm, twirling her around so he could gawk at her firm ass. "You need to come ride with me."

"Oh, yeah? What you pushing?" Shauntae's sac-chasing ears got on high alert.

Yankee bit the side of his lip as he tried to entice her with the growing bulge in his forever sagging jeans. He knew Shauntae was all about that money, but she always loved to get a taste of the dick he was holding. "I'm out and about with my team and shit." He stuck his chest out, perpetrating the big-shot role. "Getting that money flow up. You know how I do."

"Oh, yeah? Who is ya team?" Shauntae smiled as her cat trap grew wet at the sound of cash. "And where y'all's headed—to the island?"

"Naw, been there, done that." Wahoo put his two cents in as he returned with a huge bag of drinks and a pack of Newports.

"Well, we about to roll to the crib, chill, and get beyond fucked up," Yankee announced. "You and your girls coming or what?"

Shauntae did love hanging with Yankee. No doubt he was thugged all the way out and could bang for hours, but he was never one to have spare jack-off change floating around. And right about now, at the top of her agenda, she desperately needed a new outfit to rock to the School's Out Summer Jam Concert, which, all games aside, meant finding a momma's-boy sucker or some old, unsuspecting trick in the next couple of days to sponsor that black ass.

As the group walked out the door, Yankee ushered her and her clique over toward where Stuff parked, and as predicted by Yankee, the sight of the new BMW got Shauntae even hotter. She was what Negroes in Detroit often referred to as a "Bona Fide Motor Ho." Seriously speaking, even though Yankee wasn't driving, he knew given Shauntae's whorish track record, she'd be more than willing to suck his dick and every other nigga in the parking lot just to be seen near the new whip Stuff was pushing.

Finally, the young, mischievous, overdeveloped girl inspected the expensive rims from afar. She made eye contact with Li'l T.

Damn, it's the dude from the other side of The Gates. I want him bad!

With her girls automatically trailing behind her, Shauntae seductively rubbed her hand across the warm hood of the car. "Maybe we will hang with y'all," she boldly decided for the rest of her loyal followers as she propped her ass back on the front grill so Li'l T and Stuff could get a full view of what she was working with.

"That's a bet." Yankee grinned arrogantly, unaware that his wannabe girl lusted for the next dude to hit her off with a little dick. "Now, what y'all ladies drinking on? Name it and it's yours."

"Just get us some coolers," Liza, one of the girls, finally blurted out since their self-appointed leader was preoccupied shamelessly flirting with every buster that drove up.

"Okay, then." Since he was the only one with a fake ID, Wahoo took a head count before going back into the store to cop. "So ,that's three coolers."

"No, thank you." Joi shyly spoke up with her arms folded. "I don't drink alcohol."

"All right, then. No problem." Wahoo laughed at Shauntae's sister. "Two."

Joi approached Shauntae timidly, trying to whisper into her ear. "I need to go home. I have to study tonight, and it's getting late."

"Why don't you just fall back and chill? Try having a little fun for once in your boring-ass life." Shauntae loudly chastised her younger sister, still trying to remain cute despite the steaming heat rising from the running engine under the BMW's hood. "Who in the hell goes to school in the summer anyhow?"

"Somebody who wants to get ahead and make it in the world," Joi sarcastically mumbled. "That's who."

"Whatever!" Shauntae turned around, making sure that Li'l T was watching her. "Just shut the fuck up and chill!"

"Why in the hell does Yankee and Wahoo's retarded asses have this rap video wannabe female posted on my ride?" Stuff protested. "She betta not dent my ride."

Li'l T was in a trance, watching what was going on in front of him. Still holding on to the money as he peered out the windshield, Terrell ignored his friend's comments. Straining his ears to listen to the conversation taking place between the two girls in spite of all the loud music, they had his undivided attention. There was something about the slender, dark-skinned, shoulder-length pony-tail and peach-colored Polo shirt-wearing female that caught his eye. Maybe it was the unusual slanted shape of her eyes, or maybe the way she moved, which seemed soft and slow but deliberate. Needless to say, whatever it was, Terrell felt something immediately stirring inside of him as his manhood started to throb.

"Are you listening to me?" Stuff nudged Terrell's arm in an attempt to get a response.

"Yeah. Sorry, my dude." Li'l T leaned comfortably back in the seat. "But that girl is cute as hell."

"Don't tell me you're into overpriced chicks now?"

"What you mean?"

Stuff laughed, not believing what he was hearing. "I mean, I know you don't like her," he motioned.

"Come on, guy." Li'l T cut his eyes at his boy. "Ol' girl on the hood definitely got a fat ass and all, but I'm talking about the other one to the left."

Shauntae was straight overplaying her position by constantly glancing back, assuming that Li'l T and Stuff were chopping it up about her.

He on me! Shit! They both on me!

Stuff took his sights off Shauntae, focusing in on Joi, who was now standing over to the side with another girl. "Yeah, you right. She does look nice." He nodded, taking note of her presence. "And plus, she's not rocking all that makeup packed on her face like Miss Wide Ass perched all up on my car like she pays the notes."

The fellas started laughing, making Shauntae the source of their humor, while she was even more convinced that by nightfall, she'd have Li'l T exactly where she wanted him, stretched out across somebody's bed, getting her grind on.

Fuck Yankee and his broke ass! I need to hook up with his boy! He got that sho' 'nuff bread!

Chapter Thirty-four

"Damn, this shit is packed," Elon noticed as they tried finding somewhere to park.

"Yeah, but that's a good thang," his brother enthusiastically replied. "More weedheads out in these Detroit streets for us."

As the two siblings spotted their cohorts, a couple of slightly younger cats ran out the door of the liquor store directly in front of the truck, causing Elon to slam down forcefully on his brakes. The sound of the huge tires screeching put the entire parking lot of people on elevated alert. They immediately recognized the truck, as well as the ruthless occupants, and feared trouble.

Yankee and Wahoo, who didn't give two rotten pieces of shit about who the fuck was inside, stopped dead in their tracks as they made eye contact with the notoriously known brothers. For no more than five long, drawn-out seconds, the crowd held their breath and cautiously waited, bracing up for the old shoot-'em-up, bang-bang cowboy, Western-style confrontation to jump off.

Elon instinctively gripped up on his pistol that was conveniently laying on the truck's armrest. "I should put something hot through these lightweight niggas."

Donté, the wiser of the brothers, tossed his bottle of water on the truck's floor, grabbing Elon's arm, preventing him from raising the loaded gun. "Come on, bro! Let this shit go. We need to be on our way out to the island and get this dough. Ya feel me?"

"Yeah, I guess you right." Elon continued eye-fucking Wahoo and Yankee as he hit the automatic button, making the window roll down. "Y'all little punk-ass busters getting a serious pass this time, courtesy of my brother. 'Cause if it was any other day of the year, y'all pussies be halfway to hell."

"Oh, yeah?" Yankee challenged as he and Wahoo headed toward Shauntae, who was still profiling, handing her a cooler out of the bag.

"Let it go," Donté demanded. "We got business elsewhere. This ain't no time to be catching a case."

"Them busters over there with Shauntae's good dick-slurping ass! I should shoot all they asses and that BMW they pushing."

"Come on, bro! You know she ain't nothing but a ho, so let them have the tramp. It ain't like her ass is wifey material anyhow."

"Yeah, you right." Pissed and with murder on his mind, Elon skidded off and blew his horn twice, signaling for his crew to follow. Back-to-back, they all took off down Jefferson Avenue, heading toward the bridge.

Li'l T, trying his best to see around Shauntae's huge ass that was blocking his view, observed what was going on between his friends and some strange dudes in the same big black truck he'd seen a week or so before with the I GO HARD plate. He started to bug out, remembering vividly that he and the reckless driver had some serious unfinished business lingering. He didn't know for sure what was being said, but he could tell by everyone's expressions that it wasn't at all nothing nice. The summer sun didn't make matters any better as Terrell reached for his shiny 9 mm, and his paternally inherited quick-tempered blood started to boil.

"I know these fools don't want none. We should follow them. Ain't nobody gonna be disrespecting our crew like we ain't shit."

"And then what you think gonna go down? Are you insane or what?" Stuff reasoned with his childhood friend, attempting to snatch the gun out of his hands. "You know I got your back, and I'm all for this selling weed thing for the summer, but I'm not trying to go to jail for being a part of murder, especially for those idiots," he advised as Terrell struggled to lean out the window. "And now we a crew? Dude, calm the hell down and let's go to the crib."

Terrell, realizing Stuff was 100 percent correct, gradually got himself back in check. After all, they had money to count up and a town to take over, so to speak. And finally, with Yankee and Wahoo once again in the car and the group of females riding closely behind them, Simone's house was their next stop.

Each occupant in the two automobiles was caught up in their own individual thoughts. . . .

Maybe I can see what's up on that female with that pink shirt on. Terrell tried to keep his blood pressure down. *There's something real special about her. Something different. 'Cause she sho' don't look like her friends.*

Yankee closed his eyes, tugging on his manhood, imagining banging Shauntae from the back, making her scream out his name. *Damn! I'm about to give that bitch the real dick-down business. She just don't know what I got in store for her ass.*

I need to go home and study, not go over to some strange guy's house for God knows what. Joi decisively pouted. *This is the last time I hang out with my sister. She always got some crap in the game.*

That fine-ass Gates boy Terrell is gonna be mine flat-out! Shauntae schemed and plotted. *One way or a-fucking-other. And shit! I sho' hope Elon ain't notice my black ass, but even if he did, so damn what! If the nigga like the shit that much, he should've put a ring on it.*

I hope my grandma ain't using the rent money I gave her to get high. Wahoo worried about getting evicted, looking out the window. *She needs to get some professional help before she drags our family all the way down.*

I wonder which one of them gonna like me? Liza puzzled, twisting her long weave. *They all cute.*

That crazy chick driving better not bump my damn car! Stuff fumed as he drove, looking into his rearview mirror, praying for the best. *She probably doesn't even have any type of insurance, not even No Fault!*

Chapter Thirty-five

As they passed through The Gates, slowly riding over each speed bump, Terrell knew his old-earth Simone would literally hit the roof if she saw all the people he was about to have up in the crib. "Damn, Ma, sorry." His lips barely moved as he mumbled. Yet, glancing back, knowing he could get a few minutes to kick it with his mystery girl, made the nasty taste of Simone's condescending name fade out.

Stuff pulled up in the driveway, almost touching the garage door with the bumper of his car. The females were right behind him as they roared in like they were being chased by the damn police. When Stuff finally heard the driver turn off her engine on the ancient rust bucket she was pushing, he was visually overjoyed that he'd made it safely back to Li'l T's house alive, and seemingly most important to him, without as much as a single scratch on his ride.

They then all climbed out of the cars, heading toward the front door. The fellas, who knew good and fucking damn well Simone's house rules but conveniently chose to ignore them, trampled across the freshly cut green grass without as much as a second thought. Stuff, who was getting Li'l T's wheelchair out of the trunk, leered in disbelief at their *"Fuck it! I'm trying to show the hell out in front of some broads"* routine.

"Why do you put up with them?" He rolled the chair up on the side of the car.

"Just chill for a few and help me real quick." Terrell slid over. "I need to hurry up and go around the back so I can open the front door."

"Slow down," Stuff insisted, still scrutinizing Li'l T's supposed-to-be boys. "Let their wild asses wait!"

"It ain't them a nigga trying to hurry and get in the house for."

"Oh, I feel you," Stuff said, watching Joi fall back from the rest of the group, still hesitating about hanging out with the crowd. "Now I see."

Stuff protectively followed Li'l T, who rolled around the back of the house as a shocked Shauntae and Liza, and a wide-open-mouthed compassionate Joi watched in disbelief. Terrell was used to all eyes being on him, so the strange looks that he got from the girls and many others all came along with the territory of being a young, handsome, seemingly healthy man who was slowed down by a disability. It was as if he could read their thoughts, but *fuck it* was his true mind-set. It was what it was!

Up until now, the girls never saw Terrell once get out of the car, so they were speechless. Even back when Shauntae first saw him pushing his flossed-out van at the gas station, she had no idea that he couldn't walk and was confined to a wheelchair.

"Dang." Joi was the first to comment. "That's so sad."

"Yeah, it is," Liza agreed, still twisting on her hair.

"I know it must be hard for him being so young and all," Joi sympathized. "Dang gee."

"Y'all need to stop feeling sorry for that motherfucker and show me some damn hood-ass love," Yankee demanded.

"Yeah, my dude is right." Wahoo put his arms around all three ladies. "As soon as he rolls his punk ass around the back and lets y'all up in his spot and y'all see how he's living, then, for real for real, y'all ain't gonna feel shit no more but jealous."

"Still." Joi pulled herself away from the group hug.

Lost in her conniving thoughts, Shauntae wasn't saying much of nothing. Now, hell yeah, at this point, seeing ol' boy pimping that wheelchair did kinda throw her for a loop, but nothing or nobody was gonna stop her from her goal: getting that cash from Terrell's rich ass. Blind, cripple, or crazy, eight to eighty, if a nigga's dick was working, then so was she. Now, if chick got an old trick to fall in love with her skanky hot-box ass along the way and try to wife her, then so be it. She'd milk they ass for a few months, then move the fuck on to the next unfortunate sucker. Shauntae was a pro with her tactics, inheriting those slimy characteristics from her mother, Monique, aka Clip-n-Dip Moe, who was murdered in front of her, Joi, and their baby brother when they were all small children. Rumor had it that it was revenge for setting up and robbing a now-drug kingpin back in the day.

Oh, well. I guess it's true what they say: Payback is a motherfucker! Because allegedly when the stickup foursome least expected it, a lone gunman burst down their front door in broad daylight with a ski mask on, shooting Monique and the three supposed accomplices to the dishonest deed dead in their faces. Shauntae, the oldest child, watched in utter terror as the burly killer, who had distinct, long, thick braids sticking out the sides of his mask, hawked a huge glob of spit onto her mother's body, then grinned, showing his gold tooth as he snatched a pair of Tims off one of the dead men's feet before casually strolling out the front door, jumping into a Ford F-150.

**

"Damn, it's nice in here." Shauntae was first to come inside Simone's house. "And this right here look like some fly-ass art you see in a freaking movie or something." She marveled at the side of the hand-carved wood around the oval-shaped mirror that hung in the entryway.

"Whoa, she's dumb as a bag of rocks."

"What ya just say about me?" Shauntae rolled her eyes arrogantly, swishing past him, marching into the living room in search of where her intended victim of the night, Terrell, was located.

Stuff grunted, ignoring Shauntae's sassy comment while waiting for the others to come in so he could lock the door. Even though they were behind The Gates, he still felt nervous about Yankee and Wahoo, not to mention these shady, hot-style females they forced into the mix. Stuff had a bad feeling about the whole scenario but had no choice but to wait and see how the circus shit played out. Suspicious when it came in the way of loyalties, he'd bet half his trust fund and his new car that given enough time, any underhanded motives would come to the light and surely manifest.

The first half hour, Terrell tried his best to make the girls, particularly Joi, feel at home. Being the perfect host, he made sure they all had something to drink, even offering them some food. While Yankee and Wahoo disrespectfully showed off, acting like Simone's house was their own, Stuff stood back, leaning up against the wall with his arms folded.

"So, what school do you go to?" Terrell directed his question to Joi, who, by this time, had pulled a book out of her bag and was attempting to read.

"She goes to King High," Shauntae answered for her sister.

"Oh." Li'l T was disappointed that his big icebreaker inquiry didn't work and tried again. "You must gonna be a senior in September?"

Shauntae snatched the book out of her sister's hand, tossing it on the couch, hoping to get the attention off Joi and directly on her. Looking at her fingernails, trying to be cute, she flaunted her huge breasts. "Yeah, her young ass is just getting to the twelfth. I been outta school."

Yankee wasn't crazy. Even Ray Charles could see clearly that Shauntae was trying to push up on Terrell, and he was getting ready to go on straight hate patrol. "Yeah, Shauntae. You right." He took a pull from the blunt before passing it to her. "Your dumb ass dropped out in eighth grade after they caught you fucking around with the old stank-breath janitor."

"Dang, I remember that shit." Wahoo laughed, shedding even more light on the story. "Mr. Rawlins's wife came up there, ready to stomp a mud hole in ya wild ass."

"Fuck y'all," Shauntae hissed, not even wanting to smoke, and passed the blunt to her girl Liza, who was also reminiscing.

"Girl, forget them. They just mad 'cause you was getting his paycheck and wasn't giving them shit."

Yankee's plan of belittling his fuck buddy was working like a charm. He could tell that even if a small percentage of Terrell's mind had thought about getting with Shauntae, it was definitely over now. By the expression on his face, as well as Stuff's, Shauntae was officially two steps beneath bottom barrel.

Joi, who knew full well her older sister was nasty, felt immediately embarrassed for the two of them and came to her defense. "You guys need to quit. If it wasn't for my sister's sacrifices, me and our little brother would've starved some nights, so shut up."

"We was only playing, Joi, so stop being sensitive."

"I don't care, Yankee. Just be quiet." Joi started to cry and asked Terrell if she could use the bathroom.

The mood in the room was altered, and Shauntae was now, thankfully, silent. The calm of the living room was soon interrupted once again as Wahoo's cell phone rang. After a quick conversation with his young niece, he found out that his grandmother had just been rushed to the hospital, suffering from a possible drug overdose.

"Damn, I gotta go." Wahoo leaped to his feet, heading toward the door. "Grand-Moms done fucked the fuck up again."

"You bullshitting," Yankee marveled.

"Naw, dawg, they found her stubborn ass passed out in the basement near that old unplugged washing machine in the corner. They taking her to Receiving Hospital, so I gotta bounce."

"Want me to drive you?" Liza volunteered, knowing what it was like to have a loved one OD, growing up in a house of dopefiends her damn self.

"Yeah, would you? I know ain't no cab gonna stop for me at night, and my niece said it's real bad this time."

Liza grabbed her purse, turning around to see if Shauntae was going to roll. Getting no immediate response, she and Wahoo bolted out the door, jumping in her car. Before they backed out of the driveway, Yankee ran out the front door to join his boy, knowing at this point in the game any chance of Terrell wanting Shauntae was slim to none. Stuff and Li'l T were now left in the house alone with the two sisters, who were both going through some emotional bullshit.

Chapter Thirty-six

Elon led the pack of his crew as they crossed the bridge and took over their regular spot on the strip. He and Donté were later than usual, but it was still pumped. Within ten minutes of their runners getting out and circulating through the crowd, Mitts and LoLo came back to the brothers with the same complaints:

1. *All of a sudden, the bags weren't as fat as the ones that some had copped earlier.*

2. *The weed wasn't greeny green, compared to the bags the dudes in the BMW had.*

3. *Some guy in a wheelchair was slinging two for one if you bought a twenty-five or more.*

4. *Their regular all-day customers had already spent out on the other guys.*

"Ain't this some crazy-ass bullshit." Elon clenched his fist with fury. "Some other cats done tried to bum-rush our territory."

"Calm down, bro."

"Naw, fuck that. Niggas gonna die fuckin' with me."

"Naw, Donté, he need to trip," Mitts instigated as he continued to report, making matters worse. "They out here saying that whoever these kids is pushing the BMW got that monster weed."

"Oh, yeah?" Donté pondered as he smelled half an ounce in his hands.

"Dawg, I hit a blunt some dudes I sell to from the west side bought from them, and real talk, I can't even front. That shit is righteous as a motherfucker."

"Shut the fuck up, Mitts." Elon swole up, getting all caught in his feelings. "I ain't trying to hear that."

"I was just saying." He backed up slightly, realizing that his boss was heated. "The play was all right."

"Just go back on the grind, Mitts, and do what you can do." Donté temporary defused the conflict. "And, LoLo, double up the dimes and flip 'em for ten even, no shorts."

As the brothers sat back on the truck, observing their money slowly trickle in from new people just getting to the park, any hopes of an early night were quickly fading.

"I guess we need to step up our game and maybe our connect," Donté suggested. "What ya think?"

"Yeah, or get rid of the fucking competition," Elon fumed as he wondered if the youngsters rolling in the BMW Shauntae was chilling with at the store were the same dudes that his crew was complaining about. Taking his cell phone off his hip, he dialed her number but got nothing but voice mail. "What up, doe, bitch! This Elon. Get at me!"

Shauntae was left sitting in the corner of the sofa, humiliated her supposed-to-be homeboy, Yankee, had put her on full blast in front of Terrell and Stuff. With her little sister still in the bathroom probably crying her eyes out, she pressed IGNORE on her ringing cell phone and tried her best to keep her front up. "So anyway, what y'all fellas got up for the rest of the night?"

Terrell felt bad for her, shrugging his shoulders, not knowing exactly what to say. Stuff, on the other hand, stepped out of character, seeming to become strangely sympathetic to her embarrassment. He leaned up off the wall he'd been occupying the entire evening since they got there and went over to the other end of the couch, sitting on the arm.

"It really doesn't matter what you did back in the day. For real, we've all done or said things that we've regretted."

Shauntae was shocked that the one person that seemed to look at her earlier with the most contempt was the very one to soothe her bruised ego. "I know it was wrong about the janitor, but I was too young to get a job, and my little brother and sister ain't have much of shit. The State even stepped in, taking my little brother. That's why Joi is crying. We haven't seen him in years."

"Damn, that's messed up, but that was in the past. What you do now?" Stuff inquired, really knowing that this out of control tiger hadn't changed her stripes. "Where you work at?"

"I'm kinda in between jobs right now," Shauntae confessed as she sized Stuff up, coming to the realization that he wasn't that bad looking, not to mention the fact that he was driving a brand-new BMW. "But I'm always open to new things," she flirted.

"Oh, yeah?" Stuff looked past all the makeup and slick talk, trying to see if Shauntae was worth his trouble. "What kind of things?"

Terrell, seeing that Stuff and Shauntae were occupied doing their thang, rolled in the back and knocked on the bathroom door. "Hey, are you all right in there?"

After a few brief seconds of silence, the doorknob twisted and a red-eyed Joi stepped out into the hallway with her head lowered, knowing she wasn't built for this type of constant humiliation from strangers. Taking a deep breath, she finally spoke. "Yes, I'm fine. Sorry I stayed in there so long. It's just that—"

"Don't worry. We good. I understand." Li'l T reached out, touching her in hopes of providing some sort of comfort. Joi didn't move, remaining motionless as Terrell rubbed her hand and they shared one of those corny, fake-ass

Lifetime movie enchanted moments. "Let's go in here and chill for a little while so my friend and your sister can be alone. Everybody else left. Wahoo's grandmother is sick."

Joi, feeling somewhat apprehensive, followed Li'l T into his bedroom and sat down on the chair in the far corner. Both nervous as shit, they exchanged conversation about anything that came to mind the rest of the evening. Finding out that they'd both grown up without their fathers, as well as several other strange facts that had them linked, time seemed to fly.

Chapter Thirty-seven

"I can't believe Wahoo's family acted like that at his granny's service," Joi remarked as she got out of Li'l T's van that he parked in the driveway next to Stuff's Beamer, followed by Stuff and Shauntae. "They behaved like wild animals fighting about that leftover food the church donated. I never knew things were that bad for him."

"Yeah, that was some crazy shit," Shauntae replied, tugging down on the short denim miniskirt she proudly opted to wear to the ghetto funeral. "His entire family was off the chain. And Yankee acting all low class, hitting on that lady delivering the eulogy only made things worse. He didn't even take off that damn hat."

Stuff wanted to throw his two cents in the conversation but held back his spin on the subject in fear of hurting both girls' feelings. He knew that their own family tree was barely one step up from Wahoo's, considering what he'd seen and heard over the past week since hanging out with the sisters.

"I hope the State doesn't step in and try to separate the kids. That would be so foul," Joi prayed, thinking about the disastrous chain of events that followed her own mother's sudden but well-deserved death. She and her siblings had slipped through the cracks of the child welfare system.

"You right," Li'l T sympathized, rolling toward the rear of the house. "Maybe Wahoo will really do what he said last night and look for a legitimate job so he can at least have something down on paper in the government's eyes."

In deep discussion, all four of them approached the back door, talking among themselves. They were interrupted as Li'l T noticed a light on in the kitchen and grew uneasy, shifting over in his wheelchair, pressing his ear to the door. "Shhhh . . . Y'all hold up a minute," he whispered, placing his finger up to his lips. Disturbed by the movement he heard from the other side of the door, he became instantly alarmed as his heart rate started to increase. "Somebody's in that motherfucker."

Stuff, getting a quick glance of a person's silhouette passing by the sheer curtains that adorned the kitchen window, put his arm out, pushing both females backward against the house out of harm's way. His boy leaned over, pulling out his new chrome-plated pistol from underneath his cushion.

"Dawg, we should call the police." He tried reasoning with his friend, taking his BlackBerry out of his pocket. "We don't know what they want or how many of them are in there."

"Naw, Stuff, fuck that shit! I'm about to take care of whoever this is all by my damn self." Terrell showed no sign of fear as Shauntae looked at Stuff with disgust for his cowardly response.

"Terrell, they might have a gun too." Joi shook her head, reaching for his arm while trying to talk him out of being a hero. "Stuff is right. We should call the police!"

"Will both of y'all shut the fuck up before they hear us!" Li'l T snatched his arm away from Joi's touch.

"Yeah, let him do his thang." Shauntae's pussy grew moist as she felt just as much of an adrenalin rush of the unknown jumping off as Terrell was experiencing.

Gripping the gun's handle tightly after putting one up top, he was ready to let a Negro have it if need be. Kamal's offspring, following in his father's footsteps, took a deep, long breath, eagerly licking his lips as if he were welcoming the thought of an exchange of gunfire and, hopefully, bloodshed. Then, if all of that wasn't bad enough, maybe a death, even if it was his own.

Quietly, Terrell stuck his key into the lock, turning it as slowly as possible, with Stuff and the girls, all full of apprehension, looking on, anticipating what was gonna come next. Silently, the tumblers fell into place. Li'l T twisted the knob with one hand, clutching his firearm in the other, ready to blaze out in glory. Easing the door open, he rolled inside like he was the Terminator in that bitch. Leaving his friends behind, he heard more movement in the living room and quickly made his play. Bursting through the entryway, he drew down on the person.

"What the hell!" Simone spun around, wide-eyed, as she stared down the barrel of her son's 9 mm, dropping a garbage bag of empty beer bottles onto the floor.

"Ma? Is that you?"

"Boy! Is you crazy or something?"

"When did ya ass get back in town?"

"Never mind all that bullshit you talking, asking *me* questions!" a startled Simone screamed, still trying to catch her breath from being scared half shitless. "Get that motherfucker out of my goddamn face!"

"Oh, dang, my bad. Sorry." Terrell finally lowered his pistol. "I ain't know who was up in here."

"Nigga, please." She stepped backward, exhaling.

Rushing in after hearing Simone's loud voice, Stuff stood dumbfounded, finding the mother and son at each other's throats. "Oh, boy," he mumbled, knowing the shit was about to hit the fan.

"Stuff." Simone stepped over a pile of blankets that Yankee had been calling home since she'd been gone on her mini excursion. "I know ya straight-laced ass ain't got jack to do with all this mess around here."

"Hey, Simone." H hesitantly addressed her by her first name as he was always instructed to do ever since he was a child. "How you doing this afternoon?"

"Boy, don't be patronizing me."

"Stuff, just who is this stuck-up bitch supposed to be?" Shauntae motioned, being obnoxious as usual and speaking out of turn, not waiting to find out the true situation at hand.

"*Excuse* me?" Simone turned her attention to the tacky female that was firmly holding on to Stuff's arm like he was a bar of solid gold or platinum. "You better watch your slick-talking, disrespectful, motherfucking mouth, little girl, before you mess around and get that mug wired shut. Terrell, ya better tell her."

"Stuff," Shauntae snarled, showing no visible signs of backing down as her thick set of extra-long fake eyelashes flickered. "Who is this old, wanna-still-be-young trick trying to sell wolf tickets to?"

"Whoa! Slow ya roll, girl! This is my mother, so watch your damn mouth," Li'l T interjected.

"I don't give a damn who she is," Shauntae continued on as Joi tried pulling her arm in hopes of shutting her up before she said anything else that was out of order. "She don't be coming all up in here threatening me like I'm her kid. She ya momma, not mines! So how 'bout it!"

"Little girl, you done got me all the way fucked up in my house and straight outta pocket." Taking her hands off the hips of her pink-and-yellow designer sweat suit, Simone angrily lunged at the strange female that was intent on insulting her. "Terrell, ya best get this bitch before I ride out on her ass for real."

"Don't hate all on me, old-timer, because your prime time in the sun done faded," Shauntae taunted, avoiding her attacker's grasp.

Before Terrell knew what he was doing, he'd raised his gun once more, turning it this time on Shauntae, challenging her to say another word to or against Simone. Unfortunately for her, as soon as her lips parted, the cocky female wasted no time whatsoever still trying to go hard, running off at the mouth, immediately prompting Li'l T to reach up and smash the side of his gun across her makeup-covered face.

Looking down, she saw small splatters of blood on her T-shirt from her now-busted grill. Erotically charged, Shauntae felt her pussy start to get wet all over again and her nipples harden, watching the savage look of murder dance in Terrell's cold eyes.

"Terrell, don't," Joi intervened, coming in between him and her obnoxious sister as Stuff looked on. "Please!"

"Get ya hands the fuck off me." Li'l T shoved Joi out of the way, raising his voice. "Don't nobody come in my fucking house disrespecting my momma like she ain't shit! I ain't trying to hear that!" Just like Terrell was Kamal's son, Shauntae was indeed her mother's daughter. Once more, with force, the angry Li'l T swung his gun, slamming the other side of Shauntae's face as she stood there motionless, taking the blow as only a true Detroit trooper could.

For the first time in Terrell's turbulent young life, Simone seemed actually proud of her son as he beat another teenager in the defense of her so-called honor. The fact that it was a female honestly meant little to nothing to the self-righteous, pride-swollen mother. Even though back in the day she'd hated Kamal most of the time she was with him, Simone still was turned on by the rough, deranged, and sometimes unstable behavior Li'l T's daddy showed when he felt he was being shitted on or disrespected.

"Okay, okay, Terrell, that's enough." She finally stopped her baby by taking a strong grip of the handles of his chair, rolling him backward. "Don't kill the smart-ass ghetto piece of trash."

Shauntae used her tongue, licking the blood from the corner of her mouth as her face started to swell. "Stuff," she said with authority, tugging down once again on her skirt, "take me the fuck home before I snap."

"Are you all right?" Joi ran to her big sister's aid while staring at Simone as if she was plum crazy and Terrell like he had three heads growing from his neck. The young girl couldn't believe what had just taken place. "Oh my God! Look at your face!"

"Naw, Joi." Shauntae still stood tall, seemingly not moved by the spontaneous pistol whipping she'd just suffered at the hands of her sister's new crippled boyfriend. "I'm good. That nigga hit like a bitch! But I'm going to the crib."

"I'm coming with you." Joi's tears were flowing as Simone pried her son's fingers off his gun before he lost control and shot one of them, maybe even himself the way he was acting. "I can't believe this."

"Naw, Joi. You stay here with ya man. I already done told you I'm good, so do you!" Uncharacteristically, Shauntae didn't do anything or say anything more to set off Terrell or Simone. Wanting to cry out in pain, with a fat lip, dizzy as hell, she held it deep inside. She knew to never let a motherfucker see you sweat, no matter how bad shit gets. So, quietly leaving out the same door they'd just come through, leaving her sister there to deal with the certain aftermath, she was soon in Stuff's car, heading through the black steel gates and back to her side of the streets of Detroit.

***

"Damn, I'm sorry Terrell acted like that." Stuff tried breaking the ice to his mute passenger as they drove by three or four vacant, littered-filled lots, two abandoned cars, and a group of old men arguing over the last drop of a bottle of Wild Irish Rose. "Sometimes he just nuts up and overreacts to things."

"Is that right?" Shauntae finally sarcastically responded while still refusing to shed a tear as they drove up in front of the three-bedroom, small frame house that was badly in need of a paint job she and Joi called home. "It's nothing, trust."

"I know his mother was out of order, but you did kinda provoke her." Stuff did not know what exactly to say or do. He couldn't change the fact that he'd just stood idly by watching his best friend clown on a female he'd been hanging with the past few days, so he started taking a cop. "Why didn't you just chill the hell out and all that madness probably wouldn't have jumped off? You don't know him the way I do."

"Look, I said it was nothing, so damn, leave the shit alone, all right? It ain't the first time a nigga done put they hands on me, and nine outta ten, it probably won't be the fucking goddamn last." With those great, almighty hustling ho's words of wisdom, Shauntae got out of the BMW, slamming the door shut before Stuff could say another word, and disappeared into the house to nurse her wounds.

Yearning for a man in her life that was half as thugged-out as Terrell, battered and beat, she decided to stop avoiding Elon's unanswered calls, since he was the next best thing to Terrell—crazy like she liked them.

Dumbfounded with embarrassment and speechless with confusion as to why Shauntae was so composed after the altercation, Stuff turned the car radio up, pressed down on the gas pedal, and skirted off, leaving the unsafe neighborhood, heading back to the security of his suburban home. Truth be told, he had a date with Marie Averez later that evening. She had been blowing his phone up, and since she was Juan's sister, he knew for the good of the summer hustle, he shouldn't disappoint her.

Chapter Thirty-eight

Forgetting all about her son drawing down on her, Simone snickered at finally seeing him boss up in her defense. "Are you good, boo boo?"

"Yeah, Ma, I'm tight." Li'l T looked over at Joi, who was standing posted near the front door, not knowing whether to leave or what. "But can you give me a minute?"

"Go ahead and get rid of this other tack head while I try to clean up the rest of this ridiculous mess you and your other low-life friends done made."

"Ma, shut the fuck up and give me a minute. Please."

Joi, with tears flowing from her eyes, waited to hear what her once-thought-to-be Prince Charming was gonna say in the way of an explanation for his Jekyll-and-Hyde routine. "Well, Terrell? Why?"

"Baby, I'm sorry, all right?"

"That's it?"

"What else you want me to say?"

"Maybe a little bit more than just that," Joi argued. "Did you see my sister's face when she and Stuff left?"

"Well, did you hear the way she talked to my mother?" He threw the ball back in her court. "I don't know how y'all carry it on the other side of this gate, but in this fucking house, ain't nobody dissing my ol' girl."

"I'm about to leave," Joi wisely decided, turning the knob. "You're talking crazy."

"Wait, Joi."

"For what?" She paused. "So you can put your hands on me like you just did Shauntae?"

Simone reentered the living room with a smirk of satisfaction. With no regard for what the young girl must have been feeling, she asked her son why Joi was still there and quizzed about her newly found discovery.

"Now, Terrell, just who in the hell is she, and what in the fuck is this?" Simone waited impatiently for him to reply, holding a scale and dangling some baggies in her hand. "She needs to go because we need to talk."

Knowing there would be no shutting his mother up, Terrell grabbed Joi near him and informed Simone what the deal was. "Ma, this is Joi. I met her while you were out of town, and she's been hanging out here with me."

"Oh, yeah?" Simone didn't know whether to be glad her son was turning into a man, or mad he'd violated yet another one of her non-enforced house rules. She took two steps back and looked Joi up and down, sizing up her baby boy's taste. "And just where did he meet you at?"

"Well," Joi, not shy at all, spoke up, "we met at the store on Jefferson."

"Humph, dig that. Where you live at?" Simone continued the interrogation as she held on tightly to the scale. "And where's ya momma at?"

"I live on the other side of the north side gates."

"Damn, boy, you slumming now. Sleeping with trash?"

"Ma!" Li'l T yelled. "Cut that dumb shit out."

"Look, Miss Harris." Joi wasn't trying to be rude, but she damn straight wasn't in the mood for the same treatment Shauntae had just received. "I'm in school. I maintain a good GPA, and I don't sleep around. Matter of fact, I think it's ignorant and presumptuous for you to think anyone that lives in my neighborhood is automatic garbage. And please don't mention my mother. She's deceased."

"Damn, Terrell, I see by the looks of things, you went out and got you a Prayer clone."

"Ma!" Li'l T screamed out from his wheelchair.

"And what about that other thang with the smart mouth that was here? Did I hear you say that was your sister?"

"Yes, I did, and she has a name. It's Shauntae."

"It figures it'd be some old hood rat name." She smirked.

Terrell had just about enough of Simone insulting his girlfriend and came to her defense. "Ma, Joi is a good girl and has been helping me, so leave her alone. She ain't nothing like her sister. She's special."

"Whatever, boy. You don't know these streets or the hoes out in them like I do."

"Look, her mother was killed, and her sister has been looking out for them ever since their foster parents tried to separate them."

Simone, still being a bitch, didn't let up. "Well, who killed the mother? That crazy-ass sister of hers?"

"No, some man came into our house near the projects when we were little and murdered her and three of my mother's friends."

"Hold the hell up! Was it the Truth Homes? You said when you were little." Simone immediately thought some years back. "What was your mother's name?"

"Monique." Joi lowered her head, thinking about missing out on her mom's love. "Monique Richards."

Well, ain't this about a bitch! Clip-n-Dip Moe's daughter is giving my son the pussy! I'll be double damned! Detroit is small as a motherfucker! If this little ho is anything like her slimeball set-a-nigga-up ol' girl, then I definitely need to keep an eye on this one right here! Ain't no telling what she got up her shady east-side sleeve!

Simone put on her poker face and played her next card like a pro. "Oh my God! Come give me a hug! I knew your mother!" Out of character, she reached her arms out, embracing the young, confused teenager. "Me and her used to hang out at all the same spots back in the day. I remember when that bullshit happened. They never did catch the guy that did that mess, did they?"

"No." Joi, unseasoned to the world of true gangsta game, fell right into Simone's fakeness, welcoming someone that could share any memory of her deceased mother.

"Well, any daughter of Monique's is a daughter of mine," Simone plastically proclaimed as Terrell suspiciously watched his mother front. "Except for Miss Thang that showed her natural ass. She still ain't welcomed in here."

"Yeah, all right," Terrell agreed.

"Now, little nigga, let's get back to this garbage you got all up in my house like this a stash spot!"

Chapter Thirty-nine

After convincing Joi to go watch television in the den until he calmed his momma down, Terrell finally manned up. He had to answer to Simone for the drug paraphernalia she'd found throughout the house, as well as the filthy mess that her son and his supposed friends had made while she was away at wherever with whoever.

"Damn! It's been less than two weeks, and you out here like this? No wonder Drake couldn't get in touch with you and had to call me," Simone said, looking on her expensive dining-room table that was full of ashtrays with half-smoked blunts in them. "Real talk from me to your wannabe grown ass: true enough this house and the property it sits on might ninety percent belong to you, but make no mistake about it, all the stuff that's in this joint belongs to me. I'll clean this bitch out and put my shit into storage before I let you and your uncouth thugs fuck it up."

"Wait till you see this, then let's see what ya gotta say." Rolling in the rear of the house and into his room, Li'l T made his way over to his closet, where he leaned down, removing a shoe box that was hidden under a pile of clothes and a couple of old magazines. As he placed it on his lap, taking the top off, Simone judgmentally waited for what was gonna happen. Terrell snatched out several wads of money that were wrapped in red, yellow, and green rubber bands, tossing them on his bed. "What you know about that, Ma?"

Being an official old-school G about her shit, sizing up the knots by eye, Simone could tell her son had a little over six, maybe six-and-a-half grand in total. "And?" She smirked, shrugging her shoulders. "What the fuck about it?"

"That's profit. All profit from slinging them trees."

"Boy, bye," Simone ridiculed. "I know you ain't rolling around all up in here like you some sort of a boss kingpin over this little amount of change. Nigga, I spend that much on shoes and dresses in a month."

"What?" Terrell argued, disappointed that his mother wasn't in the mood to jock him. "I came up on this cheese quick. And we ain't even really put a full-court press down yet."

Simone went out into the living room, getting a Newport out of her purse, and lit it. "Look, Li'l T, I ain't knocking you for trying to do your thang, but the hustle game ain't for everybody, especially your type."

"And *what* type you think I am?" He maneuvered his wheelchair behind her, persistent in wanting an answer. "I ain't no punk! I'm about my motherfucking business!"

Blowing smoke rings up into the air to amuse herself, Simone finally broke the facts of life, as she saw them, down to her son. "Listen up, baby boy. I done been to the mountaintop with plenty of guys out here getting they grind on making that real bread, and even the cleverest put-together crews end up getting busted sooner or later. Now, is you gonna sit there and tell me you built for doing a double-digit bid? You might look like Kamal, and ya damn straight got a temper like his crazy ass, judging from what you just did to your little girlfriend's sister, but you trying to run with the big dogs, and you still just a puppy."

Terrell brushed off what Simone had just said, following it up with his own take on his situation. "Ma, I know you think I ain't a go-getter, but I am. And if you know the game as well as you claim, then instead of being against me, why don't you turn me on and be on my side for once instead of straight hating?"

"Is that what you really want? You wanna be out here in these Detroit streets with the rest of the cutthroats? You think you ready for that life? Is *that* what the fuck you want?"

"Yeah, it is," Terrell proudly proclaimed with his chest stuck out.

Simone took two more long pulls from her cigarette, then put it out. "All right, then, so be it. But when shit gets rough out there, and trust me it will, just be able to take what knocks you got coming. Stand tall with the good and the bad and try not to bring the next nigga down with you if you fall. That's the true meaning of gangsta. And for your information, son, the white man out here giving motherfuckers that get caught with weed football numbers too—in a wheelchair or not!"

As the afternoon progressed, Joi, still naïve to Simone's all-of-a-sudden acceptance of her relationship with her son came out of the den. She happily helped with restoring the house back to the way it was before she'd hooked up with Terrell. Delusional, Joi believed they were gonna be one big, happy family from this point on, something that she had always yearned for growing up.

While that was going on, Simone was mainly occupied with giving her baby boy the full advantage of her expertise in Dope Slinging 101, and the beginner's basics in how to fuck over your workers without them noticing.

When all of that was said and done, Simone left Joi and Terrell to themselves and ran a much-needed hot bath. *Fuck! It's been a long-ass day!* Dropping her clothes to the ground and stepping in, Simone got relaxed as the bubbles surrounded her body.

That oldest daughter of Monique's got me twisted. I'm still fine as a motherfucker, she thought as she blazed up one of the blunts that was left on her table. *Damn, this is some good-ass weed!* Simone reached over for the cordless phone she'd set on the edge of the sink. *Now, let me call Big Ace and tell him who in the hell is in my crib. After all these years, I know this shit gonna trip him out! Hell, a bitch like me even wanna call Prayer and Chari! But, oh well, on second thought, this weed ain't that fucking good to make a ho shoot a move like that!*

Conniving and anticipating how she would profit from the information, Simone pushed in Big Ace's cell phone number and waited for him to answer. She couldn't wait to tell him who her baby boy had hooked up with from their equally shady past. Ironically, Simone had no idea that Big Ace's sons had also encountered Terrell, and not under favorable circumstances. When the truth of all the twisted and deadly generational connections between the various families came to light, one could only hope a peaceful reunion of sorts could take place. In the meantime, Detroit was the smallest big city in America. Everyone knew someone who knew someone else. It was only God Himself who was keeping the tainted bloodlines from mixing.

To Be Continued . . .